The Little
Guesthouse
of
New Beginnings

BOOKS BY DONNA ASHCROFT

Donna Ashcroft

The Little Guesthouse of New Beginnings

bookouture

Published by Bookouture in 2019

An imprint of StoryFire Ltd.

Carmelite House
50 Victoria Embankment
London EC4Y 0DZ
www.bookouture.com

ISBN: 978-1-78681-758-7
eBook ISBN: 978-1-78681-757-0

This book is a work of fiction. Names, characters, businesses,
organizations, places and events other than those clearly in the
public domain, are either the product of the author's imagination
or are used fictitiously. Any resemblance to actual persons, living or
dead, events or locales is entirely coincidental.

To Jackie Campbell and Julie Anderson –
I thank my lucky stars for you xxx

Chapter One

Madison Skylar stood on the deck of the Sunflower Island ferry, feeling excited and nostalgic as she watched Sunflower Island come into view. Even from this distance, Madison could see gorgeous sandy beaches and flecks of multicoloured roofs. She'd been away for almost five years, with only a few flying visits in between, and seeing the only place she'd ever called home brought an unexpected lump to her throat.

Ice-cold wind whipped Madison's long brown hair into her eyes, reminding her it was only the end of February. She pulled her flimsy jacket tighter. She'd lost her coat six months before, travelling through Thailand, and apart from the jeans and red jumper she wore, she had little more than shorts, bikinis and T-shirts in her backpack. Aside from her yoga mat, which she'd hitched to the side, this was the sum total of Madison's worldly possessions. She'd have to rely on finding any old clothes she'd left at The Sunshine Hideaway – her aunt and uncle's beautiful home and guesthouse – to stay warm until she found time to shop.

As the ferry drew closer, Madison saw the familiar dock with its wooden walkway that followed the water's edge, leading foot passengers through gleaming white railings to a variety of cosy tourist shops. Closest was Sprinkles, an ice cream parlour that served the best and most unusual desserts on earth. Next to that sat The Rock Shop, which was always crammed with colourful fare including sweets, ornaments made from seashells and postcards from around the island. A couple of buildings down, Surf & Ride was already open, and a sign outside blew back and forth in the wind, offering boat tours and water-sports gear rental – not that there was much call for it in February. In the distance, behind the shops, Madison could just make out rolling fields. In the summer those fields would be brimming with yellow sunflowers tipping their heads towards the dock. The view made her feel a combination of excitement and homesickness.

Madison squinted at the crowd on shore, hoping to see Dee Walker, The Sunshine Hideaway's cook and one of her surrogate aunties when she'd been a teen. Instead, her attention fixed on a set of broad shoulders that had her stomach somersaulting. Madison quickly looked away, determined to ignore the burn on her cheeks and the tingling sensation dancing across her skin. What was *he* doing here? Connor Robertson had always had the same effect on her – it was annoying to discover that after all this time, nothing had changed. Infuriatingly, despite multiple efforts over the years to attract his attention, Madison had received little more than a dismissive nod of the head or derisive comment, and she already knew today would be no exception.

Madison picked up her backpack without looking at the shore again, and followed the crowd towards the steps that would lead her down to the exit. The ferry made a series of deep toots and then let out a long screech, signalling that it was docking. Madison pulled out her mobile to see if by some miracle the battery had recharged itself. It hadn't – she'd have to find Dee the old-fashioned way and look for her.

'Shall I carry that for you?' A blond man Madison had chatted to on the ferry – Tom something, she couldn't remember his surname – took her large backpack from her hands before she could reply. 'Are you headed straight to your aunt and uncle's place or have you got time for a quick drink?' he asked, looking hopeful.

'Thanks for the offer… but you should know I have a boyfriend,' Madison replied. This was true, strictly speaking – it wasn't the most stable relationship, but she wasn't looking for company and the mention of a partner was usually enough to see off a would-be suitor.

'Promise you're not making him up?' Tom said with a laugh.

Madison shook her head. 'He's called Seth Matthews, works for Greenpeace. Google him if you don't believe me. We met two years ago when I was travelling through Amsterdam.'

'Then have a drink with me, just as friends?' Tom persisted. 'You can fill me in on all the best places to visit while I'm here.'

'Perhaps another time,' Madison replied, following as Tom trotted down the ferry steps with her backpack slung across his shoulder. 'I'm going straight to The Sunshine Hideaway just as soon as I find my ride,' she explained. 'People are expecting me at home.' Saying the word *home* brought an unexpected warmth to Madison's eyes and throat. She'd been away since she was eighteen and now she'd reached twenty-three, it felt like the right time to finally stake her claim somewhere.

With Tom still at her side, Madison scanned the hordes of people clustering around the ferry but didn't spot Dee, which was odd. They'd messaged the day before and Dee had promised to pick her up. Usually when Madison arrived on Sunflower Island, someone from The Hideaway was waiting, often with helium balloons and banners, welcoming her back. She stopped in the middle of the crowd so she could look around. Maybe Dee had been held up?

'Madison.' Connor's voice came from her left and she fought the desire to turn towards it. It hadn't changed – there was the same deep timbre, the same sexy tone that had her body humming like a finely tuned instrument… She could only imagine what would happen if he ever touched her for real. 'Dee said you were coming alone,' Connor said, sounding grumpy.

'We're not together, we met on the ferry. I'm Tom Jones – no relation, I can't sing,' Tom joked, dropping Madison's backpack on the floor and holding out a hand to Connor, who narrowed his blue-green eyes and stared at it.

'Ah, Tom, this is Connor. He's not really a people person,' Madison explained, joining him. She ignored Connor's irritated glare, and did her utmost not to let her eyes drop to the mouth that had given her a few sleepless nights over the years.

Madison could still remember when she'd first really noticed Connor. He'd been around eighteen, working with his father, renovating what was now the Town Hall. She'd been fifteen, and had recently moved to the island after her aunt and uncle had taken her in. He'd caught her eye as he'd stripped off his shirt, exposing a muscled chest that had turned her insides to molten lava. She'd introduced herself and Connor had told her to go away, which had pretty much set the tone for their relationship from then on.

Despite that, Madison was convinced he hid a softer side that she still wanted to get to know.

'Are you here for a reason?' Madison pushed the image of a half-naked Connor out of her mind and checked over his shoulder, but the crowd had disappeared and only a few stragglers remained. 'Or did someone hire you to scare off the tourists?'

'I'm here for you,' Connor grumbled, picking up her backpack from between Tom's feet.

'Where's Dee? Is everything okay?' Madison asked, feeling her pulse quicken.

'She's fine – she was cooking and couldn't leave the food. No one else was around to take over,' Connor muttered. 'The truck's in the car park and Jaws is waiting. Best say goodbye to this guy. For some reason, the dog hates blondes.'

Madison rolled her eyes at Connor's retreating back, even as she appreciated the way his worn Levi's stretched across his backside, moulding a bottom honed from years of physical labour working for his father's building business. She sighed before turning back to Tom, who looked faintly put out.

'Friend of yours?' he asked, his forehead creasing.

'No.' Madison shook her head vigorously. 'Friend of my aunt and uncle's. I really don't understand why, except they grew up with his dad… He's only three years older than me but you'd think it were centuries. We don't get on. He thinks I'm frivolous and uncommitted – in fact, he once used the word *flibbertigibbet*, which may be the most syllables he's ever uttered in one go.' Madison grinned, smothering the brief flash of hurt. She'd been seventeen at the time and desperately in lust. 'I'd better go.' She pointed in the direction of the car park.

'Sure you'll be okay?' Tom looked concerned.

'Oh, Connor's harmless.' Madison laughed. 'Unless you can frown someone to death. And his dog's a pussycat in disguise, truly. Enjoy your holiday.' She waved without looking back as she made her way towards the car park.

'I'll give you a call,' Tom shouted after her, making Madison regret her impulse to give him her number earlier in case he was at a loose end. But after spending so many years being pushed and pulled from pillar to post with her parents, who'd worked for the Foreign Office, it had become second nature to make friends with everybody she met.

The engine was already running in Connor's battered old truck when Madison hopped in. Her backpack sat on the back seat next to Jaws, Connor's large Boxer. The dog came to sniff her face and licked it gently before flopping down again. 'At least someone's happy to see me,' Madison joked, as Connor thumped the truck into reverse and whizzed out of the car park, glaring at the windscreen. She took the opportunity to have a good look at him.

Connor Robertson had always been physically perfect. His hands were tanned from being outside so much and his forearms were strong and lean, like the rest of him – although he had his dark leather coat on so Madison couldn't see much of his body from where she sat. His cheeks were angular and brown stubble seemed to live permanently on his chin, making him look sexy, dangerous and a little unkempt. His eyebrows were dark and his full lips were always frowning as though something – perhaps life – were dragging them down. Just once Madison wanted to see them lift just for her: was a smile really too much to ask for in life? She knew Connor hadn't had things easy, and for some reason she seemed to rub him up the wrong way. Maybe now she was back on Sunflower Island, the time had come for all that to change – and this year would be one of new beginnings for both of them?

Chapter Two

Connor tried to ignore Madison and pushed the truck into fourth. They joined the road that would take them along the beach and through a small coastal village. After that they'd join the main stretch that would take them five miles out of the main town to the other side of Sunflower Island and The Sunshine Hideaway.

She smelled good – Connor couldn't fathom how, considering by all accounts she'd been travelling for three days. But then Madison never did anything he expected. He sneaked a look at her as she patted Jaws, who was lying on the back seat staring at her like a lovesick puppy. Like the boy she'd picked up on the ferry, his dog was yet another victim of her charms. There would be more before the week was out. Madison had a knack for enchanting people, and would leave the usual trail of broken hearts when she tired of her latest visit and left Sunflower Island again.

Her hair had grown. When he'd seen her last, it had been cropped and level with her jawline. The new style was artfully sexy, ending past her shoulders. It made him think of warm sheets and wild nights – things he hadn't had time for in way too long.

'So how have you been?' Madison asked, clearly determined to make conversation.

'Busy,' Connor answered without elaborating.

'Last time I talked to my aunt, she said you've been working hard running the family business. I know it was a while ago, but I was sorry to hear about your dad,' she added, sounding genuinely upset.

'Thanks.' Connor didn't know what else to say, so he switched on the radio and turned the volume up. It was an edgy jazz track he didn't recognise, and Madison looked out of the window for a few minutes, watching the green fields roll past. The atmosphere was strangely settling and he felt himself relax.

'How's your sister?'

'Good,' Connor lied, because in all truth he had no idea. Like Madison, his half-sister Georgie Grayson was a law unto herself and he hadn't heard from her in almost a month – hopefully because she was too busy studying. His sister was in the second year of a construction management degree that Connor was helping to fund. After her third-year exams, Georgie planned to return to Sunflower Island to work with him in the family business.

'So why did Dee ask you to pick me up?' Madison changed the subject suddenly and Connor felt the tension hit between his shoulder blades.

'I told you. Because she's making dinner, and no one else was around.'

'And you, what, just happened to be close by?' Madison sounded shocked, which should have been insulting, except she was right: Connor wasn't exactly the popping-in type. His work was too busy for socialising.

'I'm working for your aunt and uncle,' Connor explained. 'Doing general repairs and fixing up the cafe in the cellar underneath the kitchen. It's barely used – they wanted to give it a revamp to make it more attractive.'

'I loved the old cafe.' Madison sounded delighted. 'They used to serve the best chocolate cake. It'll be great to have it open again.'

'Sure.' Connor swallowed, wondering how much Madison really knew about her aunt's recent illness, or if she'd been told the Skylars had decided to put The Sunshine Hideaway up for sale. Dee had made him promise to say nothing about either. 'It's an amazing project.' One Connor had been lucky to get. Since his dad had died eighteen months before and he'd had to support Georgie through university, he'd needed all the work he could pick up. So when the Skylars had asked him to quote, and then eventually to take on the project, he'd been both grateful and relieved. It wouldn't bring in loads of money, but the prestige should lead to more work on the island. He owed them a lot. Which was why he'd agreed to pick up Madison when Dee had asked and – despite his better judgement – to keep their secrets. *At least for today.*

Madison looked confused. 'I wonder why they didn't mention the work on the cafe.'

'When was the last time you spoke?'

'Not for a few months.' Madison frowned. 'It's been more dif-ficult recently, especially while I was in Thailand, because the signal was bad and the battery on my mobile keeps going flat. But I called a few days ago to say I wanted to visit – that's when Dee told me about my aunt and uncle's cruise. I thought I'd come anyway. I'll be able to help out until they return.'

'Sure you'll stick around for long enough?' Connor wished he could take the words back as soon as he said them, but at twenty-three, Madison's track record for staying in one place could rival a tennis ball at Wimbledon. After a number of brief visits, she'd come to live with her aunt and uncle on Sunflower Island when her parents had died in a freak gas explosion at the British Embassy in Italy. Within a fortnight of Madison finishing school – though Connor had begun to think she might stay – she'd hopped on the ferry for her first adventure, before returning a few months later.

Madison's aunt, Sandy Skylar, had filled him in on Madison's ever-changing life from that point. She'd done a short stint at university. After dropping out, she'd trained to be a yoga teacher before working at a vegetarian restaurant. About two years ago, she'd upped sticks and gone travelling to Thailand with a band – the lead guitarist had been a customer in the restaurant, apparently. Clearly the job hadn't worked out, or maybe it was the guitarist? Connor didn't know and he really didn't care. Or maybe he did?

'My life has been filled with adventures.' Madison chewed her bottom lip, looking both unhappy and thoughtful. 'But Sunflower Island is the only place I've ever thought of as home, so I'm planning on staying… unless things don't work out.'

Typical Madison – one foot out the door before she'd even unpacked. Connor wasn't sure why that annoyed him so much and he didn't say anything. Instead he gripped the steering wheel tighter and put his foot down. The sooner Madison Skylar was out of his truck the better.

'You look angry,' Madison observed, sounding surprised. She unnerved him, always had, with her permanent smile and natural ability to befriend strangers within minutes of meeting them. She was also unusually open, telling anyone and everyone what she was thinking, and people loved it, loved her – as if exposing your deepest thoughts and feelings were a good thing. They were so different she might as well be from the moon.

'I just need to get back to work.' Connor ground the words out from between his teeth, knowing he was being unfriendly, but seemingly unable to stop himself.

'The cafe,' Madison said. 'Of course. After I've seen Dee and caught up with everyone, I'll come and take a look.' She flashed a devilish smile he recognised from when she'd been younger. 'Maybe I'll bring you a sandwich, to say thanks for the lift.'

'No need,' Connor mumbled as he joined the leafy road leading to The Sunshine Hideaway, just stopping himself from breathing a huge sigh of relief that they were almost at their destination.

As soon as Madison Skylar was out of his hair and he was back at work the better. He could already sense himself being sucked in by her charm, feeling like a planet being pulled towards a black hole it had no control over. But he didn't have time for her, didn't have time for anything except proving his father wrong. First, he had to get his sister through university. Then together they'd rebuild the family business into the thriving company it had once been. And absolutely nothing was going to get in the way of that.

Chapter Three

When Madison saw The Sunshine Hideaway approach in the distance, tears pricked her eyes. The main building was large, white and striking, with six bay windows and a tall sky-blue front door. The guesthouse sat on a hill, surrounded by dense woodland that marked the start of the long hikes Madison's uncle, Jack Skylar, took each morning. When she'd stayed at The Hideaway, Madison had spent hours outside with her uncle, stomping through woodland. The memory brought a lump to her throat. She'd been back to visit for small stretches since she'd left for university. And every time Madison felt like she was being wrapped in a warm blanket, making her wonder why she kept leaving.

A large field sat in front of the quaint building, which in summertime filled with hundreds of the blooming yellow sunflowers that The Hideaway and island were famous for. To the right were a couple of guest cottages that the Skylars used to let out to tourists. Beyond stood a double-storey building her aunt used as an office, with a huge glass window. The views from the study were incredible and Madison couldn't wait to get out there to be alone – it was the perfect place to do an early evening yoga session and watch the sunset.

It seemed like an eternity before Connor pulled up in front of the house. Madison barely waited for the truck to stop before she opened the door and hopped down onto the gravel driveway. Jaws followed, eliciting an irritated grunt from Connor. Madison didn't wait to pick up her luggage – she'd get that in a minute. Instead she half ran up to the blue front door. Dee must have been waiting, because it flew open before Madison arrived and suddenly she was being enveloped in hugs, cheered on by excited barks from Jaws.

'I can't believe you've finally come home.' Dee smelled of popcorn and chocolate, just like always. Madison hugged the cook back, letting her chin rest on the top of her head. At five foot three, Dee was a good five inches shorter than Madison, but at least twice as round. 'My goodness, you look just the same, although I swear you've lost weight.' Dee took a step back to study Madison critically. Despite entering her sixth decade last year, Dee's shiny auburn hair was styled into a sharp trendy bob that contrasted with her flowery, frilly apron. 'How were your travels this time?' Dee asked, tugging Madison through the hallway before opening the door on the right, leading to the sunroom, without waiting for her answer.

'Sit yourself down, love,' Dee said, as Madison took a few seconds to look around the room. It was scruffier than when she'd left and the walls definitely needed a paint. But the four cosy red sofas were still in the same spot she remembered, positioned around the large fireplace. The floor was polished oak, aside from a few deep scratches. A couple of thick rugs with a Mexican pattern covered the spaces between the furniture – Madison knew first-hand they were silky and perfect for sinking your toes into. Faded scatter cushions and soft blankets slung over the arms of the sofas completed the scene and made everything snug and welcoming.

Madison sat and picked at a piece of stray cotton on one of the sofa cushions. 'How long are my aunt and uncle gone for?' she asked, studying a crack in the wall above the fireplace that hadn't been there before. No wonder Connor had been hired to redecorate: the place certainly needed some TLC.

'Another six weeks. They'll be disappointed they missed you.'

'Oh, I'm not going anywhere.' Madison got up and moved to the mantelpiece. There was a picture of her with her aunt and uncle by the front door of The Hideaway that had been taken when she'd been just sixteen. Madison stood in between them, her face beaming. They'd just been on a trip to Sprinkles for ice cream and Madison had dripped some onto her favourite T-shirt. Instead of being angry, which Madison had expected, her aunt and uncle had laughed. Her aunt's long hair was tied back and she wore her usual jeans twinned with a silky shirt and pearls. Her uncle looked so much like Madison's father she felt her heart squeeze. 'Not if you'll have me,' Madison added shyly. 'I'm hoping to stay for a bit, Dee. I've been wanting to come back for a while.' She turned just in time to see Dee's expression darken, before the cook smiled.

'Is something wrong?' Maybe she wasn't welcome. Perhaps she'd be in the way? When you moved around as much as Madison did, it was easy to spot the clues that you weren't wanted.

'Of course not.' Dee marched across the room and gave Madison a swift hug. 'It's wonderful to have you, for as long as you want to be here.' She quickly changed the subject. 'What have you been doing with yourself – why did you decide to visit now?'

Madison hugged herself, stroking away the uncomfortable feeling she was missing something. 'I travelled with a band in Thailand, then got a job on one of the islands teaching yoga.' In truth she'd left the band because she'd started to feel like she was in the way. And even when she'd got her job, she'd begun to dream of The Hideaway. Strange how sometimes your deepest desires only came to you in the night. 'Three days ago, I went to work and the studio had been closed. The owner disappeared – I didn't even get my wages. I know it's the way of things there, but I'm fed up of moving around. Tired of having no base.' She sighed. 'It was what I needed because I called here the same day – maybe it's fate.'

'You never know.' Dee gave Madison's arm an affectionate squeeze, sounding overly bright. 'I'm very pleased to see you. Your room is made up and I left out toiletries. Go upstairs and unpack, make yourself at home.'

'Thanks, Dee.' Madison grinned, feeling grateful and a little tearful. 'Is the lovely Amy Walters still working here?'

Dee checked her watch. 'Of course. She should be starting her shift in a few minutes, and if I know that girl, she'll be around the kitchen helping herself to coffee around now.' Dee frowned. 'You two have lots to catch up on. Let's get you settled first. Come on.' Dee jostled Madison through the sunroom door back into the hall.

Madison half expected to find Connor still waiting in the hallway, but the front door was closed and her backpack was sitting next to it. Dammit, she'd meant to get it for herself. She didn't need to give him any more reasons to disapprove of her. She picked it up and headed towards the stairs. On the second floor of the house, there were six guest bedrooms, each with their own bathroom. The family lived above in the large attic that had been separated years ago into two bedrooms with their own en-suites, a sitting room and kitchen.

'Can I help out while I'm here?' Madison asked, taking a couple of steps upwards.

'We can talk about it with Amy later. Things have been a bit quiet…' Dee mounted the stairs with a huff. 'You get yourself settled first.'

'How many people are staying?' Madison looked around as they reached the second floor. The doors to each guest room were closed and no one was around. Usually the place was filled with noise – sometimes music, but always chatter and laughter. Today the hallway was quiet.

'There's Stanley Banks. You'll meet him later. He's been staying for months. We've got three couples booked in from tomorrow, which is a blessing. If you really want to help, you can make sure Connor doesn't need anything. Maybe get him to take a break, or feed him? He works too hard and you have a gift for getting people to relax.' Dee frowned. 'Sometimes he's here from seven in the morning until late at night. I don't know when the man has time to have a life.'

He probably didn't. Connor had always kept himself to himself on Sunflower Island. He'd lived here his whole life, but Madison knew very little about him – except that he'd fallen out with his father when he'd been twenty-one and had moved into a flat near town, on the other side of the six-mile-wide island, to live alone. Connor had returned to the family home years later to take care of his dad when he'd fallen sick. And despite women dropping like flies around him, Madison had never heard of Connor having any kind of long-time relationship or bringing anyone home. His only real connection was his half-sister Georgie, whom Madison had never met – and his dog, Jaws.

'No problem,' Madison promised, remembering Connor's expression when she'd offered to take him a sandwich earlier. She wasn't used to people finding her company annoying – maybe if she offered him good food he'd warm to her a little?

☆

Ten minutes later Madison and Dee headed back downstairs and walked through the hotel dining room, which had already been set for dinner. The room was large, with huge bay windows that looked out onto fields and beyond a beach with white sand framed by grey cliffs. The dining tables were laid with chequered tablecloths. But only one had the customary salt and pepper pots, shiny cutlery and water glass. It was five o'clock and dinner was served at seven sharp. In the past the room would be fully laid, ready for a combination of Hideaway guests and locals coming in for a home-cooked meal. Tonight, it looked like dinner for one.

As Madison stood leaning on the door frame between the dining room and kitchen, she fought another wave of homesickness. This had always been her favourite spot, where she'd spent hours chatting to and confiding in Dee, Amy or her Aunt Sandy. When she'd first come to The Hideaway, Madison had tried her hand at baking too – mostly burning things – before she'd given up, content to eat the spoils instead of making them.

'Are you hungry?' Dee walked into the kitchen and pointed to a side of beef resting on the counter.

'Still vegetarian.' Madison shuddered, following so she could give Dee another quick hug. 'And I've missed you and this place *soooo* much.'

'We've missed you too, love.' Dee hugged her back tightly. 'Connor's looking good, don't you think?' Dee's blue eyes lit up mischievously and she waggled her eyebrows.

'I didn't notice,' Madison lied, pulling up one of the wooden bar stools so she could sit at the breakfast bar, which doubled as a preparation area, to chat.

Dee winked. 'I seem to remember a conversation or two about him over the years. Maybe even an iceberg-sized crush.'

'I've moved on.' *Sort of.* Madison flicked her hair out of her eyes, pushing Connor from her mind as she looked around the kitchen. It was immaculate – there were a couple of cakes cooling on racks, and small portions of potatoes, broccoli and beans that had been sliced, diced and peeled sat ready by the side of the large-range cooker. Above the counters, wooden farmhouse-style cupboards loomed. Madison knew they'd all be bulging with equipment and ingredients in an order only Dee understood.

'He's still single, and I'm pretty sure he's not been seeing anyone recently, not since before his dad died. I don't like to speak ill of the dead, but Charles Robertson was as cold as they come.' Dee picked up a knife and began to peel a carrot. 'And the poor mite never really knew his mother. He was very young when she passed. It's a wonder that boy turned out so fine. You should take him a sandwich…' Dee's expression turned sly. 'I've got roast beef. And I have it on good authority red meat's an aphrodisiac.'

'I'll make him something with cheese.' Madison ignored her. 'With cucumber for vitamins, and a banana because of the mood enhancers – I'm pretty sure he needs them. Have you any soya milk?'

Dee grinned. 'The fridge is filled with your favourites. Connor likes cow's milk and tea so strong the spoon stands up on its own. I'm happy to make a pot if you like?'

'I'll do it. I owe him a thank you for the lift.' Madison hopped down from the stool and swiped some wholemeal out of the bread bin just as Amy opened the door and strode in.

'I'm not swearing, but fickity-fick. I need coffee and chocolate, a double helping if you've got it.' The wrinkles in Amy's forehead disappeared as soon as she spotted Madison, and she skipped across the kitchen to sweep her into a huge hug.

'You're here!' Amy hopped up and down a couple of times and beamed. She wore a dark blue suit and her red hair had been straightened, making her look sleek and professional. Amy did all of the admin for The Hideaway, managed the temporary staff, helped out in the restaurant and often greeted guests when they arrived, especially if the Skylars were busy. 'I can't believe my best friend is finally back on Sunflower Island. You've no idea how good it is to see you, Mads. I can't believe we've been so rubbish at keeping in touch. I *desperately* needed someone to cheer me up. I wished on a star for something good and then Dee told me this morning you were coming – and here you are.' Amy's amber eyes darkened. 'Today would have been perfect, if it hadn't been for the call I just picked up.'

'What's wrong?' Dee asked, thumping a large cup of coffee and a huge slice of chocolate cake on the breakfast bar before pointing to a stool. 'Pull it up and spill. There's nothing a bit of caffeine and sugar won't fix.'

Amy sighed deeply and picked up a fork before stabbing it into the cake. 'The call was a cancelled booking.' She shook her head. 'The party of six arriving tomorrow and staying into next week are very sorry.' Amy made a yappy face with one of her hands. 'They've decided to stay at Lake Lodge on the other side of the island instead, because there's a swimming pool and it's closer to the ferry, plus they offered them a huge discount. I've no idea how that place can afford to keep stealing our guests.'

'But I've made all the food.' Dee's face dropped. 'I cooked all day.' She pointed to the beef on the counter. 'I was going to do a curry with the rest of that ready for tomorrow, and there are three cakes made for when they arrive.'

'Their deposit will cover the food. But…' Amy shook her head and sipped from the mug as the room fell silent. Some of her red hair hung around the edges of her face, masking her devastated expression, but not before Madison caught it.

'What's happening?' Madison moved closer to her friend as Dee busied herself by the fridge. 'Is The Hideaway in trouble?' Madison reached out to touch Amy's hand. 'And why do you look so unhappy?'

'Oh… well, Jesse and I split up. Long story, not for now.' Amy frowned. 'When I tell you what happened, I'm going to need cocktails, hundreds of them, complete with pretty pink straws topped with flamingos to stab any passing man with.'

'I…' Amy and Jesse O'Brien had got together just before Madison had left for university, and from what she'd seen they were made for each other. 'We'll need those cocktails tonight because I'm not waiting long to find out what happened. Can you tell me what's going on at The Hideaway?' Madison's voice dropped to a whisper.

'I don't know.' Amy shrugged. 'Things started slowing down a while ago. I hardly noticed it at first. We had a few cancelled bookings, you expect that. But then families who'd been coming for years stopped calling. I revamped the website. Dee changed the menu. Your aunt and uncle did some advertising in the local paper and online.' She shook her head. 'Nothing changed. I blame it on Lake Lodge – it was after it opened last year that things started to drop off.'

'Are my aunt and uncle worried?'

'They don't seem it,' Amy admitted. 'They hired Connor to redecorate – they want to give the cafe a revamp to attract more guests.' She stared into her coffee. 'But it's taking time. Connor's got other work on and there's only him and Jesse doing everything. Your uncle offered to help but your aunt's been so tired recently.'

'She has?' Madison's breath caught as she looked at Dee. 'Is something wrong?'

'Nothing the cruise won't fix,' Dee answered quickly, her eyes darting to Amy. 'Your aunt and uncle weren't going to go but I insisted. Sandy's tired – both of them are. It's hard work running The Hideaway and even harder admitting it's not the place it was.' Dee looked sad. 'Whatever happens they'll do what they can to keep it going.'

'But… what can I do?' Madison asked, feeling guilty. Had she left it too late to come back? She'd been restless for a while, wanting to settle somewhere. All of her thoughts had led to The Hideaway but it had taken her months to admit it, or to believe there might be a place for her here, and even longer to come. Now she was here, was the whole thing about to slip through her fingers?

Chapter Four

Connor wiped a hand across his forehead and swept off a layer of dust. He was at least an hour behind because of picking up Madison and would have to make up the time, or the schedule was screwed. Still, that was the end of the sanding. He'd only had to take a couple of layers of varnish off the bar counter, but there was a hell of a mess. Everything had been covered in a thin layer of grime and he wanted to clear it before leaving. Thank God he'd asked Jesse – his right-hand man – to take Jaws for a walk this afternoon. It was going to be another late one.

Connor heard a quiet knock at the entrance to the cafe and didn't respond, but somehow knew it was Madison even before the dark walking boots and shapely jean-clad legs came into view. He dragged his eyes away and unplugged the sander, keeping himself busy.

'I brought you a sandwich and a banana,' Madison said, looking around the dusty room, holding a plate in one hand and a mug in the other. The temporary lights Connor had erected ran along the top of the ceiling and into each crevice, meaning there was plenty to see – which was good for working, but not if you wanted to discourage visitors.

Madison held out the plate, looking strangely confident and vulnerable at the same time. 'You don't want it? I worked in a restaurant for…' She counted her bright pink fingernails. 'Five months, so I'm pretty sure it won't poison you. Mind you, that tea might. You really should try camomile…'

Connor shuddered. 'I'm just not hungry.' His stomach rumbled, giving away his lie. When Madison raised an eyebrow, he wiped his hands on his jeans and took the plate before looking around the room for somewhere to put it. There was just enough space on his workbench, but as soon as he'd placed it there she handed him the mug too. 'Honestly—'

'You're not hungry, not thirsty and not looking for company. I know,' Madison said cheerfully, walking further inside before stopping to look around. The room was large, with beautiful arches across the back wall framing the bar, which had been cleared of everything but the old shelving. The whole thing was a gift to work with, and the space would be beautiful once he'd redecorated.

If he was left alone for long enough to finish it.

Connor took a bite of the sandwich. Dammit, he hated cheese – wasn't a fan of fruit either – but was hungry enough to eat both. He sipped some tea, which burned his throat and was exactly what he needed. 'Thanks,' he mumbled, feeling awkward and crowded.

'This is beautiful. What colour is it going to be?' Madison asked, showing no sign of wanting to leave. Instead she slipped nimbly under one of the arches, behind the bar, so she could look at the other side of the counter.

Connor followed despite himself, although he deliberately checked his watch so Madison could see. Not that she took any notice. 'I'll use a varnish,' he answered bluntly.

Madison frowned. 'But what about colours for the walls? Do you have a plan I can look at? I'm here to help. I'm sure yellow would work – and I was thinking, if you need it, I could assist with choosing the paint and things…' She trailed off, probably because she saw his expression.

'I've still got to change the lights, redo the bathrooms and kitchen, sand the floors. We're not ready to paint yet.' And Madison would probably be halfway across Europe before they were. Connor gulped another mouthful of tea as she moved underneath one of the overhead lights, which lit her long brown hair and made her look almost magical. He half choked on the drink and span round so he could put the mug down and gather himself. 'Won't be if I don't get on.' Connor turned again to find Madison standing over the table he'd erected in the corner, where he'd drawn up his plans for the space.

'Ah…' Madison ran a finger across the creased paper. 'I see, so you're redoing the kitchen and opening out the bar more. I can already imagine it.' She pointed to the right with a dreamy expression. 'The whole place will look amazing. Dee said my aunt and uncle are hoping it'll attract extra visitors.' She frowned again. 'I can't believe it's so quiet. Last time I came the place was fully booked.'

'Things change, especially the things we wish wouldn't.'

'Not this much.' Madison looked unhappy.

'You've been living away for almost five years – what did you expect?'

Madison shrugged, looking awkward. 'That everything would be the same. My aunt and uncle would be here and The Hideaway would be heaving with guests. Stupid, I suppose…' Connor had an unexpected urge to comfort her, which he quickly discarded. 'I'm hoping I can help.'

'Not sure how,' Connor said gently, but only because he felt guilty.

Madison shrugged. 'I'll figure something out – perhaps you have some ideas? Amy and I are going to The Moon and Mermaid tonight for cocktails. I wondered if you'd like to join us?' She grinned, looking up at him, her face animated, and Connor felt a tug. The same tug he'd always felt around her. Like he was being pulled into her orbit, caught up in that smile. A smile he didn't have time for and one that wouldn't be here in a few weeks.

'I'm busy.' He looked around the room, taking in the piles of dust from the recent sanding, the pots of varnish and paintbrushes stacked next to his sander: a sharp contrast to the fresh-faced beauty of Madison Skylar.

'And you need to get on.' Madison misread his face and nodded, moving back into the centre of the room, somehow stepping over his tools without looking at them.

Connor cleared his throat. 'It's not going to finish itself.' Had he really just said that? It was exactly the kind of thing his dad would have said. Except his dad wouldn't have tolerated her being here at all.

Madison sighed, watching him with those big brown eyes you could get lost in. Her full mouth was turned down as she studied him. 'You don't like me and I've never really understood why.'

Connor rocked back on his heels, shocked by the honesty of the statement. In his world feelings like that were best avoided. You got on with your work, made a success of your life. Found someone to share it with when you had time. You certainly didn't *talk* about it, or about who you did or didn't like. 'That's… I've never said that,' Connor murmured, feeling like he'd been put on the spot, not knowing what to do about it. This was why he didn't let people into his workspace or life. They got into his head, messed with the schedule. *Fed him.*

'Some things don't need to be said,' Madison continued, watching him. 'It's okay. Because we're going to be seeing each other a lot over the next few weeks and I'm pretty sure I'll be able to wear you down. I'm very good at making friends.' She flashed a smile that had his heart accelerating. 'Besides, this is a year of new beginnings for me, and aside from finding a permanent home, getting you to like me is pretty much the first on my list.'

'Great,' Connor said, not meaning it but intrigued nonetheless, wondering exactly how long Madison would spend trying to make friends with him. From past experience, he knew it wouldn't be long before a more interesting person or place came along that she decided to focus on instead. Knowing a small part of him, a very small one, would be disappointed when she did.

☆

Twenty minutes later, Connor had cleared most of the debris into a pile when he heard footsteps and braced himself for Madison again. She'd taken his plate and mug already, but could be returning to torture him with more fruit – or to make good on her threat of camomile tea.

Dee appeared on the stairs and Connor felt his shoulders relax.

'Looks good.' The cook inspected the space with a smile and glanced at the pile of dust. 'Tidy too. I remember your father being a stickler for that.'

His father had been a stickler for a lot of things. 'I'll be finishing off the edges tomorrow, then there's the new units to put in.' Connor pointed towards the kitchen. They still had the bathrooms to replace and floors to sand before painting, but it was coming along well and he could already see the end result in his head.

Dee bobbed her head in agreement. She wasn't one for details, which Connor appreciated. It was easier doing your job without having someone breathing down your neck, checking every aspect for flaws.

'So I wanted to talk to you about Madison.'

'Yep.' Connor nodded, wishing he had a cup of tea to drink and hide his expression in. Madison had only been home a few hours but was already messing with his head.

'I'm so happy to have her home again, but she's unlikely to be here for long. We both know she was raised on a diet of hotels, parties and travel across continents – and regardless of what she thinks, it'll be hard for her to stay put.' Dee grimaced as she paced the room, checking under one of the arches, nodding her approval. 'Despite that, she's a lot more sensitive and vulnerable than she makes out – and I know she's already upset about the state of The Hideaway. I'm hoping we can keep the fact that it's up for sale between us? I guess she'll have to know eventually, but telling her now doesn't feel right. Also, I'm thinking it's not really our news to share… that task belongs to Sandy and Jack, and they haven't even told Amy. I suppose because they're hoping we'll all be able to keep our jobs.'

Connor wondered if Dee even knew Madison. From what he'd seen the woman was about as vulnerable as a tiger shark. She came and went as she pleased, seemingly at ease with her total lack of responsibilities. Despite her obvious attachment to the place, he was sure she'd take the news about The Hideaway in her stride. Madison didn't seem to be the type of person to be bothered by roots or emotional ties. Like her addresses, her friends were numerous, eclectic and disappeared as quickly as they arrived. And she always seemed so happy to move on. As if consistency and duty meant nothing at all. 'I don't like lying,' Connor said, feeling uncomfortable.

'Think of it as a good deed, helping to keep Madison here until the Skylars return.'

'If you think that's right,' Connor said, keeping his feelings to himself.

'And I don't want her to hear anything about Sandy's heart attack. I know you don't agree.' Connor started to shake his head but Dee held up a hand. 'It's fine that you don't. I even understand your point of view. But there's no need for Madison to worry. They caught the problem early. The doctors are happy with her progress – she just needs to recuperate. If we tell Madison about it she'll fret, and I'd like her visit here to be a good one. She lost her parents young. Sandy's like a mother to her and I'm not sure how she'll handle the news, or whether it'll make her leave again.' Dee glanced at the space. 'It looks better in here already. I'm glad you got the project, I can see how much it means to you.'

Connor nodded because he didn't know what else to say. Emotion caught in his throat because Dee was right. Working on The Hideaway did mean a lot to him. 'I appreciate being offered the work,' he said gruffly.

'Final request, then I promise I'll be gone.' Dee stepped closer, looking serious despite her frilly apron. Her eyes were the same blue as his father's, Connor realised, but the similarity ended there. For starters Dee was always smiling, full of charm and friendliness. Secondly, the cook actually seemed to like him.

'Okay,' Connor agreed hesitantly. He didn't spend a lot of time around people so couldn't always read their intentions. But something about Dee's tone told him he wasn't going to like what she said next.

'I knew your father from school. I know he believed in working hard, and that happiness came from success rather than love, or people. I never saw another side to him. I damn well hope there was one.'

Connor didn't say anything, which probably said it all.

'It's none of my business, but I'm going to give you some advice anyway. Seeing Sandy, my best friend, almost die in front of me, facing the reality of living without her, and watching Jack do the same, has taught me the value of every single moment. I'm just asking you to consider that. You work hard.' She looked around the room. 'Damn hard. And you're probably the best builder there is on the island. But don't forget the things that matter.'

When Connor looked at her blankly, Dee continued.

'Friends, lovers, walks on the beach, ice cream sundaes, hot chocolate, a good bottle of red.' She snorted. 'I wish you could see how disgusted you look right now.'

Connor shook his head, trying to school his expression into something neutral. He didn't want to offend Dee, but what the hell did this have to do with the renovating?

'I'm just saying take time for life, Connor, because I'm sensing you don't. Perhaps even take a couple of pages out of Madison's book. She may not have figured out what her path in life is yet, but she knows how to stop and smell the roses, and I admire her for it. You only get a certain amount of time – use it wisely. You never know when it'll all be spent.'

'Sure.' Connor nodded his head even as it filled with his to-do list. There'd be plenty of time for making friends and having fun once the business was thriving. He had something to prove to his father and himself. He wasn't going to waste time on sunsets or suchlike until he'd done it.

Chapter Five

The Moon and Mermaid was quiet, probably because it was only six o'clock in the evening. Madison nudged her way inside the pub, taking in the bright yellow walls and light polished-wood floors. The tables had all been painted white and there were pictures of sunflowers in various media on the walls – watercolours, oils, pastels, even a few artfully shot photographs. A long bar painted green and topped with a dark granite counter followed the back wall, and in front sat six bar stools. Madison made her way across the room so she could check out the optics, trying to remember the name of the cocktail Amy liked. Unlike The Hideaway, nothing had changed since the last time she'd popped by during a flying visit to see her aunt and uncle. The familiarity made her warm and fuzzy.

'You're already here,' Amy panted, appearing behind Madison. 'Sorry I'm late, another Hideaway booking cancelled and I spent ten minutes trying to talk them out of it.' Amy shook her head, her red hair falling around her shoulders. 'That makes two in the last day. I'm really worried, Mads. I've tried talking to Dee but she just says it's going to be all right. But how does she know? I'm already resigned to the fact that I'll probably lose my job. The Hideaway doesn't need that many staff. Dee and your aunt and uncle can keep it going. But I love the place and I want things to be okay.' Amy nibbled her fingernail as she scanned the bar.

'So do I,' Madison said softly, putting a hand over her friend's just as Finn Jackson appeared from the back room and flashed them both a grin. Finn was in his mid-twenties, six foot two, with brown hair streaked blond that ended at his chin. The combination made him look more surfer dude than pub landlord. Finn and Madison had enjoyed a brief dalliance when Madison had been seventeen, which had helped take the sting out of Connor's repeated rejections, but neither of them had taken it seriously. 'Mads, you're back.' Finn grinned and leaned over the counter to give Madison a quick kiss on the cheek, teasing her skin with his five o'clock shadow. 'How long's the visit for this time?' he asked.

'I'm not sure,' Madison said tentatively. If The Hideaway kept losing income at the rate it was, she realised her visit was unlikely to be permanent. She'd been back less than twelve hours and already her dream of a forever home here was disappearing.

'Two Pink Flamingos please, Finn.' Amy put her black bag on the counter and handed Finn her debit card. 'Fill 'em up and keep them coming. Mads and I have lots to catch up on.'

'Will do.' Finn winked. 'Take a seat and I'll bring your drinks over. We should get together while you're back, Madison. I'd love to hear more about the travelling.'

'Sure,' Madison replied, following Amy to a small table by the window. Her friend was already staring glumly outside as Madison pulled up a chair. 'Do you want to get it over with? Tell me what happened with Jesse. It'll be like pulling a plaster, quick and pain-less,' she added.

Amy summoned a ghost of a smile. 'It's brilliant to have you back, Mads. It's been too long since we last caught up.'

'I'm sorry.' Madison frowned at the table. She'd stayed away for too long this time, had been too afraid to get in touch with everyone on Sunflower Island in case they'd forgotten her. Instead she'd ignored and avoided her adopted family.

'I'm just glad you're back. You're my best friend, Mads, and you always will be – no matter where you live.' Amy's face clouded. 'But I missed having you here, especially recently.'

'Tell me what happened with Jesse,' Madison asked again, gently.

Amy sighed. 'I'm worried that if I burden you with my troubles you're not going to want to stick around.'

'Don't be silly.' Madison was used to people making jibes about her nomadic lifestyle but the comment still stung. 'I don't leave because the going gets tough, it's just…' It wasn't like she could tell Amy the reason she kept leaving was because she didn't feel like she fitted in and was worried she'd get in the way. She'd spent too many years with her disinterested, career-focused parents learning how not to put down roots, moving on the minute she began to settle and make friends. Meaning when it came to wanting to stay anywhere she was clueless. 'Tell me about Jesse.' Madison changed the subject and sat back as Finn presented them with two huge glasses filled with pink liquid, topped off with quartered limes, straws and pink flamingo cocktail stirrers. A couple of people walked in the front door and he headed back to the bar.

'Perfect.' Amy pulled her drink closer and took a long sip through her straw. 'Okay, you asked for it. You know we were together for over five years, moved in together. I love Jesse, but he's always spent more time on his sports than me. I guess I thought that would change and over time he'd grow up a little. But six months ago Jesse inherited his grandfather's car. It's gorgeous – an old Morgan. But… he changed when he got it. It's almost like he fell out of love with me and in love with the car. He's obsessed. It was our anniversary a couple of months ago and I saw an envelope from a travel agent. I thought he was taking me away, maybe to propose. Turns out he was going to a classic car event in Scotland. He completely forgot our anniversary, and disappeared for the whole weekend.' Amy shook her head, looking sad. 'You know my mum went through similar, except with Dad it was other women. I want a man who'll put me first, who sees me and wants me without being distracted by four wheels and excellent bodywork.'

Madison pondered the information for a few seconds. 'What did Jesse say?'

Amy shrugged. 'He wants to get back together. He's no idea what he's done wrong. He thinks it's about missing our anniversary but it's not. I deserve more, Mads. I want someone who adores me more than sport or a bloody car. Who can't wait to see me at the end of the day. Jesse spends most of his free time under a bonnet – I just need more.' A tear slid down Amy's cheek and she swiped at it with the back of her hand before taking another gulp of her cocktail and finishing it. 'Sorry, I needed that. It's been a long day. I feel like things are falling apart around me and I hate not having control over it.'

'Have you told Jesse how you feel?' Madison rested a hand on Amy's.

'No.' Amy's amber eyes filled with tears. 'In some ways this has been going on for years, Mads. The car's just replaced the sport. I think if he really loved me he'd figure it out.'

'What are you going to do?'

'Finn's asked me out a few times.' Amy smiled sadly as the man in question blew her a kiss from the bar. 'I'm really not sure, but it could help take my mind off things – getting back out there again just to feel wanted. We've known each other for years, so neither of us would take it seriously. Besides, it's Finn – and maybe a fling is just what I need?'

'You don't sound that sure.' Madison took another sip of her cocktail. She knew all about not taking relationships seriously and it was a lot more complicated than it sounded.

'I've been with Jesse for a while. It's not going to be easy moving on. But I don't want to spend the rest of my life alone.' The bar door slammed and Amy made a distressed sound. Madison looked around. Jesse was standing at the pub entrance, staring at them.

'He's not meant to come in here on a Tuesday. That's my night. We agreed,' Amy squeaked. 'Typical. Ignoring my needs and doing exactly what he wants regardless.'

'I'll talk to him.' Madison pushed her chair back.

Jesse was still standing by the doorway staring at Amy when Madison approached. He dragged his eyes away to greet her, but his handsome face barely stretched into a smile. Jesse was tall with dark brown hair that ended at his chin. On some, the style would be effeminate, but Jesse had always managed to pull it off. He studied Madison, looking miserable. He'd lost weight and his usually bright brown eyes looked dull.

'It's good to see you again, Madison,' Jesse said without smiling. 'It's been a while. I'm guessing Amy's filled you in.' He jerked his head in the direction of their table.

'Pretty much.' Madison gave him a quick hug. 'I'm sorry to hear it. I thought you two were made for each other.'

'I still do.' Jesse blew out a long breath. 'I don't understand what I've done and Amy won't explain. She says if I can figure out how to fix a car, I should be able to figure her out. But I can't.'

'Want to talk about it?'

Jesse shook his head. 'Not unless you can explain it. Why's Amy here anyway? She made these stupid rules about us not being able to go to the same places. Tuesday's supposed to be my night.'

'She says it's hers.'

'*Ahhhh.*' Jesse looked even more miserable. 'Perhaps she's right. I can barely remember anything anymore.'

'Are you keeping yourself busy?'

'I'm working with Connor in the cafe and a few other jobs. I try not to come into The Hideaway – I'm hoping some distance will help us both. Perhaps while you're back you could visit? I'd love to catch up.'

'I'll bring you both a sandwich. I'm under orders from Dee to keep Connor fed. I checked on the cafe earlier. The place is looking good.'

'It was my day off. Perhaps I'll see you tomorrow.' Jesse frowned at the bar. 'I'll buy some beer and crisps and head home. I'm staying with Connor,' he added. 'Amy wanted me to move out.' He swallowed before giving Madison a goodbye hug. 'I won't keep you. I don't want you to get in trouble for talking to the enemy. Especially if I'm not sup-posed to be here.' He headed for the bar as Madison returned to Amy.

'Jesse's not staying,' Madison explained as Amy began to rise. 'He thought Tuesday was his night. He's buying some drinks to take away.'

'Good.' Amy's mouth set in a mulish line as she watched Jesse.

'He's unhappy,' Madison said quietly.

'Aren't we all. Besides, it's all of his own making,' Amy snapped. 'I'm sorry. I'm bored of hearing about my sorry excuse for a life. Distract me with your adventures. Have you got a boyfriend?'

'I travelled with someone in Thailand, but it was never serious. And there's a man I see off and on.'

'What's he called?' Amy sat straighter, looking interested.

'Seth. It's not what you think. Our relationship is more of an open thing. I know he sees other people…' Madison paused at Amy's shocked expression. 'Me too, and don't look at me like that. It suits us both.'

'Maybe I should take a leaf out of your book. It sounds so much simpler than falling in love. Tell me about him.'

'Seth works for Greenpeace and travels all over the world,' Madison explained. 'Sometimes we meet up. I saw him at Christmas – he popped over to Thailand.' They'd had fun, but Seth had to leave after a couple of days and for the first time, Madison had begun to feel a sense of emptiness before he'd left. Not because she'd miss him, but because being around him made her feel lonely. Which was odd.

'Perhaps I should try the same with Finn.' Amy sighed. 'I was looking for love and commitment for so long, it might be better to just have fun.'

Madison didn't get a chance to tell Amy not to follow in her footsteps, because her friend stood suddenly and waved at someone. 'Stanley Banks!'

'Amy, darling.' A man in his mid- to late fifties, with peppered grey hair and a well-groomed beard, walked towards them. He wore dark chinos and a chunky cable-knit sweater that, despite his leanness, made him look cuddly. 'I didn't realise you weren't working this evening. I wanted Dee to accompany me for a drink, but she turned me down. I've been trying to get her apple pie recipe for months – I thought a couple of wines might loosen her tongue,' he confessed. 'And who are you?'

'This is Madison. Jack and Sandy's niece,' Amy replied. 'She's been away and we're just catching up on news. Mads, this is Stanley. He's been staying at The Hideaway for the last three months. Why don't you join us?'

'I'd love to. I might pass on the cocktail and have a beer. Would you like a refill?'

'Definitely,' Amy answered for both of them, and Stanley headed back to the bar.

'I hope you don't mind?' Amy asked Madison. 'Stanley's wife died a couple of years ago and his daughter moved to Australia in October. After that he said life got lonely at home. He rented out his house in Dorset and moved in with us. He goes out walking and paints incredible pictures, and I think he's got a secret crush on Dee.' Amy winked. 'Not that she'll acknowledge it. Mind you, I think she likes him too.'

After a few minutes Stanley returned with a pint of beer. 'Finn's going to bring you both a refill.' He pulled up a chair. 'Madison, your aunt mentioned you're a yoga teacher?'

'I was,' Madison replied, feeling embarrassed. 'I've been a lot of things.'

'Madison wanted to be a lawyer,' Amy added. 'But it didn't work out.'

'I didn't like the course,' Madison lied.

Stanley sipped his beer. 'I had my own business for years, consulting. You wouldn't believe how many people I met who told me they wished they were doing something else. It's hard to find your place in life sometimes.'

'Have you found yours?' Madison asked quietly.

'I've had a very happy life.' Stanley looked thoughtful. 'But to quote that famous song, I'd say my home was wherever my wife laid her hat. I was adrift for a while after she died, but I love The Sunshine Hideaway – we used to holiday here together. It's peaceful and beautiful and I'm enjoying my painting.' He leaned forwards. 'It would be nice to have a few more guests to chat with though. Dee mentioned last week you had new people arriving today. Are they coming later?'

Amy blushed. 'They cancelled. We've had a lot of people doing that lately.'

'Any idea why?' Stanley looked serious.

'We're just a guesthouse with lovely food, welcoming staff and amazing views. That used to be enough – but now people want swimming pools and massages, gyms and non-stop activities,' Amy grumbled.

'And The Hideaway can't provide that?' Stanley asked.

'We're revamping the cafe which should encourage more visitors, but I've no idea if a new paint job will be enough.' Amy's forehead crinkled as she stared at her drink. 'We'll need to do something soon, or I'm worried The Hideaway won't survive. And I shouldn't have told you that. Too many of these loosen my tongue.' Amy pointed to her cocktail just as Finn took the empty glass and handed her a full one.

'Don't worry, dear.' Stanley patted Amy's hand. 'I've suspected as much. It's been dinner for one for a couple of weeks now and I've been wondering how the place manages.' He sighed. 'I consulted with a lot of companies before I retired, some of them hotels. I'll do a bit of research and see if I can come up with a few ideas. It would be a shame to see the place close. You understand that might mean changes, don't you?'

'It's okay, I'm resigned to the fact that I might need to move on. I just want to see The Hideaway survive.' Amy lifted her glass and tapped it against Stanley's, and Madison did the same.

'The Hideaway wouldn't be the same without you, Amy. I'm sure we can all think of something… Perhaps in return you could persuade Dee to agree to have a drink with me?' Stanley teased. 'The woman's stubborn, but I'm hoping to wear her down.'

'It's a deal.' Amy laughed.

Madison sat back and watched as they chatted, her feelings mixed. Perhaps with Stanley on board, The Hideaway would survive, but it didn't look as if her dream of a new beginning here would become a reality after all. She'd spent too much of her childhood feeling in the way, surplus to requirements. She wasn't about to let it happen again.

Chapter Six

Connor paced his kitchen holding the mobile phone to his ear, wondering if this time his sister might answer. He let it ring a couple of times, expecting it to cut to answerphone, but instead she picked up. 'Georgie,' he grumbled. 'Where the hell have you been? I've been trying to get in touch.'

'Here… I mean, working.' His sister sounded groggy, as if she'd been sleeping. Connor checked the clock. Okay, so it was after eleven thirty at night. He'd been working on the cafe and hadn't realised the time.

'Sorry it's late,' Connor mumbled, feeling guilty, but not bad enough to hang up. Georgie had been avoiding his calls, not ringing back, and now he finally had her on the line they were going to talk. 'How's the studying?' Georgie's second-year exams were fast approaching but Connor knew his sister sometimes lacked focus. Although if she'd been working until late she might finally be taking the whole thing seriously?

'Connor…'

'What? Have you run out of money again?' Connor grimaced. Keeping track of finances wasn't one of Georgie's gifts either, and he didn't have a lot of spare cash to send. Still, if she needed money he'd find it. *Somehow.*

Connor rolled his shoulders, trying to ease some of the tension that never seemed to leave, then leaned on the oak counter just in front of the kitchen window and looked outside. A thousand stars twinkled in the black sky and a full moon threw strands of white light, illuminating the fields and trees beyond. The effect was almost magical. Had he missed the whole thing on his journey home from the cafe tonight – too distracted calculating how much varnish he was going to need for the wooden counter? Was he in danger of turning into his father? A man who'd built a house ensuring the windows were carefully positioned for the best views – with sunsets in the kitchen and sunrises in the sitting room – but who'd never taken the time to sit back and watch even one?

Connor moved away from the view and grabbed himself a beer from the fridge, before putting it back in favour of water. He hadn't eaten since Madison's sandwich and banana and couldn't be bothered now. Alcohol on an empty stomach wasn't a good idea, especially as he planned to go into town to pick up supplies early tomorrow.

'I… Connor, look, I need to talk to you about something.' Georgie yawned. 'I'm sorry, I was asleep – can we do this tomorrow?'

'I'd rather do it now,' Connor answered, feeling irritated, which was never a good thing. Getting annoyed with Georgie generally resulted in her becoming upset, which meant he wouldn't hear from her again for weeks. 'Please,' he added, because for some reason he had a need for connection and she was the only other person awake.

'I… Connor, I've been talking to Mum.'

Dammit. Connor clenched his fists. Georgie had been raised by her mother, Jo Grayson, in her hometown near Norwich. At the age of twelve, Georgie had found out about their dad and had insisted Jo help her find him. She was his half-sister, the result of a dalliance Charles Robertson had enjoyed years after Connor's mother had died. In truth, Connor could hardly imagine it. His dad had barely managed to crack a smile in his life – how he'd attracted a beautiful woman to his bed was a mystery. Mind you, Charles hadn't managed to keep Jo for long – she'd fallen pregnant and then disappeared without telling him.

'What did your mum say?' Connor asked, already knowing he wouldn't like it. His sister was an interesting combination of her father and mother. Yin and yang personified. Where Jo was all light, Charles had been shadows, and Georgie spent much of her life fighting an internal battle with both of them.

'She's not sure this course is right for me…' Before Connor could respond she added, 'I'm not sure either, Con. I thought I'd come to see you, so we could talk. I love the idea of working together, but I'm only twenty and there are so many other places and things I'd like to try first.'

'But you're almost halfway through it,' Connor said, feeling exasperated. 'Can't we talk when it's done?'

'There's so much work – and I was thinking I could defer,' Georgie whined. 'Take a trip, see the world, decide what I really want to do.'

Connor closed his eyes, fighting his impatience. He'd already spent six grand on Georgie's fees, not to mention living expenses. Wasn't it just a little late to be having this conversation? 'Last time we talked, you couldn't wait to come and live on Sunflower Island. I thought the idea of working here in the business with me was something you wanted. As a legacy to Dad?' he added, even though he knew it was beneath him.

'I do… did. Hell, I don't know, Con. It feels more like your dream than mine. I'm just not sure anymore. I've seen how hard you work. I'm not sure that's the future I want. And I've met someone and he wants to take me travelling, but he's leaving soon and well, you're only young once…'

Were you? If so, Connor damn well couldn't remember it.

'I know you're determined to prove Dad wrong. What he said in the will was… well, so very him. But we both know you're more than capable of making a success of the business, despite what he predicted. And it's not your fault the company is in debt. That's down to Dad and his ability to piss everyone off, so in the end no one wanted to hire him. You're so capable, you work so hard, and you will make this work – you really don't need me. I'm not sure you need anyone.'

Didn't he? Connor got the beer back out of the fridge and opened it before taking a long sip, examining the food options. Jesse had obviously been to the pub, because there was a whole shelf of beer. Aside from that he found three slices of dried-out pepperoni pizza he'd picked up in town a few days before, a jar of extra-strong pickled onions and two packets of salt and vinegar crisps. Connor grabbed the pizza and took a bite, wincing at the dry texture. Still, it was better than lunch – even if he did have to put up with the barest layer of cheese.

'I thought I could come for a weekend. Stay for a few days. It's been yonks since I've seen you and we could talk properly. You know you didn't have any time when I popped over at Christmas.'

'Sorry,' Connor muttered through a mouthful of pizza. He'd meant to take some time off, but he'd been working on one of the guest rooms over at Lake Lodge and the manager had said it was urgent. And it wasn't like he could afford to turn work down, not if he wanted the business to stay afloat. 'The week after next is great. But don't drop out of the course in the meantime, Georgie. Give yourself time to make a decision, give me time to understand it.' *Or to talk you out of it.* 'You owe me that.' Making his sister feel guilty wasn't the way to win her over, but he was desperate.

Connor had been relying on Georgie working with him in a couple of years to ease some of the pressure on finances – because she'd be cheaper than hiring contractors – and to maybe allow him to take on more jobs. If she decided to drop out… well, he had Jesse, but the two of them weren't enough. Not if he was going to prove anything to his father. Not if he was going to pay off the company's debts and stop the business from sinking into bankruptcy.

'Okay, sure.' Georgie sounded tired. 'I really need to sleep, Con. I'll book my ferry in a few weeks and let you know which one I'm on. Sleep tight and don't work too hard, big brother. I miss you.'

'Miss you too,' Connor ground out after a couple of seconds' silence. He wasn't used to Georgie's easy affection. Even though she'd been in his life for eight years, he still found it difficult to be comfortable with her. Too many years of living with his father, he supposed, of being pushed aside and criticised. It wasn't easy to change – his father certainly never had. Connor put down the mobile and pulled out one of the chairs around the kitchen table, finishing his beer and putting that down too. He had at least an hour of paperwork to do before he headed for bed. Maybe he'd finish the pizza?

He wandered into the hallway and then down to the huge sitting room at the end of the house. The room had a long window across the back wall that looked out over the sea – the house was at the top of a steep cliff so you could see for miles. The fire had been lit but the embers had burned to a dark orange. On the sofa Jesse snored, and in front of the fire Jaws did the same – until his ears pricked and the dog hopped up to greet Connor briefly, before sloping off to the warmth again. Connor studied the row of empty beer bottles on his coffee table and shook his head. The boy would have a headache in the morning. No doubt a surly temper too. Still, as long as he turned up at work there wasn't much Connor could do. He had enough of his own problems to worry about.

Chapter Seven

Madison sat on her bed and sipped some camomile tea to help wear off the effects of four Pink Flamingos and a conversation that had left her feeling both lonely and left out. Stanley hadn't stayed long after their last drink, but for a few minutes he'd chatted with Amy about staffing and overheads, reminding Madison there was little to spare from the kitty for uninvited guests. Not that anyone would actually come out and say it.

Madison stroked the white lace duvet cover that had been her favourite as a child. Her Aunt Sandy had redecorated the bedroom when she'd come to stay after her parents had died. It had taken Madison months to settle, and she'd never shaken the feeling that she'd been thrust upon her aunt and uncle – regardless of the fact that they'd always made her feel so welcome.

Despite that, even now, Madison remembered seeing her bedroom for the first time, having her own space. A place she could come back to again and again. It had felt both overwhelming and strangely right – she'd never forgotten it. After all these years, when Madison visited The Hideaway, she'd lie on her bed for as long as possible with her eyes closed, smelling the familiar fabric conditioner, stretching out on the comfy mattress she knew so well.

Madison eased open the top drawer of her bedside cabinet and pulled out an envelope before sliding out a wad of money. Insurance, she called it – enough for a flight anywhere in the world, so she always had the option of leaving. An escape if things got too much, or she'd outstayed her welcome. Madison's phone pinged suddenly, making her jump.

Had so much fun tonight. Fab to have you home. A xxx
Me too. M xxx

Madison tapped the reply before opening up her wardrobe, where the few pieces of clothing she'd brought with her hung. She took a nightshirt off its hanger and a red cardigan tumbled onto the floor of the wardrobe, landing on a purple photo album decorated with hearts.

Madison picked it up and sat on her bed. Her aunt had given her the album a few months after she'd first moved in. It was filled with pictures of her parents. Aunt Sandy had probably meant for it to comfort Madison as she grieved – instead it had made her realise how little she'd really known them. She opened the album to the first page: a black-and-white photograph of her as a baby. She lay in a cot, dressed in a spotty Babygro while her parents gazed down at her. Madison looked closer, as she had a million times, searching their faces for some clue of emotion – and as she had a million times before, found nothing.

Madison flicked to another page, then another. The photographs were all formal, usually of her and her parents at embassy parties, unsmiling and smartly dressed. She turned the page over and let it rest as her heart thumped. In this photo, Madison wore a yellow and brown uniform. Her hair was brushed severely from her face and she was frowning. It had been taken when she was seven, on her first day at boarding school.

Madison still remembered that day like it was yesterday. She'd been living in New York with her parents, looking forward to her best friend Katy Brown's birthday party, which they'd been planning for months. Madison had chosen her outfit – a green sequinned dress and patent shoes. But a day before the party, she'd arrived home from school to find her bags packed. Five hours later, she'd been on a plane with her mother, heading to a boarding school she'd never heard of.

At the time Madison had believed she was being punished for accidently breaking her mother's favourite vase that morning. Until she learned her parents had known she was leaving for weeks – they just hadn't told her. She could still remember crying at the airport. 'Don't be silly,' her mother had snapped, without looking up from her magazine. 'You should be grateful we've found somewhere so nice for you to live. It's an excellent school.'

'D-don't make me go,' Madison had begged. Tears had run down her cheeks onto her dress, but her mother hadn't wiped them away.

'You have to go to school, Madison,' her mother had said patiently. 'Embassy life is no place for a child. We really don't have the time to deal with all the things you need. You'll fit better into our world when you're older.'

Which, roughly translated, meant she was an inconvenience, in the way.

Madison hadn't asked if she could stay after that. Instead she'd lived at the school until she turned thirteen, when her parents had decided she was old enough to join them – and her life of travelling and parties had resumed.

Madison stood and put down the album, shaking away her feelings, before heading quietly down the stairs remembering how it had felt when her aunt and uncle were home. She wished they were now. Wished she could speak to them – but according to Dee they hadn't taken their phones on holiday because they wanted a complete break. Besides, it wouldn't be fair. Not now she was leaving.

The Hideaway was so still tonight. She tiptoed through the dining room and into the kitchen, pausing at the doorway to take in the shiny surfaces and smell of chocolate permeating the air. It all felt so familiar, and yet so out of her reach. If The Hideaway had been heaving with guests, she knew she would have tried to stay, carved out a place for herself within the guesthouse and finally put down roots. But things were quiet and there was no Madison-shaped hole waiting to be filled. Her aunt and uncle were good people, and nothing like Madison's parents: they were far too kind to tell her she needed to move on. Which meant she'd have to do it herself.

Madison's mobile pinged again with an emoji heart from Amy, and she smiled sadly before scrolling through her emails. There was one from a travel company telling her about cheap flights to Mozambique. Another from Seth asking if she had time to visit him in Amsterdam when the Greenpeace boat docked.

There were a thousand places she could go if she wanted. Madison looked around the kitchen sadly. And a thousand more even if she didn't. Whatever happened, she wasn't going to stay and become a burden. Tomorrow she'd head into town to take one last look around before researching times for the ferry.

Chapter Eight

Connor's head hurt. God knows why – he'd only had one beer but he hadn't made it to bed until after one, because the paperwork had got the better of him. Then he'd been up at five thirty for his daily run with Jaws: a habit so ingrained into him by his father that he simply couldn't shake it.

Connor pulled his truck into a large parking space on the High Street, a few shops along from The Red Velvet Bakery, which opened early and did the best meat pies in the world. One of those with a strong cup of tea, and another for lunch later, would soon put the world to rights. Then he could head for the builder's yard to pick up the supplies before joining Jesse at The Hideaway – hopefully the boy had made it off the sofa by now and into work with Jaws. He already knew it was going to be a very long day if they meant to get back on schedule.

Connor had barely made it out of his truck and onto the pavement before he spotted Madison staring into the colourful window of Merlin's Travel Agents. The High Street looked empty and Connor took a second to check her out. She was dressed in jeans and a light green coat he didn't recognise. Her long brown hair was piled up on the top of her head and she looked an endearing combination of unsure and unhappy, which made his heart hammer unhelpfully.

'Planning your escape already?' Connor grumbled, coming up behind her and catching a whiff of lemongrass from her hair. He was probably being unfair but the conversation with Georgie last night had put him in a bad mood. 'I thought you'd stay at least a week this time.'

'Oh, it's you.' Madison stumbled backwards as she turned, her face going crimson. 'I… I was just thinking…' She waved a piece of paper in front of her face and Connor's heart sank as he recognised it.

'Ferry times? I thought you'd have them memorised by now.' He felt angry. Stupid really. He'd known she was bound to leave eventually – he just wasn't expecting it to happen so soon. And it rankled. The Hideaway was in trouble, Madison seemed keen to help out, but the next day she was looking for routes off the island. In some ways she reminded him of Georgie, which after their recent chat really didn't help.

'I… I don't know, this one's out of date and I checked online, but the information's unclear. I wanted to talk to someone.' She looked uncomfortable, her eyes darting up the High Street, across the rows of shops spanning each side.

'It's nothing to do with me.' Connor held up his hands. Maybe he'd have two pies for breakfast to make up for his crappy mood. 'But what happened to new beginnings, making a fresh start? Or have you decided to just skip this one and head for the next?'

'I'm just in the way.' Madison shook her head. 'You don't know how that feels.'

Didn't he? 'I've a fair idea,' Connor muttered, thinking about how it had been living with his father. 'And how are you in the way? Dee was delighted to see you, so was Amy – and your aunt and uncle feel the same way. Everyone's busy – it's not like they've had time to throw you a party, but that doesn't mean they don't care.' His voice was probably sharper than he'd intended, but what did she expect?

'I don't need a party, Connor,' Madison snapped before blushing. 'I'm sorry, I didn't sleep very well and you've caught me in a bad mood. The four Pink Flamingos I drank last night were probably a bad idea. But before you judge me you need to understand I want to stay. I just... can't.'

'Why not? You've a roof over your head, and people who want you around, which is a lot more than most. What's complicated about that?'

'You make it sound so easy.' Madison sighed, running a tanned hand across her forehead.

'Probably because it is. Look.' Connor closed his eyes briefly before opening them again. 'It's none of my business. I need breakfast, and some of us have work to do.' He waved a finger at the timetable in her hand. 'Good luck with the trip to wherever you're going and have a nice life.' With that he turned and marched down the High Street, passing the post office, Happy Paws Pet Shop, Sunflower Supermarket and the Little Card Shop before he heard Madison shout.

'Wait!'

Connor heard Madison behind him and stopped when he reached the glass entrance of The Red Velvet Bakery, turning just as she reached him.

'You're being unfair,' she said, frowning at him. 'Jumping to conclusions. You've made a decision about me – the wrong one. You've no idea what I'm like.'

Connor just stopped himself from snapping back at her. 'I'm sorry, you're right,' he admitted instead, running a hand through his hair, watching Madison's eyes flicker as they followed his reflex reaction. 'I didn't sleep well either and I haven't eaten. I apologise.' The words came out hollow, but in truth he was disappointed. In himself, in Madison. God knows why: she wasn't his business. But somehow, between yesterday and today he'd realised he liked her being around. She brought light and laughter, not to mention a large dollop of irritation, into what had begun to feel like a very boring life. Maybe he understood Dee's words more than he thought?

'And I accept. In truth, I'm hungry too. So maybe we should both eat before talking again?' Madison suggested, still looking unhappy.

Connor nodded and opened the door to the bakery, inhaling the mouth-watering fragrances of sugary treats and savoury pies. Madison walked in, bumping straight into a young woman with short brown hair that Connor recognised as the owner of Magic Charm Jewellers. 'Claire Spring, how's the shop?' Madison asked, hugging her while somehow avoiding the cup of coffee Claire had in her hand.

'Great thanks, Madison. I didn't know you were home?' Claire said warmly. 'We must get together, I've barely seen you since school.'

'You remember Connor?' Madison stepped back to draw him into the conversation.

'Of course.' Claire nodded. 'How serendipitous. I need some painting done in the shop and I've been looking for someone. I have to admit, I hadn't thought of you. Do you have a card?'

'Sure.' Surprised, Connor pulled one from his pocket.

'I'll give you a call about the work – and let's get a date in, Madison,' Claire said before heading out of the door.

'If you frowned less, you'd probably find that happened more,' Madison said to Connor, walking across the shiny tiled floor towards the glass counter where all kinds of pastries were displayed. The smells were incredible and Connor's stomach grumbled as he scanned the meat pies and sausage rolls, huge slices of pizza as well as doughnuts, croissants and large cream cakes.

'Do you have any salads, please?' Madison asked the woman in the white hat and apron with a pair of silver tongs ready to serve. Connor recognised the woman – he came here most days – but despite that he couldn't remember her name. She'd told him once in a flirtatious tone, but he'd been in a hurry and hadn't wanted to prolong the conversation.

'We have carrot cake.' The woman flashed a slight smile.

'It looks lovely too.' Madison grinned back, her face transforming. 'I'm Madison Skylar, I don't think we've met. Do you make all this food yourself? It looks fantastic.' Madison offered a hand over the counter and to Connor's surprise the woman took it.

'I'm Gillian Rogers, I moved to the island a year ago. Not all of the food, but a fair amount. We do sandwiches at lunchtimes, but we've never had salad on the menu. There's just not much call for it here.'

'Fair enough. Salad's probably not the best thing to have for breakfast anyway.' Madison chuckled to herself and Gillian grinned. Madison was doing it again, Connor thought, working her magic like she always did. Getting people to like her with just a few words. How did she do it? It was a gift he honestly hadn't managed to understand, let alone cultivate. Not that he'd spent much time trying. 'Have you got anything vegetarian?' Madison asked, biting her top lip as she looked at the display. Connor's stomach grumbled again and he hoped she'd get on with it, but in the interests of a peaceful relationship decided not to complain.

'A cheese pasty, unless you fancy something sweet?' Gillian replied. 'My sister's a veggie and I promise those pasties are completely meat-free.'

'Sounds perfect,' Madison said. 'Do you happen to have any bananas or camomile tea?'

Gillian smiled again. She had piercing blue eyes and was quite pretty when you looked closely. Connor just hadn't noticed before. 'I've some fruit out back and camomile teabags. We don't sell them, but I drink it in the afternoons. I'll get you a cup and sort out that pasty and banana.' Gillian's eyes darted to Connor. 'Do you want your usual nuked heart attack complete with builder's tea?'

'Um… yes,' Connor replied, taken aback by her teasing tone.

'He means please,' Madison added with a swift smile. 'He always does, it's just with Connor the manners are silent.'

'I'll find us a seat.' Connor shook his head and went to sit at one of the white wooden tables at the window. He looked out onto the High Street. It was still early but a few people had begun to mill about. On the other side of the road, the postman collected mail from a gleaming red postbox and a woman he vaguely recognised cleaned the windows outside the laundrette. Connor massaged his fingers over his temples as Madison took the seat opposite.

'Headache?' she asked.

'I'll be fine after eating.'

'If we get a quiet moment sometime we could do some yoga. There's nothing like a bit of stretching to take the tension out of your body. The dragon pose would suit you.' Gillian brought their food and drinks and placed them on the table before disappearing to serve another customer. Connor sipped his tea, wondering if Madison was joking.

'I thought you were leaving?'

'Oh.' Madison looked surprised and then unhappy. 'I'd forgotten.' She put the timetable underneath her plate. 'So, no dragon pose for you – you should be grateful.' She picked up the knife and fork Gillian had brought and cut a slice of the pasty before taking a bite. 'That's amazing.' Madison closed her eyes as she chewed. She seemed so entranced by the flavours Connor couldn't help but watch before looking down at his meat pie – he'd already eaten half of it and had barely noticed.

'So tell me again why you're leaving?' Connor took another bite of his pasty and this time he took a moment to savour it. It tasted salty, beefy and very, very good.

Madison's forehead creased. 'I went out with Amy last night and she was talking about The Hideaway. It's not doing so well. You must know that?'

Feeling guilty, Connor jerked his head and took another bite of pie so he didn't have to answer.

'She's worried about her job and now I'm worried too. I didn't come home to be a burden. I was expecting to work – but without any guests there's not much I can do.' Madison shrugged before eating another small forkful. 'And no one is going to tell me I'm in the way, they're too afraid of hurting my feelings…' She paused. 'Aside from you. But if I can't help out, then I'm just another mouth to feed and it won't be long before Amy and Dee, or my aunt and uncle, start to resent it. And I couldn't bear that, not here.' She stopped talking and stared at her plate for a few moments.

'So it's work at The Hideaway, or leave – you can't think of any alternatives?' Connor asked, incredulous.

'I can go on another trip. There's a mindfulness course in India I've thought about, or I have a… friend in Amsterdam who'd like to catch up, so there are other options.'

'When I said alternatives, I wasn't suggesting leaving. I mean, what about finding another job on Sunflower Island?'

Madison looked taken aback. 'With you? I thought you didn't need any help with choosing the paint yet?'

'No.' *God, no.* He didn't want Madison around him all the time, messing with his feelings, distracting him. Connor looked at the uneaten banana on his plate. *Definitely not.* 'Not with me. I'm not looking for more staff, but I've heard on the grapevine – actually Jesse heard – Lake Lodge is hiring. Perhaps you could do something there?' When Madison frowned he added, 'Depends on how much you want to stay.'

'A lot. But won't that be a bit like consorting with the enemy?'

'It's a job, Madison,' Connor said firmly. 'Besides, you could think of yourself as a spy. Steal all their secrets, and implement them at The Hideaway.'

'Oh, I like that.' Madison's face brightened and Connor instantly regretted the joke. He didn't want her thinking she could save the place. Her aunt and uncle were already talking to people about selling – with Sandy's health problems and dropping guest numbers they didn't have the money or energy to do anything else.

'You could go now? Lake Lodge is near the builder's yard, I can drop you on my way,' Connor suggested, keen for the conversation to be over. He didn't like lying – to himself or anyone else.

'I'm not really dressed for an interview.' Madison glanced down at her outfit. 'But I guess I could pop in and ask if they're hiring. Pick up an application form. I don't even have a CV.'

'So write one. I'm sure you can think of something to put in it…'

'Has travelled, is game for anything.' Madison gave Connor a wry smile. 'I guess. Thanks. When Dee gave me a lift into town this morning, I didn't have the heart to tell her I was planning on leaving, and now there might be a chance I can stay. Thanks to you.'

Connor avoided her eyes, unsure whether he'd just created a whole host of problems for himself. If Madison stayed, she'd find out The Hideaway was for sale and perhaps that he'd known all along. 'You've got to get a job first,' he answered gruffly, looking at his plate. 'Do I have to eat this banana?' He quickly changed the subject.

'Yes.' Madison's laughter rang through the bakery, a light tinkle that lifted the whole atmosphere. 'And someday soon, I'll get you to try the dragon pose. We're friends now, Connor Robertson. I've got an awful lot to thank you for.'

'Don't mention it,' Connor said, his feelings mixed as he eyed the banana suspiciously. Wondering what Madison would say once she discovered he'd been keeping secrets from her all along.

Chapter Nine

Connor pulled off his jacket as he arrived home from the builder's yard and dropped it over a chair in the kitchen. There was a hook in the hall, but out of some sense of rebellion, or perhaps because – even after eighteen months – he was still laying claim to this space, he couldn't bring himself to use it. Besides, while it was petty and beneath him, Connor knew the simple act would have driven his father crazy.

In the sitting room, through the hall to the left of the kitchen, Connor heard the low hum of the TV and headed for it. It was after nine in the morning, the blinds were still shut and the room smelled faintly of beer. Connor yawned and opened the shutters, letting in some of the dull light from outside. It had been an early start and a busy morning lugging the supplies he'd bought in the builder's yard to his truck, not to mention breakfast with Madison. He already needed another shower and really wasn't in the mood for this.

He headed for the oak coffee table that sat parallel to the dark leather sofa he'd shipped from his rented flat in town when he'd moved home to care for his father two years before. The table was filled with bottles of beer, all of them empty, and on the sofa a young man snored.

'Jesse.' Connor gave his new lodger-stroke-employee a gentle poke, eliciting a grunt and then a long groan. 'I'm guessing you didn't make it to bed.' He didn't wait for an answer. Instead he picked up the bottles and headed for the kitchen, tossing them into the recycling. He returned with a glass of water, wondering what the hell had got into him. He wasn't usually one for missions of mercy, and the boy deserved the stinking hangover he no doubt had.

'You're supposed to be at The Hideaway,' Connor said mildly, sinking into a leather armchair – the only other seat in the room – and rolling his shoulders, trying to ease out some of the knots. Jaws came to sit beside him, and they both stared at Jesse as he pulled himself into a sitting position and sipped from the glass of water.

Jesse's eyes were bleary and he still wore his clothes from the day before. 'I'm sorry,' he muttered, his voice hoarse. 'I had too much time to think on my day off. I saw Amy in The Moon and Mermaid last night and guess I got caught up.' Jesse frowned at the coffee table, probably looking for his empties.

Connor searched for the words Jesse probably needed to hear and failed miserably. 'I saw how many bottles you got caught up with and I've got to say, that's a lonely path. It'll be lonelier still if you don't get to work on time again because I'll sack you. You should have been at The Hideaway at 6 a.m. so you owe me three hours. More if you've not sobered up.'

'I'm sober.' Jesse blinked, looking like he was going to be sick. 'And I'm sorry. I just… needed to forget for a while. It won't happen again.'

'Sorry won't make it better,' Connor said, instantly wanting to bite the words back, because he'd heard the exact same ones from his father's mouth about a million times. He ran a hand through his hair, feeling every one of his twenty-six years. Jesse might be only three years his junior, but there could have been a couple of lifetimes between them. 'I know you miss her,' he added, because he couldn't think of anything else to say.

'I feel like I've had a limb removed. I've messed up, lost her. I can't get Amy out of my head and I don't know how to make everything better,' Jesse began, his brown eyes sad. 'It doesn't seem to matter how many times I say I'm sorry for whatever I did, she won't listen to me.'

'Have you tried flowers?' Connor suggested, glancing towards the door for a way out of this conversation, even though he knew he wouldn't leave Jesse in this state.

'Amy likes tulips.' Jesse's face dropped. 'And I tried that last week. She always filled our house with flowers. I never realised how much colour she brought into my life.' He shook his head. 'I don't care about anything when she's not with me. Even the car means nothing without her.'

Connor nodded, even though he had no idea what the hell Jesse was talking about. 'Then bury it and move on. Throw yourself into work. Stay busy, because then it's easier not to feel anything.'

Jesse frowned. 'Sounds like a miserable way to live.'

Connor rose from the chair. This was why he never gave advice. He didn't understand people, even the ones he cared about. 'Beats drinking yourself into oblivion.' Connor's dad had tried it so he had first-hand knowledge it didn't work. 'Besides, work hard enough and for long enough and you'll build something worth having. Maybe that's the best way to win Amy back? Success, money – isn't that what everyone wants in the end?'

'It's not about money.' Jesse glared at the table, perhaps hoping a full bottle of beer would magically materialise. 'But you're right. This isn't the way to make myself feel better. I'll shower, get dressed and take a walk to the cellar.'

'Eat something first. I'll wait for –' Connor checked his watch – 'fifteen minutes. If you're ready by then I'll give you a lift and you'll get there quicker. Otherwise you'll be owing me even more hours.'

'I'll be quick, and thanks.' Jesse dragged himself up from the sofa before heading towards the door. 'I know you're not one for heart-to-hearts, but that helped.'

'Just don't make me do it again,' Connor muttered. It had been a long morning of advice for him and he was already exhausted. His mind wandered briefly to Madison, wondering how she'd got on at Lake Lodge, before he shook himself and nodded to Jaws. He really didn't have time to worry about other people's problems today. He needed to get his own life on track.

Chapter Ten

Lake Lodge was huge and impressive. Madison stepped onto the dark blue carpet in the entrance foyer and looked around the reception area. There was a long white counter at the front, complete with a computer and a couple of efficient-looking suited women. To either side were blue and white tables and chairs strategically placed for guests, which looked stylish and uncomfortable. Flicking her eyes forwards and running a hand over her no doubt very untidy hair, Madison marched forwards, putting on a brave face. She'd spent her life meeting new people, usually taking it all in her stride, but somehow this felt different. Perhaps because so much was riding on her getting a job?

'Good morning.' One of the women behind the counter looked up from the computer and flashed a professional smile as Madison approached. Her hair was short and brown, styled in wispy curls that framed her face. 'Are you here to check in?'

'I wish,' Madison answered, looking around. 'I love your hair,' she added.

The woman touched her fringe. 'Thank you. I had it cut yesterday… Can I help?'

Madison flashed her friendliest smile. 'I'm looking for a job – are there any going here?'

The woman smiled, still fiddling with her hair. 'There might be some vacancies in housekeeping. If you take a seat, I'll check.' She pointed to the chairs to the right of the desk as the phone rang and she picked it up.

Madison wandered towards the seating area and took the first chair she got to, facing outwards towards the entrance. She looked around. There were a few people milling around and you could tell the place was busy. Madison sighed. The Hideaway had a lot to offer, but would it be enough? Next to this gleaming and polished reception area, would everything look shabby and old? Feeling disheartened, Madison stood and wandered towards the enormous glass windows that looked out over the Lodge's car park, which was filled with about a hundred multicoloured cars. A long road, which Madison knew led to the port and the town centre, wound from the car park into a dense forest of trees. To the left, a blue lake framed with pine trees glistened in the winter sunshine, while a couple of boats bobbed on the surface. As she watched them, someone cleared their throat.

'Madison?'

She turned. Stanley Banks was sitting cross-legged at one of the tables. He wore dark glasses and a fake moustache that was darker than his hair. He glanced at the other tables to make sure no one was watching, before motioning at Madison to join him.

'Oh,' she gasped, taken aback. 'Are you thinking of leaving us?' She was dismayed – if they lost their only guest there really was no hope for The Hideaway. Even if she got a job at Lake Lodge, there would be nothing for Dee or Amy to do – which meant her home and adopted family would soon fall apart.

'Certainly not.' Stanley laughed, pointing again at the chair opposite, which Madison swiftly took. 'I'm probably here for the same reason as you. I'm scoping the place out, seeing what's on offer.' He lifted his glasses and glanced at his open laptop, which sat on the table between them. 'I've been up most of the night researching. If we want to work out what The Hideaway needs, we have to see what the *enemy* is offering.' He leaned forwards and whispered, 'The coffee's good and so are the pastries, but they're not a patch on Dee's – and I'm not just saying that. I used to travel a lot when I had my consulting business, so I'm a bit of a connoisseur.'

'Did you learn anything else?' Madison leaned in too.

'They're efficient and the place is clean. They have a decent pool, excellent gym and offer beauty treatments and massages. But these seats are bloody uncomfortable.'

Madison chuckled, shifting in hers. 'They really are.' A group of four people walked into the entrance and headed towards reception. 'That doesn't seem to be putting anyone off.'

'They do special weekend offers so I wondered about you doing the same at The Hideaway,' Stanley suggested. 'The place needs a lick of paint but your aunt and uncle are dealing with it. Young Connor is fixing up the cafe and he's already said he's going to repaint the bedrooms.' He looked thoughtful. 'We just need a hook, an angle, a reason for people to come. I've had a few ideas and you're an important part of them.'

'I am?' Madison asked, feeling excited. She wasn't used to being central to anyone's plans.

Stanley nodded. 'Yoga. You teach?'

'Yes.'

'And you're qualified?'

'And insured – I keep it up to date, just in case. It's a good way to earn extra cash if I need it.'

Stanley tapped something into his laptop and twisted it around. 'It's the latest thing. Yoga and walking retreats. A yoga lesson in the morning, a walk in the afternoon. We could get the cafe open as well, to pull in daytime visitors – do a Grand Opening to attract lots of local PR. With Dee's incredible food and the Skylars' hospitality, we could be onto a winner.'

'I love the idea of a Grand Opening for the cafe. That could work. Let's have a chat with Amy and Dee later and start planning. As for the yoga…' Madison looked at Stanley's laptop screen and scrolled through some of the pictures. There were immaculate studios and professional-looking teachers. Could they compete? 'Where would I run the lessons? There's not an obvious space.'

'I've an idea about that. Your aunt has an office she rarely uses, beyond the house. It's got beautiful views over the fields. I know because I've walked around it a couple of times. It's almost empty. We could move the furniture and paperwork out. Maybe get Connor to help with some decorating. The floor is carpeted and the place looks clean. You'd just need some yoga mats and I guess that would be that – unless there's other equipment you think is important?' Stanley asked.

'No.' Madison shook her head, considering. 'I can pick up the mats – I'm guessing we won't need loads. We could fit probably six there for a class – and if we got too busy I could run two sessions. What about the walks?'

Stanley chuckled. 'You've got legs and I'm guessing you knew your way around the place when you lived here?'

'I can follow a map on my phone.' If it meant Madison could help save The Hideaway and stay, she'd be up for anything. 'But how will we get the guests in? I don't think there's money for advertising. I've got a little saved, but I'll need some for the mats, and paying my way.'

'I can make a leaflet on this.' Stanley tapped a finger on his laptop. 'And Amy has a printer. We can give a few to the tourist information office in town. I'll update the website, maybe mail existing customers if we have their permission. It won't cost much – I'm happy to give my time for free. I'm guessing you know a few people on Sunflower Island you could mention it to?'

Madison nodded. She was good at making friends. An afternoon walking the streets, handing out leaflets, would probably drum up some business.

Suddenly someone touched her on the shoulder, and Madison turned as the receptionist waved a piece of paper in front of her nose. 'Thank you for waiting. We have vacancies in housekeeping. Here's an application form. You can fill it in now, or bring it back later. Good luck.' The woman squeezed Madison's shoulder. 'Can I get you anything else, sir?' She turned to Stanley with a warm smile.

'I'm good, thank you.' He grinned back, stroking his moustache. 'I think we're about done.'

'Thank you.' Madison took the piece of paper. She wasn't planning on using it, but it was worth keeping her options open just in case they needed to do more research. After her conversation with Connor, she was determined to stay on Sunflower Island and do everything she could to help save The Hideaway.

Chapter Eleven

Madison wandered through the small guesthouse that doubled as her aunt's office, pacing the floor. There was more furniture to lose than she'd anticipated, but they could probably find a spot in one of the upstairs rooms of the two-storey building. There was a little space in the bedroom – failing that, a few bits could be moved to the sitting room in The Hideaway.

Madison studied the large oak desk piled high with papers, the big leather chair and three tall bookshelves packed with leather-bound books. There were pictures of her, Aunt Sandy and Uncle Jack everywhere. On the bookshelves, the desk, even piled on the floor along with four of her aunt's favourite lavender hand creams. She'd checked the bathroom, which only required a quick wipe around, and the carpet needed a hoover. The big mirror almost covering the wall on the right of the room would be perfect for her classes to watch themselves in.

Then there was the window – it took up the whole back of the first floor, offering incredible views over the fields and hills, giving a glimpse of the sparkling blue sea beyond it. Madison already knew you could watch sunsets from here – she'd done it a few times with her aunt. It was one of the reasons they'd never bothered hanging curtains. Once cleared out and after a lick of paint, the room would be perfect for yoga sessions. The small kitchen opposite the bathroom could be closed off and no one would bother going upstairs. She grinned as Amy wandered in.

'Are you getting a feel for the space?' Amy asked.

'Yes.'

'I can't believe we never thought of offering yoga lessons at The Hideaway. Then again, we had no one here to teach.' Amy swung an arm around Madison's shoulder. 'And a Grand Opening for the cafe is inspired. I'm so glad you decided to come home. I'm feeling positive for the first time in yonks, and Dee's baking Stanley's favourite apple pie as a thank you – which tells me she's excited beyond words.'

'We need to get some guests before we start celebrating,' Madison cautioned, looking at the furniture again, trying to figure out what to move first. 'That desk is too heavy for us to shift ourselves.'

'We could ask Connor?' Amy suggested. 'If he brings Jesse, I'll make myself scarce. But we could clear all the papers, books and the lighter furniture ready for him. You don't think your aunt will mind?'

Madison shook her head. 'I hope not. She rarely used the office, but did yoga here quite a lot.' For a while they'd done sessions together and Sandy had given Madison an early passion for the practice.

'Not recently. Not since she got sick…'

'She was ill?' Madison asked.

Amy looked away. 'I don't know all the details, but I will say Sandy looked fine after a week's rest so you shouldn't worry. I think the main reason your aunt and uncle booked the cruise was to get away from it all. It's been stressful here.'

'I wish I could speak to them, but Dee said they didn't even take their mobiles.' Madison nibbled her lip. If her aunt was ill, why hadn't anyone told her?

'Try an email? It might get there. Just tell your aunt you're here and missing them,' Amy advised. 'Don't mention the work. That way, when they return to a guesthouse full of people, it'll be an even bigger surprise.'

Madison watched Connor inspect the empty desk with a frown. A large tool belt, filled with heavy implements, was slung across his waist and he looked dusty, tired and irritated. In contrast, Jaws ran around the large room sniffing the furniture, before coming to lie in front of Madison to beg for a tummy rub.

'You need me to what?' Connor asked, ignoring his dog and the view out of the window in favour of a chip in the paintwork to the right of the window frame. He ran his finger across it and whipped out some sandpaper from his tool belt, his muscles flexing as he worked.

'Help me move the desk out of the room. Amy and I managed to shift the chair and bookshelves, but this is too heavy. Then can you freshen the walls up with a lick of paint? I don't know what you've been hired to do, but if it doesn't include the office, I'll pay you.' Madison rubbed Jaws's stomach and bit her lip, wondering if she'd offended Connor when he turned from the sanding to narrow his eyes at her. 'I've an idea about colours. Something calming. I plan to run yoga sessions here,' she explained, feeling the bubbles of excitement that had been building since she'd had her conversation with Stanley evaporate at Connor's lack of enthusiasm.

'What happened to getting a job?' Connor's frown deepened. How did he look at that face in the mirror every day and not want to smile?

Madison shook her head. 'I've got an application form for a housekeeping position. But I bumped into Stanley at Lake Lodge and he's got some great ideas for The Hideaway. We're going to start offering yoga sessions and afternoon walks to see if we can drum up business. And Stanley thinks we'll attract even more guests if we do a big Grand Opening for the cafe.'

As Madison tried to meet Connor's eyes, he looked away. 'I can't leave the cafe at the moment but I can fit in some painting in the evenings if you're determined to do this. I don't want money – your aunt and uncle are paying me and the guesthouse was included. But I've got to say, you'd be better off getting another income. It might be foolish putting all your eggs in one basket if you really want to stay.'

'You don't think we can do it?' Madison straightened up, feeling oddly hurt. Jaws hopped up to sniff the desk again.

Connor sighed. 'I didn't say that. It's just turning a business around is hard work. It takes commitment and endurance.'

'Which you don't think I have?' Madison put her hands on her hips. 'I thought we'd moved past that poor opinion of me this morning?'

'I'm not trying to insult you.' Connor looked pained. 'I'm simply pointing out that turning a business around is a lot more work than it might seem. I've been trying for the last year and it's tough, often thankless, and doesn't leave time for much else. Besides, your aunt and uncle might have other plans for the place…'

'They've been living here for years, I know how much The Hideaway means to them.' Madison took in the lines around Connor's face for the first time, the tension in his shoulders. He looked wrung out – not that he'd admit it – which probably explained the crappy mood. 'The fact that they've hired you to do up the cafe and redecorate shows their commitment to making it work. Imagine their surprise when they come home from the cruise in six weeks to a thriving business.' She grinned, feeling it fade when Connor didn't so much as smile back at her.

'I'm imagining it.' He winced, stroking a hand over his temples.

'Headache again?' Madison's irritation was instantly forgotten as she walked towards him. 'I learned some massage techniques from a friend in Thailand. If you sit on the floor I could help?'

'Another friend?' Connor shook his head, backing away, so Madison dropped her hands to her sides. 'I've no time for a massage. I've left Jesse-of-the-sore-head varnishing the cafe counter and I don't want to leave him for long. I'm not sure if he's in more danger of falling asleep or going in search of booze.'

'Is he okay?'

Connor shrugged. 'He's breathing and working, so I'd say so. If he stops doing either, I'll let you know.'

'I'll pop by and see him later,' Madison promised, as Connor undid his tool belt and dropped it on the floor.

'So where did you want this?' Connor walked around the desk.

'You want to move it now?' Madison had been expecting Connor to complain before agreeing to do it later. 'What about your headache?'

'It'll disappear if I work through it,' he muttered, folding his arms. 'Besides, I'd rather get the desk moved now so I can focus on the painting later. Unless you're planning on changing your mind?'

Irritated, Madison huffed. 'Upstairs in the bedroom, if we can get it there. I've measured the hallway and it'll just about fit.'

Connor stared at her. 'We?'

'I'm stronger than I look.' Madison walked to the right of the desk and put her hands on either side. 'If we shift it sideways we'll be able to do it.'

Connor frowned. 'I don't need your help. I can do it alone.'

'Your mantra of choice, I'm guessing, but you don't have to.' Madison flashed him a bright smile she didn't quite feel. 'I'm trying to prove myself here, Connor, show I can stick at something regardless of how tough or –' she let her eyes flick to the desk – 'heavy it is. Don't throw the gesture back in my face without giving me a chance to try it.'

Connor's mouth set into a grim line.

'If I go first you'll take all the weight – I'll just be guiding the desk into the bedroom,' Madison pleaded. When Connor didn't say anything, she added, 'If you don't let me help, I'll ask Amy or do it myself.'

'I'm guessing you might just be stubborn enough to try it.' Connor shook his head, grasping the other side of the desk. 'Which is a side of you I hadn't expected. Fine, but if you hurt yourself you're going to find it difficult to teach the yoga you're so sure is going to turn this place around. So let me take the weight and – I know it's hard – but try to follow my instructions.' With that he picked up the desk and flipped it to the side without giving Madison the chance to assist. She lifted the bottom and tried to take some of the weight, though it was obvious Connor was carrying the brunt of it. The desk was still heavy though, and she leaned into it.

'If you walk around, you can get it through the door and into the hallway,' Connor ordered, nodding to the right as his breath shortened with the exertion. 'Take it slowly and don't let yourself trip. I'm guessing dropping the thing could make a horrible mess of your toes.'

'Let me take some of the weight, Connor,' Madison begged, watching the flush creep further up his face. 'It's too heavy for one.'

'It's fine,' Connor replied mildly. 'But it would be good if we could get it done quickly.' He eased her backwards through the door and into the hallway. The next turn was tight, but Madison got a foot on the carpeted stairs and began to back upwards.

'You're going to injure yourself,' Madison grumbled, watching the muscles underneath Connor's shirt strain against the weight. She tried to speed up and move faster, but it was difficult. The damn thing was really heavy – even if Connor was carrying most of it – and she began to regret her decision to help him alone. 'Can we put it down for a second?' she asked, ignoring Connor's frustrated expression. 'Just here on the stairs – we can take a short break, give our bodies a chance to recover.'

Connor sighed loudly and let the desk drop onto the stairs as Madison did the same. He was still holding it with the side of his body, but she could see the relief around his mouth.

'Did we bite off more than we can chew?' Madison looked down at the desk, wondering if she could possibly lift it again. 'Because it's heavier than it looks.'

'Do you always give up this easily?' Connor asked, incredulous. 'We're only a few steps from the top of the stairs, and I'm guessing the bedroom isn't far beyond it. The secret to getting things done,

Madison, is pushing forwards, heading in one direction – no distractions and no giving up. My dad didn't teach me much worth remembering, but for a life lesson, that was top of the list.'

'It's a good one,' Madison said, grateful for the small insight into the man she found so difficult to read. 'But if by pushing you mean hurting yourself, I'm not sure I'm completely on board. I get the lesson about sticking with things. I'm trying to learn that one myself, but we're not machines – sometimes our bodies and minds need time out if we don't want to break them.' Sighing, she squatted down, taking care not to push the desk with her knees, and picked it up again, groaning with the effort.

'Work can be relaxing.' Connor gritted his teeth as he took the weight into his shoulders. 'Building things, making stuff happen. There's an art to it, perhaps even a joy. I don't get that feeling from much else.'

Digesting the comment, feeling sad about it, Madison stepped backwards, stumbling a little on the top step before heading towards the small bedroom. 'Almost there,' she said, relieved – although the comment was more for herself than Connor, who now looked perfectly at ease. 'I thought we could put it next to the bed to use as a dressing table. There's enough space to walk around and I can even add a mirror.' Her mind wandered to the work she still needed to do in the yoga studio.

They were almost through the bedroom doorway when Madison felt something furry tickle her leg and jumped, startled. 'Jaws?' she yelped, losing her footing suddenly, tripping over the bundle of fur and bones that had decided to place itself directly in her path. Madison tried desperately to stay upright – she knew in her head she should let go of the desk and just fall, but instinct took over and her hands grabbed at the wood, determined to stop her inevitable crash to the ground.

'Let go,' Connor yelled as Madison began to topple backwards, her arms flailing as she did as she was told. She heard Connor grunt with the strain of holding the desk alone as her feet went out from under her. Then she was lying on the floor looking up at the ceiling, and Jaws was standing beside her licking her face.

'Are you okay?' Connor shouted, sounding worried.

'I'm fine, just… a little winded.' Madison heard Connor grunt again as the desk thumped down on the floor in front of her. He'd moved backwards, carrying the whole weight, and it was now sitting in the middle of the doorway.

'Ouch, bugger,' Connor grumbled as Madison picked herself up, stroking Jaws, who was looking at her adoringly.

'What's wrong?' Madison frowned as Connor slid to the floor with a hand at his shoulder.

'Nothing.' His voice sounded wrong.

'You've hurt yourself.' Madison bounced onto the desk and slid over it, ignoring the excited bark from Jaws as she dropped to her knees, taking in Connor's pale complexion and cursing herself for being so stupid. 'I'm sorry, it's all my fault. You should have let go – let it drop.'

'On top of you?' Connor shook his head. 'I may not be great with people, Madison, but I draw the line at crushing them. I'm fine,' he added as she began to fuss. 'It's an old injury – I did it years ago helping my father knock down a ceiling, and was back at work the next day.' He tried to roll his shoulder and his face went white. 'Dammit. I haven't got time for this.'

'Stay still.' Madison pressed a hand over Connor's, ignoring the slight shiver that shot up her arm. 'I'll get some ice packs and painkillers from Dee. Stay there, I won't be long.'

'I need to get back to work,' Connor repeated, although he didn't look in any hurry to stand. 'I feel dizzy,' he added feebly.

'I'd suggest putting your head between your knees, but I'm not sure you'd be capable of it. If I help slide you onto your back would that help?' Madison suggested.

'Hard to say.' Connor blinked, shifting himself to the side, away from the wall and the desk, letting Madison ease him to the floor.

She knelt, fighting the urge to stroke a stray curl of dark hair off his forehead, to run a finger across the five o'clock shadow on his jaw. 'I got my wish,' she joked. 'It's not the dragon pose, but you're almost in my studio.'

'It's not funny,' Connor murmured, although the edges of his mouth did twitch. 'You promised me painkillers and ice.'

Madison jumped to her feet. 'I'll bring a banana too. For the—'

'Mood enhancers? Dee mentioned something about that last time I was in the kitchen. If you think it'll help you'd better bring two.'

'Is that a joke?' Madison headed for the stairs. 'Did you bang your head?'

'Painkillers,' Connor murmured.

'I'm sorry.' Madison broke into a run as she headed for The Hideaway and Dee's well-stocked first aid kit, feeling guilty for injuring Connor, but strangely light – because now Connor was starting to open up, there was a small chance she'd be able to make him like her too.

Chapter Twelve

Connor sat on a chair in his kitchen and tried to gently rotate his shoulder, but it hurt. Not a gentle stab either, more like something out of *Psycho*. He cursed as he tried again, attempting to ignore Madison as she whizzed around making something deeply suspicious on the stove.

'It's camomile tea. I know you're not keen, but one cup won't hurt you. It's a great stress reliever and muscle relaxant. Combined with the painkillers and a few gentle exercises, I'm guessing it'll help.' She put a steaming mug of what looked like cat's pee under his nose. 'And I still don't understand why you won't see a doctor.'

'I'll be fine by tomorrow.' Connor sniffed the liquid and groaned.

'See, it's working already, you're almost back to your old self,' Madison joked, as she opened his fridge and stood staring into it. 'Do you keep your vegetables somewhere else?'

'No.' Connor rolled his eyes and tried to get up, but Madison turned and fixed him with a scary expression he hadn't seen before. There were a lot of sides to Madison Skylar he was getting to know this afternoon – not all of them pleasant.

'You promised you wouldn't move – at least for a few hours – and in return I said I wouldn't take you to the hospital.'

'I don't have time—'

'I know.' Madison held up a hand, looking both amused and exasperated. 'So I'll feed you and figure out some exercises and we'll see if this is anything more serious than a strain. But I've got to say, Connor, you don't look fit for anything, let alone varnishing – or whatever else you're meant to be doing for my uncle and aunt today.'

'Putting a new toilet in the cafe.' Connor fought the sigh. He'd lost an hour already this afternoon helping Madison move that bloody desk. Who knew how many more would be gone before he could get back to work. The woman was distracting in so many ways, but he had no idea why he couldn't pull himself away.

'So no vegetables.' Madison sighed. 'What is it you eat exactly?' She opened one of his cupboards to search and Jaws came to stand beside her, begging for a head rub which Madison delivered.

'Pizza, pies and the occasional packet of crisps.' Connor knew the stark list would drive Madison crazy and he was right. Her eyes widened and she looked so taken aback he almost laughed. If it weren't for his idiot shoulder he might have followed through.

'That's ridiculous.' Madison pulled her mobile from the back pocket of the stretchy dark blue yoga pants she'd been wearing all afternoon – they hid a lot of things, aside from the lean curviness of her figure, and Connor dragged his eyes to the window so he could distract himself. 'Dee,' Madison barked into the phone. 'I've got an emergency at Connor's…' She paused. 'No, he's not fainted, but his fridge is empty aside from a packet of crisps and about a hundred bottles of beer. There's nothing green or leafy in the whole house, except for a half-dead plant on the windowsill… Okay, thank you.' Madison smiled as she hung up. 'Dee's going to pop over some vegetables so I can make soup.' Connor grimaced. 'Indulge me and I promise I'll leave you alone just as soon as you've eaten… oh, and tried a couple of yoga poses,' she added with a mischievous smile.

'I think my shoulder's feeling better.' Connor tried to move it without wincing and failed.

Madison snorted, sipping from her own cup before nodding at his. 'You might as well drink some – I'm not going until you have. It's my fault you're injured so I'll do whatever I can to make you better.'

'Great.' Connor shook his head, picking up the large mug with his left hand before trying the liquid. It tasted exactly as he'd expected and he fought the desire to spit it out. 'Don't you have things to do? If you're determined to drum up business for The Hideaway, shouldn't you be dropping leaflets or, I don't know… planning your next trip?' Anything other than sitting here staring at him with those big eyes, making him feel things he'd never intended.

'I'm going to ignore the comment about travelling and blame your poor memory on painkillers.' Madison shrugged, smiling at him. 'Stanley's making the leaflets now and I said I'd drop them in town tomorrow. And since we're currently guestless there's not much else I can do for The Hideaway at the moment. Aside from help you out… which means you're stuck with me, at least for now.'

'Great,' Connor repeated, annoyed because, despite himself, he was enjoying Madison's attention. 'I can't sit here for long. Jesse's on his own and even if I can't put the toilet in today, I can paint.' He didn't try his shoulder again but he had a perfectly good left arm.

'Then I'll help.'

When Connor tried to reject the suggestion, Madison's mouth set into a thin line. Wow, there were a lot of hidden sides to this woman.

He was starting to realise you couldn't always judge a person by their past. Especially one you'd never taken the time to get to know.

There was a knock at the front door and Madison went to answer it, leaving Connor staring at the tea, wondering if he had time to pour it down the sink before she came back. His question was answered when Dee marched into the kitchen, carrying a shopping bag filled with all sorts of green stuff. She wore her regulation frilly white apron over a pair of dark jeans and a blue sweatshirt.

'Whatever have you done to yourself?' Dee asked Connor, dumping the bag on the counter so she could give him a hug he wasn't expecting but accepted anyway. He wasn't used to physical contact – it wasn't something his father had dished out, unless it was the punishment kind. His mother had died when he was young and he barely remembered her at all.

'Connor saved me from being crushed by my aunt's desk,' Madison answered for him, shuffling through the bag and pulling out a leek and carrots. She searched his cupboards without asking, and grabbed a large pan and a vegetable peeler he didn't even know he had. 'He's a hero actually, not that he'd admit it.'

Connor shook his head, watching the two women chat, moving around his kitchen with an ease he'd never experienced. He felt a strange mixture of baffled and relaxed. Jaws came to stand beside him, and Connor tried his shoulder once more – surely the painkillers would kick in soon? *Ouch.* Not yet.

'I don't want to panic you, Madison, but we had a call just before I left,' Dee said, taking the carrots Madison had just peeled and expertly chopping them into small chunks. 'Seems Stanley moves fast. He got the leaflets printed earlier and dropped them at the tourist information office because you were busy with the studio. We've got a booking for the day after tomorrow – a couple staying for a week who want to experience our yoga and walking retreat. Your plan seems to be working already.'

'Wow.' Madison grinned before her face dropped. 'I can't believe it's happening so quickly. We're not ready for them. The yoga mats should arrive in plenty of time – I paid for express delivery – but my aunt's study is a mess.' She frowned at Connor. 'You're in no state to paint. Should we cancel the booking?'

'And give up?' Dee asked, incredulous.

'I… well.'

Madison looked so conflicted Connor jumped in. 'There's no need to cancel anything. I can paint with my left arm.' Even if he didn't feel better later, he wasn't completely useless. Jesse could continue in the cafe and he'd be able to handle the lighter jobs. 'Besides, I'm sure I'll feel okay after some soup.'

'If you don't I can help,' Madison said, searching through the bag again. 'Have you any garlic, Dee?'

'If it's not in there, I'll have left it outside.' Dee handed Madison the car keys.

'We have to tell Sandy and Jack what Madison's planning,' Connor whispered to Dee as soon as Madison was out of earshot. 'It doesn't feel right letting her do all this work when the place is up for sale.'

'I thought the same.' Dee looked troubled. 'But Madison's happy and perhaps the new buyer will like her ideas? Besides, when Jack left he gave me strict instructions not to contact them unless it was an emergency. I know for a fact they're not checking emails. Sandy needs a complete rest – God knows the woman hasn't had one in years. I've thought about what Madison's doing and she's happy helping. We both know she'll be off on that ferry as soon as the whim takes her. Why upset her while she's here?'

'I don't like lying,' Connor explained, feeling strangely put out. Why he cared about hurting Madison he didn't know – but this whole thing didn't sit right with him.

'Neither do I,' Dee admitted. 'And I feel just as bad not telling Amy. She's fretting about not having a job soon and she's been working at The Hideaway for years. But a promise is a promise, Connor, and neither of us has the right to break it. If Jack gets in touch, I'll mention something. Otherwise let's continue as we have.'

'Mmmm,' Connor grunted, because there wasn't much else he could do. He stopped talking as Madison whizzed back into the kitchen, holding a bunch of garlic and sporting a smile that made his chest thump.

'It's so sunny today – we should take a walk later.' She grinned at Connor. 'I forgot how pretty Sunflower Island is. Honestly, there's no place on earth like it.'

'If you want that yoga studio to be ready for your new guests, you won't have time for a walk,' Connor grumbled, staring into his tea instead of giving in to the urge to watch her.

'There's always time for a walk, Connor, just ask Jaws.' Madison grinned back at him. 'And there's always time for yoga. After the soup, we'll pop into town for that paint and then I'll prove it to you.'

'Great,' Connor repeated for the third time, closing his eyes for a second and wishing his life could return to some level of normality, but knowing that, now he knew Madison so much better, it probably never would.

Chapter Thirteen

'Step away from the brush, Madison,' Connor said, his voice more frustrated than it had a right to be. Stepping forwards, he used his left arm to pick up the large yellow paint pot they'd spent half an hour arguing over, before moving it into the kitchen. Jaws bounded after him and then whizzed back to sniff the carpet. 'There's a certain order to painting,' Connor explained.

'Does any of it involve a brush?' Madison slid a hand over her face, feeling exhausted. 'Because it's almost nine o'clock and our new guests are arriving the day after tomorrow. If we're going to get this room painted –' she swept an arm around her, pointing to the four dirty grey walls of her aunt's now empty office – 'then I'm thinking we should start.'

'There's sandpaper in my truck. We'll need to rub away any marks and wash the paintwork before starting.'

'Now?' Madison asked, incredulous. 'Can't we cut a corner or two, get it done? I'm sure the paint isn't going to mind a bit of dust. Besides, you're still injured.' She glared at Connor's arm. He'd declared himself fit and well after suffering a bowl of vegetable soup. And there'd been no time for the walk either. Although he had let her drive the truck to the builder's yard, which proved he wasn't completely better. How they'd manage to prepare and paint the whole room tonight and finish off tomorrow with just the two of them was a mystery.

'We'll do it properly.' Connor frowned. 'Or not at all.'

Madison didn't say anything. Connor had been surly and disagreeable all afternoon and his bad mood showed no sign of abating. She should probably leave him to it – she was obviously in the way. They'd even argued in the builder's yard when he'd suggested grey paint and she'd insisted on yellow – she'd only won the argument because they were short on time. Her mission to make him like her was clearly doomed to fail unless she did something to change it. 'Where's the sandpaper and what do we need to wash everything?' she asked. She wasn't giving up on him yet.

'In the back of the truck. I'll get it,' Connor muttered, disappearing out of the door with his dog before Madison could offer to help. Instead of following, she paced the room, imagining it filled with yoga mats and clients. She'd missed running classes, and doing them here would be a dream come true.

The paintwork was truly awful. Madison ran a finger along one of the walls, taking in the black marks she and Amy had scratched into the plaster while moving the bookshelves earlier. Beside the window frame – which also needed some TLC – were black notches etched into the grey. She took a step closer and followed one of the lines. There were three horizontal stripes about an inch apart, with numbers next to them.

'Heights?' Madison asked, as Connor walked into the room with a bucket.

'I guess. A family rented this place years ago, I can't remember when. They had a child, so it's probably something to do with them.'

'Did your dad do the same for you?' Aside from when she'd been at boarding school, Madison had never stayed in one place for long enough to grow a few millimetres, let alone had a place to mark it. Not that her parents would have bothered – too busy with their life and work. And by the time she'd moved into The Hideaway, she'd been fully grown.

Connor shook his head. 'My father marked the passing of time with tax returns. Why?'

'Nothing. It'll be a shame to paint over it. It's like covering up a piece of history. Someone's roots.' Madison ran a finger over the marks again, feeling strangely put out.

'I didn't have you down as sentimental.'

Madison shrugged. 'It's a chapter in a life. It feels important.'

'The marks aren't even yours.' Connor came to stand beside Madison and she fought the urge to turn around.

'I know, and if we leave them the room will look unfinished, which will probably give you hives. It's fine.' Madison stared down at the bucket on the floor, which was filled with water and a large sponge. 'I guess if I start cleaning the walls, you could do the sanding. If your shoulder is up to it?'

'My shoulder is on the mend.' Connor picked up some sandpaper with his left hand. 'No yoga required.'

After ten minutes of cleaning, following Connor as he sandpapered, Madison wiped a hand over her forehead. They hadn't turned the heating on, but she felt warm from all the physical exertion. She checked her watch. 'If we start the first coat at ten o'clock, it's going to be after midnight by the time we finish – are you sure you're up for that? I'm guessing you had an early start?'

'Didn't you too?'

Madison watched the muscles across Connor's back flex as he worked. He'd taken off his jacket when they'd first entered the house and was now just dressed in jeans and a dark blue T-shirt, which had seen better days but somehow worked.

Connor turned and caught her watching. 'Is it past your bedtime?' His voice had deepened. Was he flirting with her?

Madison cleared her throat. 'I don't have a set routine for sleeping. It all depends on what I'm doing. To be honest I don't have a set routine for anything – my life changes too much for that.'

'Does it bother you never knowing what's coming next?' Connor turned away again, proving he wasn't comfortable asking questions. Perhaps because conversations weren't something he concerned himself with much. Jaws stopped sniffing the carpet and went to stand beside Connor, and he scratched the top of the dog's head, wincing as he moved his shoulder.

Madison considered the question. 'I grew up never knowing – we moved around so much, often without notice, and I didn't get a say in it. And even when I was at boarding school it never felt permanent, and I had no idea how long I'd stay there for. Moving around feels normal to me. But if you're asking if I'd prefer having a routine, a place to call my own, I think so – at least, I'd like a chance to find out.'

'Don't you think you'll get bored?' Connor asked, curious.

'I don't think so.' Madison's reply was firm. 'I'm fed up of moving from place to place, of making friends I won't keep – who barely know me. You'd be surprised how lonely constantly moving can be.'

'How does someone surrounded by people get lonely?' Connor looked stunned.

'Sometimes a busy room is the loneliest room of all. Especially if that room is full of people who know each other well, or have a history – I've only just started to understand how empty it feels.' Feeling exposed and wondering why she'd just opened her heart to a man who didn't even seem to like her, Madison changed the subject. 'Shall I text Amy to see if she wants to help with the painting?'

Connor's mobile chose that exact moment to ring. 'Georgie?' He asked.

Madison quickly texted Amy to see if she was free to help, trying not to listen to Connor's conversation, but the confined space made ignoring it impossible.

'You're arriving on the ferry on Friday and staying for how long? I thought we decided you'd wait?' Out of the corner of her eye, Madison saw Connor shake his head. 'You said you agreed with me… Won't you be missing lots of lectures?' He leaned his head onto one of the walls and Madison watched him close his eyes, looking tense – but when he spoke again his voice stayed level. 'I know you want to talk to me, and it doesn't sound like I have much choice. Sure you can stay at the house, it's half yours. I don't understand why you need to do this now… Okay.' He looked resigned. 'Then I'll see you soon.' He hung up and turned to face Madison before wincing. 'Dammit, I've got a meeting about a job at one on Friday. I can't pick Georgie up. Unless I cancel…' He tapped his phone, looking at his diary.

'I'll get her,' Madison offered. 'I could use your truck or Dee will lend me her car?'

'It's fine.' Connor shook his head.

'I'm sure it is, but why not accept help when it's offered? If you've a meeting, I'm sure you'd rather be there, and I'd love to finally meet your sister.'

'That's not the best idea. Georgie's thinking of dropping out of her course to go travelling and I'm trying to persuade her not to—' Connor stopped talking abruptly and Madison waited for him to continue before the penny dropped.

'You think I'd be a bad influence? Seriously, Connor, what do you think I'll do? Give her a full commentary on my incredible life of leisure, or put her back on the ferry with a round-the-world plane ticket?'

'I don't know.' Connor flushed. 'But I want her to finish the course. You've been all over the world, which will sound romantic to her. She's easily led and I don't want you putting ideas in her head.'

'Wow, you really don't think much of me, do you?' Ridiculously hurt, Madison turned away and picked up the bucket so she could stomp to the kitchen to pour the water out. On the counter sat the pot of yellow paint alongside Connor's bag of rollers and dust sheets. He followed her and leaned an arm on the counter so he could look into her face.

'Go away,' Madison said, turning aside.

'I'm not saying you'd do it deliberately,' Connor murmured. 'It's just Georgie is easily influenced.'

'Sounds like you have a low opinion of her too.' Madison got a knife out of one of the drawers under the white counter and began to pry the paint pot open, stabbing her finger in annoyance. Tears welled in her eyes but she was determined not to let them fall. Connor didn't deserve to know how much he'd hurt her.

'I didn't mean to offend you.' Connor put a hand on Madison's shoulder, but she shook it off as someone tapped on the front door. She went to open it, and instantly threw herself at Amy, who was standing in the doorway. Jaws barked a couple of times before settling down.

'You okay?' Amy asked, as Madison enveloped her in a big hug.

'You're wearing heels?' Feeling a little better, Madison ignored the question and stepped back to stare at her friend's shoes. Amy was dressed in dark blue overalls, and her hair was tied away from her face ready for painting, but the sparkly black heels looked out of place.

'I know the outfit's ridiculous, but I bought the shoes today and didn't want to take them off.' Amy kicked the heels to one side and walked into the small hallway, taking in Madison's expression. 'You look annoyed?'

'Argument with a paint pot,' Madison answered smoothly, in no rush to confide in her friend, who might have thought the same about her as Connor did, but was too polite to say so. 'I'll get over it. Thanks for coming.' She led Amy past the kitchen, ignoring Connor's surprised expression, and into the yoga room, pointing to the walls. 'We need to get the first coat on tonight, so it can all be finished tomorrow, ready if the new guests want to do a yoga session when they arrive on Friday.'

'I'm not a great painter, but I'm guessing six hands are better than four.' Amy waved hers in the air with a grin. 'Besides, I was only kicking about the house by myself, admiring my new shoes.' She paced the room, looking at the walls as Connor laid dust sheets on the carpet.

'I'll do the ceiling and edges later,' Connor explained, putting a paint tray on the floor and handing them each a roller. Madison avoided his eyes and turned to look at Amy, who was watching them both with a concerned expression. 'The walls are in reasonable shape, so I haven't had to fill any holes,' Connor continued. 'If you can concentrate on the middle and leave me the edges.'

'Looks like a late one, which is fine with me – beats spending the evening by myself again.' Amy picked up her roller and filled it with paint before swiping some onto the wall. The colour looked good. It was bright yellow, which would work in summer when the sunflowers were in full bloom and in winter when the room needed a lift. Madison watched Connor fill a brush using his left arm before painting around the doorway. He was a determined man, one she couldn't help appreciating in spite of their differences.

'Where's Jesse?' Madison asked without thinking, in an effort to fill the silence. 'I'm sorry, I shouldn't have asked,' she added, remembering.

'Don't mind me,' Amy sang, sounding more cheerful than she'd been the day before. 'I've got a date with Finn next Friday so it's all good – after our conversation in the pub, Madison, I decided it's time to move on, hence the shoes. I'm done waiting for Jesse to work out what went wrong. I've realised I've spent too many years waiting for him to grow up and take our relationship to the next level. Too many years wondering when he'll decide to put me first. I've been a golf, darts, football and running widow – I'm not prepared to play second fiddle to a car.'

'I'm not sure how the boy will feel about that.' Connor finished the edges of the doorway before starting on the paintwork next to the skirting boards. 'And you'll be doing me a favour if you don't mention this date. If Jesse finds out, he'll be even more useless than he already is.'

'He's useless?' Amy frowned.

'Your ex will be fine when he takes his nose out of the bottle and puts it into work.' Connor didn't turn around, oblivious to the chaos he'd created with those few words.

'He's drinking?' Amy squeaked, looking devastated.

'We were drinking Pink Flamingos the other night,' Madison soothed. 'And I'm guessing Jesse has to find his own way through this. A broken heart takes time to mend.'

Amy frowned as she bashed the roller over the walls, swishing this way and that without concentrating. Madison was no perfectionist, but even she itched to snatch the roller away and had no idea how Connor managed to restrain himself.

'It does when there's no reason for it,' Jesse said from the doorway, dropping his coat and backpack in the hall, ignoring Jaws, who barked briefly. 'If you're going to ask me to leave, I'd suggest you think again,' Jesse added, looking a whole lot more confident than he had in The Moon and Mermaid. 'Because I know we divided up the pub, but no one said anything about The Hideaway, and this is my job so I'm not going anywhere.' Proving it, Jesse marched across the room and dipped a fresh roller into the paint before turning his back on everyone else. The room fell silent as they watched him work. 'We need to learn to spend time in the same space – avoiding each other isn't going to solve anything.'

'I'm not going anywhere.' Amy cleared her throat. 'And I'm not hiding either, so I guess we're going to have to learn to live with each other.'

'I did learn how to live with you and I liked it,' Jesse said quietly. 'I know I missed our anniversary – and I want to make it up to you.'

'It's too late…' Amy waved her roller in the air, splattering drops of yellow paint onto the dust sheets. 'And it's more than the anniversary. I need more than you're willing to give. I need someone who sees me and loves me more than anything else…' Madison could hear the hurt in Amy's voice and ached to step in, but knew from her own experiences that some things you had to fix yourself.

'I do love you,' Jesse replied eagerly. 'Let me prove it.'

'Where's the Morgan?' Amy turned around, splattering more paint on the floor as she glared at Jesse.

'My car – what?' Jesse looked confused.

'Where is it?'

'She's outside,' Jesse said. 'I didn't want to leave her alone at Connor's. I can give you a lift home if you like?'

Amy hissed out a long breath. 'I'm not changing my mind, Jesse. I'm sorry but it's time to move on.'

Jesse closed his eyes. 'I don't understand… Whatever I've done wrong, I know I can make it right.'

Amy dropped her roller into the paint tray before marching towards the door. 'I'm sorry, Mads, I'm done for the night. I'll help again when the company improves.'

'I'll join you if you like? I could do with a walk,' Madison offered, knowing Amy probably needed to talk.

Her friend shook her head. 'My car's outside too and I'd like to be alone.'

'I got it wrong again,' Jesse said sadly as the door slammed, plunging the room into another uneasy silence. 'Every time I talk to Amy, I mess up.'

'You hurt her,' Madison said. 'She can't see past that.'

'But how do I make it right?'

'Amy needs you to figure that out yourself.' Madison wished she could help, but knew Amy would hate her if she tried. Besides, if Jesse couldn't see what he'd done wrong now, maybe he never would.

Chapter Fourteen

Connor's eyes hurt, perhaps because he hadn't slept for more than four hours in the last two days. Madison had left late on Wednesday after finishing the first coat of paint, and he and Jesse had stayed on to do the ceiling. He'd done another late one with Jesse last night, putting on a second coat and glossing, until the new yoga space gleamed.

He was exhausted, but had decided to go for a run anyway. Probably because the morning jog was so ingrained into his routine it had become part of his DNA. Ahead of him, Jaws trotted along the dark pathway lined with tall pine trees that would take them to the beach near his house. The dog had a blue torch on his collar and Connor had the same on his head – together they lit the ground well enough to see. It was a tricky, rocky descent that wound itself downwards like a zigzag for about forty metres, before hitting sand. Connor's father had shown it to him when he'd been a child and he used to pick his way at a snail's pace, afraid of tripping and getting injured in case it meant he couldn't work. This morning he felt reckless, so he took it at a speedy jog.

Connor was uncomfortable and it had nothing to do with the ache in his shoulder, which jarred as he ran. He'd hurt Madison. So much that the usually chatty, opinionated pain in his neck had been silent for most of Wednesday night and had avoided him completely yesterday. He should have been happy, but in many ways he felt like he'd stomped on a butterfly, which reminded him of the way his father had handled all of his relationships. He'd spent his whole life trying not to be like his father – why then did he turn into such an ass when Madison was around?

Reaching the beach, he stood for a couple of seconds deciding his route. The moon was low, but threw enough light along the shoreline to help him follow it. He knew the tide was going out so there would be no danger of them getting caught somewhere. And he needed to run, to work off the frustration and irritation that had taken up residence in his mind and body like a virus. In front of him, Jaws went to sniff at the breaking waves. The foam and spray tickled his nose but didn't scare the dog away.

Connor had put his father in that same spot eighteen months before. Stood with his sister at the water's edge and dropped the ashes into the foam before watching them float away. Sometimes he wondered if it had been a mistake, leaving his father in the one place he came to clear his head – the only spot on Sunflower Island that wasn't tied up in or wedded to the family business.

'You thinking of going in?' Finn asked from behind him. 'Because be warned, I've no intention of saving you. It's cold and my head hurts, and even if it didn't, I've never been a hero. But if you are, can you take that running jacket off first? I must admit, I've always admired it.'

'What are you doing here?' Connor turned, frowning. He ran this way most days and never bumped into anyone. He'd been at school with Finn, but didn't frequent the pub so their paths rarely crossed.

'I discovered this part of the beach a couple of weeks ago, thought I'd check it out again – I couldn't sleep,' Finn explained. He wore black jeans, a fleece and a grey woolly hat that he'd pulled down to cover his ears. 'What are you doing here?' he echoed.

'Running. Thinking,' Connor answered, turning back to look at the waves.

'About what?'

Connor let the question hang in the air, reluctant to share. But in the end tiredness – or perhaps an unexpected need to connect – got the better of him. He kicked a stone into the water, watching it bounce before sinking. 'Do you think souls stay in the place you leave them?'

'No,' Finn said sharply, sounding unhappy. He came to stand beside Connor and they looked out into the horizon. 'And it's way too early for a philosophical discussion, especially without beer. Why are you asking about souls anyway? And just to be clear, I'm only checking because I'm a barman – getting people to open up is in the job description.'

Connor shrugged, letting his eyes run across the water, stopping at the black, jagged rocks jutting out of the sea. The waves hit them, spraying an arc of foam into the air. 'I sprinkled my father's ashes here after he died. I'm not sentimental, but since he had such a low opinion of me, I wonder if he's hanging around so he can say I told you so if I screw up.'

Finn cocked a hand against his ear. 'Now you mention it, I *can* hear something. There it is again, I can just make it out… yep, he's saying *sucker*.' Connor barked out a loud laugh, caught unawares by Finn's unexpected humour as the man in question scratched his chin. 'We all know your dad was a bastard, Connor. I'm not sure why you still care about his opinion.'

'I don't.' Connor moved to stand on a stray branch buried in the sand, cracking a piece off before picking it up to toss it for Jaws. Tall cliffs framed the beach, throwing squiggly shadows over the sand. Jaws chased the stick, disappearing into the darkness. 'He said I was born to fail – I'm proving him wrong.'

'But?'

'Nothing. *Jeez*, I'm just thinking out loud. I'm not even sure why I told you that.' Connor rolled his eyes.

'It's the barman in me.' Finn looked smug. Jaws headed back and dropped the branch at Connor's feet, but Finn picked it up instead and threw it back into the shadows. 'And if I'm honest you gave it up way too easily – usually I have to get my customers drunk first. On a more serious note, if you need to talk, come to the pub,' he offered. 'The beer's not free, but the ear is. Sometimes death dumps a whole heap of baggage on you, which falls into a black hole initially, then turns up years later. It's best not to ignore it – just unpack the whole case and see if any of it still fits.'

'I don't need to unpack anything,' Connor said, feeling uncom-fortable and surprised at himself for sharing with someone he'd barely spoken to since school. Maybe it was just a sad, sorry testa-ment to his life and how few people he had in it since his father had died – and even before, he'd hardly been overrun with friends. 'I came for a run, so I could clear my head.' He waved at the sand. 'A few hours' work –' not to mention getting the house ready for

Georgie – 'and I'll be fine. My father was wrong… and I'm going to prove it. He's not here.' Connor nodded at the waves, dismissing them and the sentimental claptrap he'd just been thinking.

'Well, I can't see him.' Finn looked thoughtful. 'But the offer still stands. I'm not sure you've ever been to The Moon and Mermaid. It's a good place to visit – for company or beer, and the ear's not a requirement.'

'I'll bear that in mind.' Connor began to jog on the spot, warming his legs, ready to take off and end this conversation, until something occurred to him. Maybe another conversational itch he needed to scratch that wasn't going away. 'You know Madison Skylar, right?'

'Sure.' Finn took a step backwards, almost tripping over Jaws, who'd returned with the stick. 'Not intimately – just in case you're sweet on her and are looking to beat me up?'

Connor shook his head, ignoring the voice inside that disagreed.

Finn looked relieved but he still took another step backwards, stepping on Jaws's stick, which he threw again as the dog began to growl. 'We dated once, I can't remember when. I'm more of a love 'em and leave 'em type, but I think in this case she may have left me. That's the way of a wanderer. She's back – you've seen her?'

'I have.' The words were loaded with a weight even Connor could hear. 'I may have upset her. In your capacity as a barman, and in your clearly vast experience of lending an ear, what would you do about a woman like Madison if you'd hurt her?'

'My go-to is flowers.' Finn scratched his head, his eyes roaming the beach again as he considered the question. 'But that won't work with a woman who cares more for seeing the world and for people than possessions. How did you hurt her? Because Madison's a friend of mine, so I might have a mind to rescind that invitation to my pub.'

Connor sighed. 'I told Madison I didn't want her to meet my sister Georgie – I'm worried she might lead her astray.'

'Ouch. Your interpersonal skills haven't improved since school, have they? Georgie.' Finn nodded. 'I remember from when she first turned up on your doorstep. Since starting uni she's been to the pub a few times – blonde, pretty, funny and very friendly. She's nothing like you, right?'

Connor raised an eyebrow.

'Have you thought about apologising to Madison? I'm thinking words would have more of an impact. Perhaps let her meet your sister if she wants to? It's not like you can stop them bumping into each other – at least this way you might have some control over the conversation.' He paused. 'I'm guessing control is a big thing for you.'

'Isn't it for everyone?' Connor asked, but Finn didn't answer. 'Flowers would be easier, but I think you're right. They won't work on Madison.' He looked out to sea again. He usually didn't care how other people felt, but there was an ache in his chest that was worse than the one in his shoulder and he needed to fix it. 'Thanks for the advice. I'll think about it on my run.' He checked his watch. 'It's getting late, and I've got work to do.'

'Good luck with Madison.' Finn flipped a hand in the air as he walked in the opposite direction down the beach. He cut a lonely figure, and for a moment Connor wondered if he needed to talk himself before dismissing the thought. A man like Finn had a million people to confide in. *He* didn't need a stranger to offload to.

Connor began to jog again. He'd do a quick sprint up the beach before returning home to shower. He had work to do this morning, a meeting in town and an unhappy woman to appease.

Chapter Fifteen

'You don't need to cook breakfast for me,' Madison said to Dee, feeling a combination of exasperation and gratefulness. She wasn't used to anyone looking out for her – it would be easy to get used to, but years of holding back from people had made her careful.

'It's my job.' Dee fussed around the breakfast bar as she whisked eggs for an omelette. It was a nice day and rays of sunshine hit the blinds on the window, spraying shafts of light onto the kitchen cabinets and counter. 'Besides, I've only had to cook for Stanley for the last few weeks and that's going to change, thanks to you.' Dee squeezed Madison's shoulder, making her insides warm with emotion.

'I hope it works,' Madison confided, as Dee placed a cup of peppermint tea on the counter and pointed to it.

'Sit, tell me what you were up to the night before last. There's paint in your hair so I'm guessing it had something to do with Connor.' Dee waggled her eyebrows suggestively.

Madison ran her fingers through her hair and found a couple of lumps that hadn't washed out when she'd showered. She picked them out. 'I helped him paint our new yoga studio so it's ready to go when the guests arrive. Nothing else to report.'

Dee's face fell but she didn't ask any more questions. Instead, she put some vegetables into the pan on the hob and the air filled with the sound of frying and the sweet scent of onions. They sat silently until the kitchen door banged behind them.

'Connor,' Dee exclaimed. 'Are you here for breakfast? I can pop something on the hob.'

'Tea please, I don't need anything to eat.' Connor pulled up a bar stool and Madison felt his large body beside her, but didn't turn to look even though she wanted to. His comments from the other night still stung and she wasn't ready to forgive him yet.

'I came to apologise and to take you up on your offer,' Connor explained quietly, leaning closer as Dee bustled around the kitchen making tea and stirring the frying vegetables. In the end Madison gave in and looked at him. His hair was still wet, probably from a shower because it wasn't raining, he had a light dusting of dark stubble on his chin and he smelled of sawdust and paint, which was strangely sexy. 'I have that meeting at lunchtime, so if you could pick Georgie up from the ferry I'd appreciate it.'

'Well… I… Okay.' Madison nodded her head, surprised but oddly touched. 'If Dee will lend me her car, that's fine.'

'That's it?' Connor sounded mildly put out. 'You're not going to tell me how bad I made you feel the other night, or ask me why I changed my mind?'

'You did hurt me, but I think you know that,' Madison said simply. 'If you want to tell me why, you're welcome to. I don't get the impression you enjoy talking about your feelings, and I've learned people normally keep their thoughts to themselves for a reason. I'm just trying to make it easier.' She sipped some of her drink as Connor stared at her. 'Although if I'm honest, I would like to know.' She allowed herself an embarrassed smile.

Dee placed a cup of tea the colour of a dark swamp in front of Connor and a plate filled with omelette and salad in front of Madison, before heading for the dining room. 'I won't be long,' she sang as the door slid shut, leaving them alone.

Connor picked up his cup. 'I'm not good with people. I'd say it's my father's curse but that would be too easy,' he added quietly. 'I'm a grown-up, I make my own choices and take responsibility for them. Sometimes I say the first thing that comes into my head without thinking.' He blew out a long breath. 'And I rarely care – or notice – if I hurt the person I'm talking to.' He paused to take a sip of tea, perhaps because he wasn't sure what to say next. Stunned, Madison picked up her fork so she could dig into the omelette, but curiosity got the better of her.

'You care that you hurt me?' Hope bloomed in her chest but she tried not to show it. Was this the new beginning with Connor she'd been hoping for?

'Yes,' Connor said simply. 'And I have no idea why. Perhaps because I was unfair the other night and that reminds me of my father. Whatever I am, I've never set out to be like him.'

'Seems to me you're following your own path.' Madison stabbed at the omelette again, feeling lighter. 'And I'd be happy to pick up your sister – do you want to tell me which subjects to avoid first?' she joked.

'Oh.' Connor's blue-green eyes turned serious. 'Travel… countries you've been to… the world?'

'My whole life then?' Madison choked. 'I guess we could talk about you?'

Connor paled. 'I'm not sure what you'd say.'

Madison laughed. 'Oh, I've a fair idea. Your obsession with pies for a start, then there's that phobia of vegetables and the deeply disturbing colour of your tea. Perhaps if I get Georgie on board, I might even persuade you to try some yoga?'

'I may be regretting my change of heart.' Connor shook his head, looking more amused than upset, which inexplicably made Madison want to smile. 'That said, she might open up to you.'

'Why?'

Connor frowned. 'For some reason, people talk to you.'

'Perhaps because the corners of my mouth aren't constantly turned down?' Madison chuckled. 'Tell me about her.'

Connor looked thoughtful. A slight crease marred his perfect forehead and Madison ached to stroke it away. 'Georgie's a little directionless. I find her difficult to figure out. She's smart, but unfocused and easily led. She sometimes applies herself, but doesn't put her soul into what she does, which I don't understand. She'd rather go out partying than put her head down and do a good job. It was her idea to do a degree, to come and work with me, but sometimes I wonder if it's because our dad told her not to. Whatever, she's almost halfway through, dropping out now...'

'You think I'd encourage her to do that?' Madison stabbed the omelette with her fork, none too gently.

'You dropped out of your degree. I think you've done the things she'd like to do – perhaps I believe that talking to you might encourage her to go in a direction I don't approve of.'

'Which is?'

'Away from Sunflower Island. Georgie has a chance to be something here, to work alongside me and build a business and career. I don't want her to waste the opportunity.' Connor's knuckles whitened as he clenched his mug. 'If she's here with me, we can work together. I can show her everything I know. There's so much to learn and so much to do. If she leaves…'

'What if it's what she wants?' Madison asked quietly.

'Then I want her to wait. She's only a year and a half from graduating. What's the rush?'

'I don't know,' Madison said. 'But perhaps that's what you need to find out.'

Madison unwrapped the first of her new blue yoga mats and placed it on the freshly hoovered carpet. The room looked good – the paint job had refreshed the space, helping draw attention to the incredible views from the large windows. She'd opened them earlier to help clear the smell of paint, and placed a couple of incense burners in the corners.

She put another mat on the floor and stood back to admire the landscape. There was a huge hill, which in summer bloomed with yellow sunflowers, and beyond it rolling green fields made their way to cliffs and dark, choppy waves. In Thailand, Madison's yoga studio had looked over a white sandy beach, but that view wasn't a patch on this one.

The Hideaway guests weren't arriving until three, so Madison had plenty of time to get the room ready, pick up Georgie from the ferry and be back in time to lead the first yoga session. She unwrapped another mat, considering whether she had time to stretch. Then her mobile buzzed in her back pocket and she pulled it out.

'Seth,' she answered, surprised. Her sometimes-boyfriend rarely called unannounced and they'd texted recently about his ship docking in Amsterdam. She hadn't admitted she wasn't going to meet him. After their last few meet-ups, she'd decided it was time for them to become just friends, forgoing any benefits – she just hadn't told him yet. She knew Seth wouldn't be upset. Their relationship had always been open, and he had plenty of friends – most of them women.

'How's The Hideaway, are you bored yet?' Seth laughed, launching straight into conversation without any small talk, which was normal for them.

'Not yet,' Madison replied, her voice light. She held the phone to her ear. 'How are you?'

'Bored. We're docking today and I wondered if you'd given any thought to meeting me in Amsterdam. We could go cycling, do some galleries, check out the odd cafe? You've been on the island for three days now – I figured you'd be tearing your hair out.'

'Not exactly.' Madison frowned at the mat on the floor and adjusted its position. She'd put out four – would that be enough? Perhaps if she unwrapped the others, she could pile them in the corner ready for more guests? Her tummy fluttered with excitement as she imagined the room full. With Stanley in charge of drumming up guests, it was looking like a very real proposition. And she could only imagine her aunt and uncle's delight when they returned to find The Hideaway booked up. This was the first time Madison had ever felt that her presence actually made a difference to somewhere she cared about – it was a revelation. 'I'm loving it here. I'm in the process of setting up a yoga studio – we've got guests arriving today and I'm planning on running classes,' Madison explained, her voice all excitement.

Seth cleared his throat. 'Are you thinking of staying long enough to make that worthwhile? There's no point in getting your aunt and uncle's hopes up.'

'They're not even here.' Madison fiddled with a stray curl of hair that had fallen into her face. 'But I'm thinking of staying,' she added tentatively.

Seth barked out a loud laugh. 'I've heard that before, and I think we both know it won't happen. Give it a few weeks and you'll be back on the road again. We're the same, you and me.' His voice deepened. 'We weren't built to stay put. You'll never be truly happy unless you're moving on, seeing the world. It's how you're made.'

Wouldn't she? Madison frowned at the mats, unsettled. She had tried to stay in places before, to put down roots, but after a few months she'd always found a reason to move on. But none of those places had been The Hideaway – none of them had ever felt like home. People cared about her here, and in many ways she already felt like part of the furniture.

'Besides, I'm sure no one will miss you if you disappear for a couple of days. Come out to visit, it feels like ages since we caught up,' Seth continued, oblivious to her feelings.

'I honestly can't leave.' Madison surveyed the room again, her good mood evaporating. 'I'm sure there are plenty of other people you can meet up with instead?'

'They're not you,' Seth replied softly, something odd in his voice. 'Give me a call when you're travelling again and we'll get together.'

They said their goodbyes, but even after she hung up Madison felt uncomfortable.

Was Seth right: would she be bored of The Hideaway in a few months? Was the need to travel ingrained into her DNA, a design flaw embedded during her nomadic childhood? She looked at the mats, at the view out of the window, shaking her head. Seth was wrong. She'd been working up to this for years and was definitely ready to settle down. So she'd stay and stick things out – whatever Connor, Seth or anyone else thought.

Chapter Sixteen

Madison watched as the ferry docked and a multitude of people began to stream off, spilling onto the busy walkway. She'd borrowed Dee's old Renault Clio, but hadn't thought to ask Connor what his sister looked like. Madison had never met Georgie, because Connor's sister had only visited Sunflower Island in the holidays – exactly the time of year Madison had gone travelling, trying to ensure her aunt and uncle had some space. But she'd seen her from a distance once and could still remember a mass of blonde hair, a colourful dress sense and a smile so out of place with the Robertson men.

Madison waved at a couple of people she recognised as they exited the ferry and watched a young blonde woman, who looked about twenty, wander onto the dock, pulling a small purple suitcase behind her. The woman glanced at the sea of faces a few times, looking confused.

'Georgie?' Madison asked, marching up and holding out a hand, taking a few moments to study her. Connor's sister was pretty, with clear skin and large blue oval-shaped eyes. She looked small – around five three – and was pale and very slender. In short, she'd inherited very few of the Robertson genes – although she was stunning. 'I'm Madison Skylar from The Sunshine Hideaway. Are you Connor's sister?' Madison asked, when Georgie looked at her hand quizzically.

'My brother didn't come?' Georgie sounded irritated.

'He had a meeting that he couldn't get out of. He's dying to see you though,' Madison added, because she knew how horrible it felt to arrive somewhere and feel out of place and unwelcome. 'And Jaws is in the car if you're in need of a familiar face.'

'I'm thinking I should be grateful. Once, Connor got caught up at work and forgot me entirely.' Georgie sighed, shaking her head, before smiling. 'He felt awful when he remembered. I'm not sure he's ever forgiven himself. Thank you for stepping in. I don't think we've ever met, but I have heard of you. Do you work with my brother now?' Georgie followed Madison as they slowly headed for the ferry car park.

'No. You probably know my aunt and uncle own The Sunshine Hideaway – he's working there at the moment, redecorating and doing up the cafe.'

'Really? How's it going?'

Georgie's expression was warm and friendly, and Madison felt an instant connection with her. 'Okay. Good.' Madison nodded, opening up. 'We're trying to appeal to some of the guests who've defected to Lake Lodge. They've been undercutting our prices, and business at The Hideaway has been dropping off.'

'Connor hasn't mentioned any of it, obviously.' Georgie sighed, pulling her trolley alongside her as they walked. 'What are you doing, aside from decorating?'

'We're offering yoga lessons and afternoon walks now. Plus, a Grand Opening of the cafe will be a big part of making it more appealing.'

'I visited Lake Lodge when I was over last. It's a little sterile for me, but there's a lot for guests to do. You should see if there's anything up there you could copy,' Georgie said, as they entered the car park and Madison guided them towards Dee's car.

'One of our guests has been spying on them – it was his idea to offer yoga,' Madison admitted. 'We probably need to take another trip there soon, just in case it sparks off any more ideas.'

'You should invite Connor,' Georgie suggested slyly. 'I'm hoping you're friends. I'm only asking because he doesn't have many, so that would be good news. If you're a girlfriend, I might even do a cartwheel. Connor has a bad habit of dating tourists, I'm guessing because he knows the relationship will be transient and won't interfere with his work. You've probably noticed he doesn't get out much?'

'He's very dedicated,' Madison murmured, wondering how much more she might learn from Georgie about the man who kept himself so closed off. 'We're friends, I think. Actually, sometimes I wonder. Your brother can be difficult to read.' They got to the car and Madison unlocked it before putting Georgie's suitcase in the boot. Jaws sprang from the back seat as soon as she opened the door and spent the next few minutes jumping up and down, licking Georgie's face.

'If Connor were a book it would be an ancient Greek tragedy – impenetrable, dark and incredibly hard work.' Georgie flashed a smile that lit up her face, instantly reminding Madison of Connor. 'Despite that, he's loyal and lovable – once you get to know him, which you obviously have. He must think a lot of you if he's let you look after Jaws. This dog is a handful and – much like Connor – the people he takes to are few and far between.'

'I think Jaws was for your benefit. He really was sorry he couldn't come himself.'

Georgie shrugged as she jumped into the car. 'I appreciate you lying for him, but I think we both know Connor would rather be at a meeting than here. In many ways he's exactly like our father – except even when Dad was alive he didn't have a beating heart. It's not Connor's fault – he grew up spending almost every waking hour with Dad at work, and he's never learned how to do anything else.'

Madison started the car, wondering what to say to that, but she didn't get a chance because Georgie began to chatter again. 'Can we go via the beach? I feel like I've been gone for ages and there's something about seeing the sea that makes me feel at home.'

'I feel the same,' Madison admitted, feeling like she might have met a kindred spirit. She pulled the Clio out of the car park and took a right so she could get onto the coast road. The drive would take longer than the direct route, but she had plenty of time before the guests arrived. Besides, a few more minutes might teach her a lot more about Connor Robertson.

'Are you from the island originally?' Georgie asked, making conversation as she looked out of the window at the view. To the right a green lawn of lush grass framed the edge of the road, leading about a hundred metres to the edge of a steep cliff, beyond which two red boats bobbed on the sea.

'I'm from all over,' Madison answered carefully, unwilling to break her promise to Connor. 'But I went to school on Sunflower Island from the age of fifteen and lived with my aunt and uncle, which is probably why you've heard of me.'

'I grew up in a small village in Norfolk,' Georgie admitted. 'My mum still lives there. I found out about my dad and Connor eight years ago. I'd been an only child and discovering I had more family was exciting. I insisted on meeting them, despite my mother's reservations. I fell head over heels with Connor – I've always wanted a brother. My dad was harder work.' She stopped talking abruptly.

'I didn't know Charles well…' Madison said, non-committal. 'But I've heard he was difficult.'

Georgie shrugged. 'I'll never understand what my mother saw in him. I do understand why she left. He had no need for a daughter, told me as much when I arrived on his doorstep. Connor was kinder – he insisted I was allowed to stay and embraced me into the family. Gave me a place in the business which he still wants to share. I've no idea how a man like Connor came from someone like Charles. My mum calls it the miracle of genes – how all the good ones club together.' She laughed. 'I wish that were true, but I'm fairly certain I have some of the evil ones in me.'

'Why?' Madison asked, curious. 'Does your head spin when you get annoyed?'

Georgie chuckled. 'Not that I've noticed… It's a long story.'

'We're doing the longer drive, so there's time,' Madison probed.

Georgie looked out of the window for a few moments. 'Connor's spent the last eighteen months paying my way through university. He's got this fantasy about us working together, and he needs the help. He wants to make a success of the family business – a legacy, I think, for both of us. He's working day and night to turn things around. If I was here, that might be possible. More importantly, he might actually get to take a day off.' Her gaze slid towards Madison. 'Or find time to have a girlfriend.'

'I've been trying to persuade him to do yoga.' Madison changed the subject. 'I got the feeling he could do with taking some time out, but he's not keen.'

'Oh, yoga – hot rooms and barely any clothes…' Georgie nodded. 'Most males would jump at the chance. I really do despair of my big brother.' She sighed. 'The thing is, I don't know what I want to do. I fancy travelling. I went along with Connor's plans because… well, he's my big brother and I love him. He needs help and I want to be there for him. But I'm only twenty and I want to see the world. I've met someone and he's off on an around-the-world trip next month. He's offered to pay my way. I plan to drop out of uni, or see if I can defer…'

'Can't it wait?' Madison asked gently, imagining Connor's face when Georgie told him she'd definitely decided to drop out. 'The world is there whenever you want to see it.'

Georgie sighed. 'I really like this guy… I might not get another chance. Besides, I really don't think Sunflower Island is the place for me to live permanently. I'm not even sure I want to work in the building trade. But Connor's paid for everything and he's expecting me… See what I mean about evil genes?'

'Sounds more like a case of difficult choices and being honest to me,' Madison answered carefully.

Georgie looked out of the window again, as fields and houses flew past. 'Have you ever travelled?' she asked suddenly. 'You were never here when I visited – where did you go?'

Madison swallowed the bubble of panic, wondering what to say. She didn't want to lie to Georgie, but she didn't want to make things worse either. She was finally getting somewhere with

Connor, and he'd be disappointed if he thought she'd gone back on a promise. 'I've been to a lot of places but I think of Sunflower Island as my home.'

'Where have you been?' Georgie perked up.

'Oh, all over.' Madison switched on the radio. They were probably only fifteen minutes from Connor's house, but every one of them would feel like a lifetime if Georgie kept asking questions like that.

'Sounds amazing. Where? What about Thailand?' Georgie prodded. 'It's where we're planning on visiting first.'

'I was there for a few months.'

'How about Australia?'

Reluctantly, Madison nodded.

'America, South Africa, Nigeria, Morocco, Italy, China?' Georgie continued. Madison nodded at each one, feeling terrible.

Georgie bounced on her seat. 'Oh, wow. We need to go to the pub tonight so you can tell me about everywhere you've been, give me advice on what to see. I can't believe I stumbled on you. Or that you're actually friends with my brother.'

'But wherever I go, I always wish I was here,' Madison added desperately, trying to steer Georgie in a new direction. 'I know wanderlust – I was raised on a diet of it – but I also understand the value of having a home and security. Certainly finishing your degree will go some way towards securing that.'

'Not if it's in something I don't even want to do.' Georgie pouted. 'Yet.'

When Georgie didn't say anything, Madison added, 'I understand about not knowing your place in the world. I think that's normal for some of us, but don't give up opportunities in your eagerness to escape. I started a degree in law a few years ago and dropped out after the first year.' She grimaced. 'I really regret it now…'

'I hear you.' Georgie looked thoughtful. 'But I really don't think that will happen to me. When we go to the pub tonight you can tell me more about your travels.'

Madison's hands gripped the steering wheel. She was sure Georgie would regret dropping out of university, unless she could convince her to change course tonight. And Connor would be furious when he heard what his sister was planning. Would he be mad at her too for telling Georgie about her own travelling? Dammit, she should never have offered to help out in the first place, as whatever progress she'd made with Connor had just been undone.

Chapter Seventeen

Amy gave Madison a huge, welcoming hug as soon as she arrived back at The Hideaway after dropping Georgie off at Connor's. The house had been empty, but Georgie had fished out a key from her bag and disappeared inside, with a promise of catching up over a drink later. Connor was going to murder Madison when he found out about their conversation in the car.

'Our new guests are in their rooms.' Amy grinned. 'They're just making themselves comfortable, getting changed. They wanted to take a walk this afternoon.'

'They don't fancy yoga?' Madison's heart sank when Amy shook her head. 'I haven't sorted out a route.' She'd been meaning to do it this morning, but picking up Georgie had meant she hadn't had time. 'I know a couple of walks, but I'm worried I might get us all lost and ruin everything.'

'No matter.' Stanley walked into the hall and patted Madison on the shoulder. 'You can play it by ear and I'll join you. I've been walking a lot since I arrived. I'm sure I'll recognise where we are once we get going. I'll just pack some supplies.' He headed for the kitchen.

'And there's always your phone, Mads,' Amy added. 'I can't believe we've got guests! Dee is practically yodelling in the kitchen, getting dinner ready for tonight, and I took another booking this afternoon for next week. You're a genius.' Amy threw her arms around Madison's neck, looking so excited she couldn't help but get caught up in it.

'I think we owe Stanley our thanks – he's the one who had the idea and dropped the leaflets into the tourist information office,' Madison said.

'Dee's been baking Stanley's favourite food as a thank you for the last two days – she won't admit it but I think she's falling for him.' Amy smiled.

'Maybe one of us needs to plan another spying visit to Lake Lodge to see if that sparks any more inspiration – or romances?' Madison looked down at her outfit. 'I'd better change so we can start this walk. I guess there's no time like the present.'

Half an hour later, Madison trotted down the steps into the hall where Stanley was now waiting, kitted out in his walking gear, chatting to a petite woman who looked about thirty.

'I'm Sophia Brown.' The woman stepped forwards so she could shake Madison's hand. She had cropped white-blonde hair and a huge bright smile. 'I'm here on a break with my new boyfriend. He sprang this on me yesterday, booked time off for both of us – a surprise for my birthday. He says he's been here before, but this is my first time. I've fallen in love with The Hideaway already, it's so cosy and there's so much character – so much nicer than Lake Lodge.' She wrinkled her nose. 'I can't believe I hadn't heard of it before.' Sophia swept an arm around the room, clearly oblivious to the greying paintwork and chips in the banister.

Charmed, Madison led Sophia to the front door, where a bulging green backpack sat on the polished oak floor. 'Snacks and drinks packed by Dee, along with a first aid kit – all the essentials really,' Stanley explained, picking it up before Madison got the chance. 'I reckon if we look hard enough we'll find a kitchen sink.'

'Is your boyfriend walking too?' Madison asked Sophia, as a man appeared from the sitting room.

'David O'Sullivan,' he barked, shaking Madison's hand. He was tall – around Connor's height – but thicker in the waist. His hair was thinning but his light blue eyes were sharp. He focused them on her. 'I met the owners last time I stayed. I understand they're away.' He didn't wait for Madison to respond. 'Nice place though.' He looked around the room. 'It was busier last time I came – is it just the four of us today?'

'It is. We've only just started advertising the yoga and walks – we weren't expecting anyone to book in so quickly. But it's wonderful to have you,' Madison added quickly.

'So you introduced the walks and yoga sessions? I don't remember them from before. And they're popular?' David looked at Madison intently.

'You're our first clients. I've just moved back to the area, and we're in the process of implementing some changes to The Hideaway to make it even more appealing to our customers.'

David nodded. 'Sounds like a good business plan. Places like this need an angle.' He frowned as he looked around. 'This is a very nice space, but we must all move with the times – stay competitive – if we want to succeed. There's no room for sentimentality. Where are we walking today?' he asked, his attention switching to something else.

'Ah…' Madison cleared her throat, trying to remember the last walk she'd done with her uncle. She'd probably remember the route once they started. 'Um, through the woods behind the house, across the meadow to the left of them which leads to a lovely rocky climb down to the beach.' She paused, trying to remember the rest. 'We'll walk along the sand for about half an hour before heading back up to the top of the cliffs. It's a loop walk, around six miles.' She hadn't done it for at least five years, but the landscape wouldn't have changed, and even if she lost the pathway, there were always the maps on her phone.

'Sounds great.' Sophia beamed, looking excited. 'I'm a really keen walker and I've been getting David into it recently – you'll see from the form Amy asked us to fill in. I've not been to this side of the island before… We normally stay near the ferry…' David frowned at her, seeming annoyed that she was holding them up.

'Shall we go? Or it'll be dark before we get back,' he grumbled.

'There are torches in the backpack, just in case.' Stanley jumped in. 'But you're right, we probably ought to get going.' He dipped his head towards the door in a silent message to Madison to get on with it and, feeling a lot less confident than she looked, she opened the door.

The weather was good for an afternoon in early March. The air had a chill in it, but the sun was high and the sky was blue, with just a few cotton-wool clouds spaced across it. This part of the walk was easy and Madison knew exactly where to go. She strode confidently behind the house, and took the small gravel pathway that led all the way along the long field at the back to the small woodland you could see from the kitchen and dining room. As they entered the woods, the sun was hidden by trees and the light dimmed. The gravel was replaced by a spongy bed of leaves that crunched underfoot.

'We've got a variety of trees on the island.' Madison racked her brains to remember the species, but once again Stanley helped her out.

'That's an elm, and you'll see pines further up – the island's filled with them, birds too. If you walk here in the morning you'll hear a lot of birdsong.'

'I used to come with my uncle,' Madison reminisced, remembering the early morning walks, sometimes before school, when he'd taken her out with a pair of binoculars and breakfast so they could bird-watch. She'd been a teenager, but had still savoured the time with him – he'd been so knowledgeable, so keen to teach her. Those had been some of her favourite mornings on the island. Everything had been so quiet, aside from the birds, and she'd felt settled and happy. Trees endured: you always knew where they were. Madison even recognised a couple as they walked past. 'We won't stay in the woods for long – soon we'll walk through the meadow, and beyond that are a couple of sunflower fields, which are definitely worth a visit in the summer.' She honestly couldn't remember how long it would take to get across them. 'After those, we'll get to the pathway that leads to the beach.' Assuming she remembered where it was.

'I love being outside.' Beside Madison, Sophia tipped her face upwards so she could look at the tops of the trees. 'I'm a midwife and enjoy what I do, but there's not much call for babies being born in nature. I do miss the air on my face and the smell—'

'How long will the walk take exactly?' David interrupted, looking at his watch with a frown.

'About two hours,' Madison guessed. 'We'll definitely be back before it gets dark, although we'll need to keep up our pace.' And she'd have to remember the route. Madison's stomach fluttered uncomfortably as she wondered if she'd bitten off more than she could chew, then she dismissed the thought. She'd been in plenty of situations like this and had worked her way through them – life didn't always need a plan. Sometimes you just had to wing it.

Twenty minutes later they reached the edge of the forest. The trees ended abruptly but she could see the path across the meadow that led to the top of the hill, and another track that led to the right. Madison's brow furrowed as she tried to recall which way her uncle normally walked to the beach. Her sense of direction suggested straight ahead, but it wasn't obvious. Ahead might lead to a dead end and then she'd look like an idiot. Madison sneaked a look at her phone but there was no signal, probably because they were in the valley. Once they got to higher ground she'd be able to check.

'Does anyone want a drink or a snack?' Stanley walked up beside Madison. 'I think it's straight ahead,' he whispered. 'Not sure after that, but your uncle took me this way on my first week at The Hideaway. We didn't go to the beach though, so I can't help you there.'

'I'm sure I'll recognise it when we get there. The two paths just confused me,' Madison confessed, as Sophia joined them and took a mug of hot chocolate from Stanley's flask. David refused. Instead he walked ahead and stood looking at the pathway.

'David's great once you get to know him.' Sophia looked embarrassed. 'He works too hard – things haven't been going so well at work – and he doesn't know how to de-stress. It always takes a few days for him to calm down and go with the flow.'

'I know someone a little like that,' Madison confided, wondering if Connor had talked to Georgie yet and exactly how long it would take him to come looking for her.

Once they'd finished the drinks and packed up, they marched across the field, taking it more quickly because Madison was worried about them losing light. Finding the way in daylight was hard enough – doing it in the dark would be impossible. When they got to the top of the meadow, she recognised the next field immediately.

'We need to take this path over here.' Madison pointed to the right. 'And there's another beyond it. After that we'll find the start of the trail that will take us to the beach. It's a little later than I wanted, so we need to speed up. Does anyone want one of Dee's cakes?'

Sophia nodded, but David shook his head. Stanley opened the bag, taking one for himself too. 'Sunset's at five forty-five and it's a half past four,' he said quietly.

'Then we'd better head off,' Madison replied, feeling a lot less confident than she sounded. In the end it only took thirty-five minutes to walk through the meadow and the next two fields. David strode ahead of all of them, setting the pace – to the point that Sophia was struggling to keep up with him. Madison dropped behind for a few seconds to check her phone. There was signal by the meadow and she quickly found the rest of the walk, even though the battery on her mobile was beginning to die. So when they reached the edge of the second field, which was framed with rough hedges, she had an approximate idea of where the track to the beach began.

'The pathway might be a little overgrown,' Madison guessed, leading them to a small gap. 'And it's narrow in places. You'll need to tread carefully, take it slow. It's probably best if I go ahead.' David's expression clouded. Sophia was right: he didn't know how to relax. It took almost fifteen minutes to negotiate the trail. It was rocky in places, and at times more of a scramble. She'd have to research the next walk, especially if The Hideaway's guests weren't so physically able.

The beach was empty and the tide wasn't that far out. The sky, which had been bright blue earlier, had turned a darker, less friendly colour. Madison swallowed a bubble of uneasiness and faced the group with a smile. 'So we're going to take a walk up the beach this way.' She pointed to the right. 'We might have to take the shorter route today because the sea's coming in. We'll go about a mile and then there's a path back to the top of the cliffs. It's another brisk walk of about twenty minutes back to The Hideaway from there.'

Sophia shivered. 'That might be a good thing. I should have worn more clothes, it's getting chilly.'

'There's a spare fleece in the backpack if you'd like it?' Stanley jumped in again, making Madison feel useless. Stanley was doing a far better job of leading – she was just in the way.

'I'll take it.' They waited as Sophia took off her jacket and pulled on the fleece. Madison studied the sea. It had moved into the shore by about a foot. When the tide was in, the water would reach right up to the edge of the cliffs, which meant there would be nowhere to walk. Thankfully the group sped up and they walked silently for another fifteen minutes.

'Don't worry about the sea coming in, we're almost there,' Madison commented as she noticed Sophia's worried glances. As they approached the place where the pathway was, Madison's stomach did a little somersault, because the gap she recognised as the way up to safety was now a mass of fallen white rocks.

'Looks like there's been a rock fall.' David sounded irritated.

'The path was clear last time I came.' Madison didn't mention it had been five years ago. But the route had still been marked on the map on her phone, so the rock fall couldn't have happened that long ago. Madison looked to the left and the right. The sea was coming in too quickly for them to make it back the way they'd come.

'Perhaps there's another track further up?' Stanley suggested. 'If this pathway's been closed off, walkers will have found another one.'

'Of course,' Madison agreed. 'There's one in about four miles, but we won't have time to get to it. I'm sure you're right and we'll find another one sooner.' If they didn't, they'd all be stranded on the rocks and she'd be using someone's mobile to call the coastguard. She could only imagine Amy and Dee's faces when she screwed up the first of their walks. This was such a typical Madison move – she couldn't do anything right.

'Let's continue to walk up here.' Madison pointed up the beach, and pulled the mobile out of her pocket again to check the route: there weren't any other paths she could see. Her fingers danced across the screen. Connor lived close by. She knew he walked Jaws on the beach and ran too. He might know more about hidden entrances and exits? But would he answer the phone if she called?

Madison watched as Sophia picked her way across the sand, following David who was back to marching. Stanley took up the rear. They looked a motley crew but they all trusted her and she didn't want to let them down. She dialled.

'Madison,' Connor barked. In the background Madison could hear a cheerful tune on the radio. 'What's happened? Did you get Georgie?' She heard a clatter and the music stopped.

'You haven't seen her yet?' Madison was incredulous. She'd dropped Georgie at Connor's house over three hours before.

'Dammit, is that the time?' Connor sounded annoyed. 'I'll be heading home in a minute.'

'Could you do a detour on the way, please? I have a problem.'

'Which is?'

Madison dropped back from the others and put her hand over her mouth so they couldn't hear. 'I don't have long, because the battery on my phone's almost dead. I'm out with guests, it's getting dark, we're on the beach and the tide's almost in.' She glanced towards the waves, which had inched further towards them. 'The walkway up to the top of the cliffs which brings us out near the main road is blocked.'

'Madison, that route's been closed off for almost a year.' Connor sounded exasperated. 'There was a big storm last winter and we had a lot of rock falls.'

'I… I wasn't expecting to walk this today, I thought we'd do yoga.' She closed her eyes, pushing down the panic in her chest. 'You can call me stupid later. I'll probably even agree with you. For now I need to know how to get off the beach before our guests all drown.'

'Where are you?'

'Not far from the old entrance.'

Connor sighed. 'Keep going. There's a way up in about ten minutes. It's difficult to find if you don't know it's there, so I'll come and show you the way. And Madison…'

'What?'

'Run—' Madison's phone died, and she frowned at the black screen before pointing up the beach.

'There's another exit. Someone's coming to guide us out.' She rushed over and overtook David, who'd slowed right down. He looked tired and his cheeks were bright red. 'Are you okay?' she asked.

'Fine,' he puffed. 'I wasn't expecting to have such a workout today.'

'Sorry.' Madison swallowed the guilt. 'We've got about ten minutes left – as long as we're quick we should be fine,' she bluffed. The water was almost lapping their boots. They'd probably be paddling by the time they saw Connor. She only hoped he'd be easy to find because now she didn't have a working phone.

Why did she do this? Connor was right: she was more suited to jumping on a ferry or plane than looking after other people. She'd only been home a few days and she was already making trouble. Amy and Dee would be livid when they found out what had happened, and all of their new guests were going to cancel. How long would it be before Amy and Dee were whispering behind her back, wondering when she was going to leave?

Madison continued to march. What was probably only minutes later, but felt like a couple of hours, she saw Connor emerge from the cliffs, flanked by Jaws. A vision in jeans, work boots and a dark leather coat.

'You made it,' Madison gasped, just stopping herself from throwing her arms around his neck. Only the fact that the others were there stopped her – that and the deep frown decorating Connor's face.

He glanced at the water, which was now millimetres from their feet. The beautiful wide sandy beach had become a tiny strip of sand. 'Cutting it fine, Ms Skylar?'

'Who wants predictable?' Stanley patted Madison on the back in a gesture of solidarity that made her feel a million times better. 'Life's far more exciting with a hint of danger – walks too.'

David grunted and pointed behind Connor. 'Is that the way? These are new boots. I don't fancy getting them wet.'

Connor nodded without smiling. 'Just behind the tree. It's narrow and rocky so take it slow or you're liable to fall. If you wait I'll guide you.'

'I'll be fine.' David shook his head and indicated to Sophia that she should follow. Stanley went with them, leaving Madison standing alone with Connor. Now they were safe and there was no one there to watch, her emotions got the better of her and a tear slid down her cheek.

'I'm sorry.' Madison shook her head. 'I wasn't expecting the walk. I jumped in, thought I could do this. I was wrong. Amy and Dee will be so annoyed.'

'Why?' Connor searched her face. 'You got everyone to safety, saved the day – seems to me no one is blaming you for anything. Your guests looked relieved and happy to be off the beach. Speaking of which, the sand's almost gone. We should move before I get *my* boots wet.'

He pointed to a wave as it moved in close enough to lap at their feet, and ushered her to the safety of the cliffs. The track was hidden by a tree they had to duck behind. After that the route was obvious.

'If they don't blame me it's a miracle. I'm not the right person for this,' Madison grumbled, as she negotiated the rocky path upwards. It was steep but dry, and even in the dimming light it was easy to find the way.

'Are you giving up, Madison? One setback, is that all it takes?' Connor probed, watching her.

'I wasn't saying that. It's just…' Madison almost tripped but Connor caught her coat on the way down and steadied her. 'See, I'm supposed to be guiding these people and I can't even stay upright.'

'You're doing just fine,' Connor encouraged. 'You got ahead of yourself. Didn't plan. So next time do better.'

'If there is a next time,' Madison muttered.

'If you give up now, you'll never know what you're capable of. Seems to me you came home to make changes. You either make them or you don't, but if you let one setback stop you from achieving what you set out to do, well… you're not the woman I thought you were.'

Madison turned suddenly, stopping on the pathway so she could face Connor. The light was dimming, her guests were miles ahead and she really should hurry, but she couldn't, not until she got to the bottom of what he'd said. 'The woman you thought I was? You've always considered me a waste of space, a drifter – a flibbertigibbet, you once said. Even now you're expecting me to jump on the ferry and disappear.'

'Because of your history. But is it only me who believes you'll leave, Madison? Seems to me if you're looking for your biggest critic you should look closer to home.' Connor fixed his eyes on her in the dimming light, almost as if he couldn't tear them away. 'I don't know what you're planning to do next. You're as predictable as lottery numbers. But I know you came home to do something, and you've said you want to stay. If you only stick around when things go right, you're going to spend your whole life moving on every few months. Which is exactly what you've done so far.'

'I don't want to be in the way. I never wanted to be a burden.'

'Who said you were a burden? Do you think only those who are perfect measure up and get to stay? Because those are very high expectations to live up to, even higher than mine.'

'Well, you are perfect…' Madison was only partly joking. 'Just look at you.' She waved a hand, feeling her cheeks flush. 'You look like that even when you've been working all day. You're always on time, you'd never get lost because you'd probably have stayed up into the early hours planning your route. You've never messed up anything in your life.' Her heart hammered.

Connor laughed. 'Aside from every day of my life since I was born, according to my father. And you did actually meet my sister today?'

Madison reddened, remembering her conversation with Georgie. Yet another example of her screwing up.

'Because I'm sure Georgie shared my list of faults,' Connor continued. 'She adds to them regularly – number one is the time I forgot to pick her up from the ferry.'

'She told me about that,' Madison admitted with a laugh. 'She didn't share the others, but we're planning on going for a drink later.'

'Ah.' Connor's smile faded. 'I expect you'll get the full lowdown then.'

'Not if you join us.' Madison indicated that they should continue walking before one of her party came looking for her. It was definitely dusk – she could barely see the path now as they picked their way through the rocks. She might even have to ask Connor to drop the walkers back at The Hideaway when they got to the top.

Madison knew her way home from Connor's house but it wasn't an easy route in the darkness. She almost tripped again, and this time Connor grasped her hand before she ended up flat on her face. He held on, leading her quietly upwards. She didn't comment, too afraid that he'd drop it or pull away, but having him touch her felt strangely right.

'I've still got a couple of hours' work to do tonight,' Connor began. Had his voice deepened? They reached an easier bit of the path and Madison reluctantly let go of his hand as they got closer to the guests waiting at the top.

'Doesn't socialise, spend time with his sister or do yoga. You're right, those faults are endless. Perhaps I'll help Georgie add to them later,' Madison joked.

'Okay.' Connor shook his head, turning back to look at her with a slight smile. 'In the interests of keeping my list of faults short, I'll come… for a while. But I'll have to get back to work afterwards or I'll fall behind.'

'Sure,' Madison said, knowing she was lying. Because once she had Connor Robertson where she wanted him – away from work, relaxed, with at least one drink inside him – she'd do everything in her power to keep him there.

Chapter Eighteen

Connor walked into The Moon and Mermaid with Georgie and looked around, trying not to notice the time, or think about how much he still had to do before going to bed. The place was full, and a quiet tune played in the background, making him think of dancing and the kinds of careless days and nights he'd never had.

'Madison!' Georgie screeched, racing across the pub to greet her. Connor tried not to notice the way Madison looked. She'd changed out of her walking gear into jeans that made her lean legs look endless, and a pink shimmery top that dipped just low enough to expose lightly tanned skin. 'You came.' Georgie swung Madison up into a big hug as Connor went to the bar.

'So you finally decided to visit.' Finn tipped his head and studied Connor without smiling. 'You here for a drink, or that ear?'

'A drink – if the ear's obligatory I'll be off.'

Finn laughed. 'The ear's optional, but don't dismiss it entirely – you may need it one of these days. As for the drink, what'll it be? Actually, don't tell me, let me guess – bitter, maybe Castling? It's brewed in Castle Cove, which isn't far from here, and I know how you like to stay local.'

Connor shook his head. 'I'll have a Coke – I need a clear head. I've accounts to do later.'

'Give him the bitter, please, Finn,' Georgie interrupted from behind, patting Connor on the back. 'One won't kill you and I doubt even a barrel of the stuff would keep you from your paperwork. Two Pink Flamingos to go with it, please – one for me and one for my lovely new friend, Madison.'

'Good to see you again, Georgie.' Finn leaned across the bar to give Connor's sister a kiss that was dangerously close to her lips.

'And that alone was worth the trip here.' Georgie giggled, making Connor roll his eyes. Seriously, was everyone losing their heads today?

'I aim to please.' Finn flashed a wicked smile in Georgie's direction as he poured the drinks and handed them over. Connor pulled out his wallet but Finn shook his head. 'That round's on the house, because it's your first visit and I'm hoping it won't be the last. From the amount of interest you've attracted from the locals, I'm guessing takings will be up tonight.'

'I aim to please.' Connor echoed Finn's words, picking up his beer and following Georgie as she headed to the table by the window that Madison had already nabbed.

Connor sat down as Georgie put the drink in front of Madison. He tried not to stare at the pink gloss Madison had applied to her lips, or the way her cheeks still glowed from the walk. 'I'll buy the next round,' Madison promised. 'I owe you for rescuing us today, Connor, and I'm not sure I thanked you properly.'

'You only put me an hour behind.' When Georgie tutted, Connor added, 'Besides, Jaws appreciated the time out. Did Dee and Amy forgive you for almost drowning your guests, or have you booked your ticket off the island?'

Madison shook her head with a wry smile. 'Would you believe Stanley and Sophia loved it – they said it was the most fun they'd had in ages. It was only Sophia's boyfriend, David, who wasn't impressed. Although he cheered up over dinner because Dee cooked roast lamb. Stanley wants to rename them "adventure walks"– he reckons people will enjoy the hint of adventure. Tomorrow he's asked if I can just follow my nose.'

'I can't promise to be available to find you every time you run into trouble. Too much—'

'Work. Brother, you're so predictable,' Georgie interrupted, shaking her head as Connor picked up his pint.

'I'm thinking it might be sensible to have a secret plan,' Madison admitted. 'Perhaps I can get us lost a couple of times on the way to spice things up. I'll try to keep rescue missions to a minimum.' She paused. 'Thank you for coming to our rescue today. If you hadn't, we might have been swept out to sea.'

'That's okay.' Connor took a sip from his pint so he didn't have to say anything else. Madison's intense brown eyes and the quiet intimacy of the conversation made him feel awkward and a little embarrassed – not to mention doing things to his body and mind he hadn't felt in a long time. The music in the pub changed, growing louder, and Connor scanned the room. Somehow, despite living on the island his whole life, he'd never been here before. The place felt friendlier than he'd expected and it was very busy. A man Connor vaguely recognised cleared glasses from a table beside them. As he passed them, his face lit up.

'Madison!' He approached, juggling four pint glasses and three beer bottles between his thumbs. 'It's Tom.' He nodded at Connor, his expression guarded. 'I think we met on the dock when you picked up Madison.'

'Tom! How's the trip to Sunflower Island?' Madison asked. 'This is Georgie, Connor's sister – she's visiting too.'

Tom grinned. 'Nice to meet you. Being here's brilliant. I'm enjoying the wildlife and scenery, and the locals are friendly – I've picked up some work here in exchange for a room.'

'Which you'll be losing if you don't get back to work,' Finn joked, as he delivered drinks to a table beside them.

Tom laughed. 'I'll get back to it, boss. I'll call you.' He nodded to Madison. 'Maybe we can go out?'

'Sure,' Madison said lightly.

Connor fought a wave of jealousy and sipped his pint again.

'So, Madison, tell me more about the places you've travelled to. Connor's kept you a secret for far too long,' Georgie began.

Connor thumped his glass back onto the table, slopping some of the dark liquid over the sides, as annoyance and a dose of disappointment shot through his system. 'You told her?' he asked Madison, incredulous.

'No... not exactly.' Madison blushed, looking vulnerable. 'Georgie asked and I didn't want to lie.'

'What's the problem?' Georgie looked back and forth between them.

'I didn't want her putting ideas into your head,' Connor ground out, wishing he'd just picked his sister up himself instead of asking Madison.

'My ideas are my own, whether you approve of them or not – and Madison's not to blame for what I'm about to say either, so you can wipe that irritated expression off your face,' Georgie snapped, before downing her Pink Flamingo in one. 'Okay, so here goes. I've decided I'm definitely dropping out of university, Connor… I'm sorry, but I don't want to move to Sunflower Island and I don't think the building trade's for me. I want to travel, and as you know I've a chance to leave now. I know it's not what you want to hear and I don't want to hurt you, but that's it…' She looked a lot less confident than her words had been.

'You *what*?' Connor processed what she'd said, trying hard to hold on to his temper. He didn't know who to be most angry at now: Madison for indulging his sister's whims, or Georgie for having them in the first place. 'That's not what we agreed – you said you'd wait.' He tried to temper his angry tone but failed miserably. 'You wanted to live here.' He shook his head, fighting back the sinking feeling that he was always going to be alone in this. Alone in trying to turn the family business around, alone in proving how wrong his father had been. His whole life stretched out before him, the day-by-day grind, the loneliness of doing everything himself. And the money he'd spent on Georgie's tuition fees, on living expenses – he could barely think about it.

'It's only, what, four more months until the end of term, Georgie?' Madison started, her tone a little unsure. Connor wanted to tell her to stop talking, but for some reason he let her continue, waiting to see what she'd say next. He rested his pint on the table and watched.

'Yes,' Georgie harrumphed. There was no other word for it but Connor could see his sister was about to embark on one of her legendary moods.

'So what's the hurry?' Madison asked, surprising Connor so much he continued to stay quiet. He wasn't used to anyone having his back. And he definitely hadn't expected Madison to try to talk Georgie out of travelling. 'Can't you finish this year? Wait and join your friend in the summer?'

'I don't want to wait,' Georgie whined. Connor could see the mood building. In a minute he knew his sister would probably storm out of the pub and head home. 'The world is out there now for the taking, studying is boring and I've no idea what I want to do with my life.'

Madison shrugged. 'You've years to find out. If you get this degree your options are open. Seems to me you might owe your brother something too.'

About six thousand pounds by all accounts, but Connor didn't say anything. Instead he sipped his beer, wondering if Finn had slipped something into it and he was hallucinating that Madison was on his side. At the bar someone put on 'Let's Go Fly a Kite' from *Mary Poppins*, and a crowd of drunk young men began to sing along.

'Oh, I love this song.' Madison smiled as she watched them.

'My friend is going soon,' Georgie interrupted, sounding less confident.

'So join him later.' Madison leaned forwards so they could hear her above the singing. 'The world will still be there, but the opportunities you have now won't. I can only tell you about my own experiences. I've travelled to a million places, I've lived a million lives, but I've never felt like I belonged anywhere. Imagine what you could do with a degree. What you could build. Giving up on things, dropping out, won't help you find your place in the world.'

'So how come you got to travel so much? How come you're so lucky?' Georgie asked, missing Madison's point entirely.

'I wouldn't say *lucky*. Both of my parents worked for the Foreign Office. Having a child was more of an expectation than a want – and once I arrived I was an inconvenience. Their careers came first. Always. Aside from a stint at boarding school, I followed their postings, trying not to get in the way. It was glamorous but we moved around a lot. I saw a lot of places but belonged to none. I never got to keep the friends I made – until I came to Sunflower Island.' She glanced back at the bar, where the men were still singing. 'I love it here. The people are friendly and the place is always filled with laughter and music…'

'Where did you go?' Georgie asked.

'All over: Australia, Russia, the Far East… every continent you can think of.'

'What an amazing life.' Georgie sighed, looking at her empty glass before waving it at Finn and signalling for two more.

'In some ways it was. The world is a beautiful place – I've seen most of it so I should know. But imagine never having a home, a school, friends you get to see every day. Imagine spending Christmas in a different place each year. Sometimes in hotels, often with strangers my parents worked with. Then my parents were killed in an accident and I moved here.'

'So why didn't you stay?' Connor asked.

'I… I don't think I was ready to settle. I'm not sure I knew how.' Madison tried to explain. 'And I never wanted to be a burden to my aunt and uncle – it's not like they chose to have me.'

'What about your degree?' Connor asked softly, digesting her words.

'I think I sabotaged it. The first day I moved into halls I knew I wouldn't fit in. Perhaps it was because I wasn't used to staying in one place. Perhaps I didn't try hard enough at the work. Everyone seemed to speak the same language, a language I didn't understand. I felt excluded. It wasn't their fault though.' Madison shrugged. 'I'm good at making friends. I was invited to parties… I'm not sure law was the right degree for me, even though my marks were okay. The whole time I felt like I was playing a part. I was me on the outside, party girl Madison, smiling my way through the lectures and the social life, but in here –' she hammered a fist on her chest – 'where it mattered – here I felt lost, in the way, alone. I was terrified of being chucked out, so I left before that could happen.'

When she put it like that, Connor almost felt sorry for Madison. She hadn't been taught to stick anywhere, to feel like she belonged. Until she arrived on Sunflower Island – and perhaps by then it had been too late? He sipped his pint, giving in to the need to just listen, to let the conversation run its course. He already knew it was difficult to change his sister's mind once it had been made up.

'That's how I feel… like I don't fit,' Georgie declared, as Finn brought fresh drinks and took their empties. 'Sort of.'

'Is it?' Madison cocked her head. 'Is that truly the problem?'

Georgie pouted, and looked into her drink before taking a long sip. 'Perhaps not entirely. I have a home with my mother and I'm happy there. At uni, I don't really know. I'm bored of studying, lectures make me want to go to sleep. This boy I've met is exciting and he's leaving now.' She drank more of her cocktail, pausing as the men at the bar stopped singing and left. 'If I don't go, by the time I do perhaps he won't want me to join him at all.'

'If that's the case, he's not worth leaving your course for,' Madison said. 'And there'll be plenty more people to travel with later. Believe me, when it comes to seeing the world, it's not difficult finding company.'

Georgie sulked. 'It might not be the same for me. And I chose this course because our dad said I shouldn't. He said the building trade was no place for a woman.' Georgie screwed up her face as she took another sip of her drink. 'He thought I'd be useless and I wanted to prove him wrong.'

'And leaving now will do that?' Connor asked, because he couldn't help himself. It was a mistake because Georgie's expression turned mulish.

'Our dad's not even here to see me sticking at it. Being away, having the time to think, has given me a new perspective. Who cares what Charles Robertson thought of you, of me or of what we can achieve? I spent years – you spent a lifetime – being told that we weren't good enough, couldn't measure up. I realised recently that he was just a mean old man, that his opinion doesn't matter. Shouldn't have then and definitely doesn't now.'

'The business matters. It's been in the family for generations. If we lose it… if we fail, then that'll make him right. That'll make us just as useless as he predicted,' Connor argued, knowing his voice held the wrong hint of challenge. The kind of tone his father had used, the tone that had driven Georgie crazy.

He was right – she shook her head so her blonde hair flew, and downed her drink before slamming the glass on the table. 'I knew you wouldn't see things my way. You're just like Dad. You want everyone to be like you – a workaholic, with no time for anything in your life, including me. And you wonder why I don't want to join you here.' Georgie's cheeks flamed and Connor saw the regret in her eyes, but she didn't retract the comment. Instead she turned to Madison. 'I'm sorry, I knew my brother wouldn't understand. It's been a long day. I've done what I came to do. Let's catch up tomorrow. Alone.' With that, she stormed out of the pub with a quick backwards wave to Finn.

Connor sat silently as Madison picked up her glass, looking guilty.

'Well, that went well…' He tried to dismiss the uncomfortable feeling that on some level Georgie's words had been right. Was he just like his father? Trying to control everything, living only for work? He didn't have much of a life. There was almost no one he connected with. Jaws probably didn't count, and Jesse was more employee than friend.

'You're nothing like your father.' Madison leaned forwards, putting a hand over his as she read Connor's mind. 'I didn't know him very well, but I know enough. He wasn't a kind man and you've kindness inside you. My guess is he'd never have supported you through university, or given you the encouragement you've given Georgie.'

'She's right about me working all the time,' Connor argued, feeling bitter and guilty. He wanted to shake off Madison's hand but couldn't bring himself to. There was something about the gentle brush of her soft skin that made him feel calm. Instead he sipped his beer until there was just a little left in the bottom, reluctant to finish it. In a minute he'd have to head off – he had a load of paperwork to tackle. But suddenly he didn't want to leave the pub, or this beautiful woman who confused him so much.

'I can't argue with that,' Madison admitted. 'But I understand the reasons for it, even if I don't know the full story. Perhaps if you look hard enough you might find a way to remedy it.'

'With yoga?' Connor asked, with a glimmer of a smile he couldn't suppress.

'Why not?' Madison smiled back, her face lighting up. 'Who knows – you might even enjoy it.'

'I don't really have the time.' Connor sighed, staring into his pint as the words echoed around his head. His father had always said the same thing. There wasn't time – to watch him play football, to turn up to his parents' evening, to talk. Mind you, there had always been time for work.

'Then make time.' Madison lifted her glass to her lips and fixed Connor with a questioning look, her brown eyes searching, perhaps hoping to read his deepest thoughts. 'I'm planning another recon mission to Lake Lodge, to see what else they might be offering to customers. It could even be fun. Perhaps you'd like to join me? It'll only take an evening, part of an afternoon at a push, so you won't need to miss much work…'

Connor began to shake his head, thinking of how much there was still to do to finish the cafe, how much paperwork was spread across his desk, the jobs he'd been asked to quote on that added up to hours of work. But instead of the predictable *no* coming out of his mouth, he found himself saying *yes*, knowing he'd regret it. Because if he wanted to prove his father wrong, spending more time with Madison Skylar was the opposite of what he should be doing.

Chapter Nineteen

The new toilet and sink were fitted in the small cafe bathroom, the floors had been sanded and the kitchen was in. Connor picked up a brush so he could join Jesse as he smoothed varnish over the huge oak counter. Behind them wooden racks – which would one day contain mugs, cups, saucers and speciality coffees and teas – already gleamed. They were making good headway. It had been a quiet week. Connor had only spotted Madison once, guiding Stanley and the new female guest to the yoga studio, and Georgie still refused to talk to him. So he'd spent the additional hours trying to get ahead. It was now a month until the Skylars were due back from their cruise, and he had a lot to finish up ready for the cafe's Grand Opening and The Hideaway officially going up for sale. Connor rolled his shoulders, trying to work out some of the kinks, as Jaws wound himself around his feet and whined.

'I think he's angling for a walk.' Jesse wiped a hand across his forehead as a bead of sweat dripped down it. They'd closed the door to the cafe earlier, after being disturbed by passing locals a couple of times, and the room had become hot. 'I'd be happy to take him for a quick walk. I could do with a break, and if I'm honest I'm hungry. I'll go find Dee, maybe see if I can run into Amy. She's still not talking to me and I need to put things right before I go mad.'

Connor checked his watch. It was after four thirty and they hadn't taken a break all day, aside from when he'd fed Jaws and taken him for a short jog. He rubbed his neck, feeling the start of another headache. 'Sure. I'd like to finish the varnishing up tonight so we can get on with the kitchen counters tomorrow. It's shaping up well.' He stood back to inspect their handiwork. 'I'm guessing in another fortnight we'll have sorted the kitchen, then it's just painting and finishing touches.'

Jesse grunted. 'Then we'll be redecorating inside The Hideaway. So Amy will find it harder to avoid me.' His mouth curved into a grim smile. He washed up the brushes and picked up Jaws's lead before calling out to Connor, 'Enjoy the rest of your evening,' with a hint of something odd in his voice.

'Aren't you planning on coming back?' Connor shouted at the empty room, but Jesse was already gone.

Five minutes later, Connor heard the light tap of feet and looked up, expecting to see either his dog or Jesse. Instead, Madison stood at the bottom of the steps with a wrapped sandwich in one hand and a large sports bag in the other.

'I've come to collect.' Madison walked around the workspace, peering into the bathroom, making approving sounds. She was dressed to impress today – in shiny red high heels and a matching dress that followed her curves to just above her knees. Connor swallowed the lump in his throat – he couldn't seem to stop his eyes from sliding to her legs.

'Collect what? Are you off out somewhere?' he asked, failing to fight the burn of jealousy inching its way up his gut. Was she going on a date? With Tom?

'We're visiting Lake Lodge.' Madison waved the bag in the air. 'Remember – recon mission? You promised you'd join me? I've booked us a swim. Georgie found your trunks – albeit reluctantly. Are you two still not talking?'

'No.' Georgie had locked herself away for most of the week and he'd been at work. 'We're not currently a family that communicates.'

Madison looked disappointed. 'There's a change of clothes in the bag. Jesse's promised to look after Jaws, and he said not to worry about work because he'll finish up.'

'Jesse's in on it?' Connor frowned – so that explained the smile. 'I can't.' He searched for excuses.

'When I asked in The Moon and Mermaid last week, you said you would. Georgie told me you'd try to duck out of it, but I said you're a man of your word.' Madison cocked her head and hit him with a searching gaze, her eyes dark and questioning. 'I'm guessing all this will still be here tomorrow. You've worked hard these last few days, I've seen you – and Georgie says you've barely eaten or been to bed. You've made amazing progress… surely one evening off won't kill you?'

'Swimming?' Connor eyed the bag in Madison's hand suspiciously as she passed him the sandwich. He unwrapped it, suddenly ravenous, and took a bite. Cheese and cucumber. He winced but swallowed anyway. 'Thanks. No banana?' He found his humour as the food went down.

'Didn't want to push my luck, considering I've also booked us a massage at seven. There's tension in your shoulders I can see from here,' Madison explained, as Connor shook his head. 'Please?' she begged. 'Sophia and David are leaving tomorrow, we've got another couple booked in from Sunday and more the week after – things are really looking up. But I've heard Lake Lodge have dropped their prices again, plus they've started offering yoga too. We need to keep fresh – not lose momentum. I want some new ideas and it would be good to see how Lake Lodge treat their customers.'

'Can't Stanley go with you?' Connor asked, feeling desperate. The thought of seeing Madison in a swimsuit was more than he could bear… Keeping his distance, fully dressed, was far safer.

'No, he can't.' Madison rolled her eyes as he finished the sandwich. 'You said you didn't want to be like your father, Connor Robertson. This is your chance to prove it. It's one evening – afternoon,' she corrected herself, after checking her watch. 'If you don't do it for yourself, do it for Georgie – to prove you can change. God knows, watching you work yourself into an early grave is hardly an advert for coming here to work with you.'

Connor looked around the cafe, considering. He could stay and do a few more hours, go home and be ignored by his sister, or take Madison up on her offer. What would his father have said?

'Okay, sure, yes,' he muttered, because dear old Dad would have said no and chased Madison out of the door.

Madison nodded. 'I was hoping we'd find time for a quick ice cream after. I've borrowed Dee's car to give your shoulder a break—'

'I'll drive. Give me five minutes to clear up.' Connor looked down at his clothes. 'Are you sure I don't need to change? You look…' The words in his head wouldn't translate onto his tongue. 'Clean.'

Madison laughed. 'Thank you for the compliment. That's one I've not heard before.' She stepped forwards, looking into his eyes, her tone turning husky, sending prickles up and down his spine.

'You could lighten your mood a little – otherwise we're good to go. There are showers, towels and everything we'll need at Lake Lodge. This is meant to be fun, Connor. Try to enjoy it.'

Connor didn't answer. Instead he dragged his eyes from Madison's mouth and took the brushes, dumped them into white spirit so they wouldn't go hard, and unplugged his power tools. It felt odd leaving now, like he was walking out of the office at lunchtime with no intention of going back. In his head his father called him idle, but he pushed the voice away as he marched up the stairs behind Madison, keeping his eyes fixed firmly on the stairs, before closing the door without locking it, because at least Jesse would be back.

As they headed for the car, Madison dropped back to walk with him. 'You look like you're heading to a funeral,' she joked. 'This afternoon is about finding more things to implement at The Hideaway. And if we're lucky, Connor Robertson, we might even have fun.'

That was what he was worried about. Connor swallowed as his brain churned, looking for an excuse or way to back out. Spending an evening in this gorgeous woman's company was a one-way trip to disaster. But even as he hopped up into the truck before firing the engine and Madison climbed in beside him, filling the car with the scent of lemongrass, his head wouldn't deliver the words. So he pulled out of The Hideaway, and took the main road that would lead them to the other side of the island, knowing, even then, that his life was about to change forever.

Chapter Twenty

The pool was stunning. It was aqua blue and framed with white tiles that stretched to walls painted with murals of mermaids and sea creatures. Beside them, inviting sun loungers were piled with fluffy white towels and squidgy cushions. Above, a ceiling made from pure glass exposed a darkening, clear sky and about a billion emerging stars. The lights around the room had been dimmed for maximum effect, and inside the pool tiny white lights glittered. Despite all these attractions the place looked empty.

Connor dumped his towel on a nearby chair and looked out into the water. He'd already showered off the day, ready for a swim. He rolled his shoulders, trying to work out the aches, realising for the first time in weeks how tired he felt. He didn't look up, even when he heard quiet footsteps behind him and felt a prickle of awareness glide across his back.

'Looks good, doesn't it?' Madison whispered, sounding put out. 'I was hoping for something a little less glamorous. Do you think you and Jesse can whip up one of these before my aunt and uncle get back?'

'Not unless you find me twenty spare contractors, a ton of equipment, oh, and around two hundred thousand pounds,' Connor admitted.

Madison sighed but Connor still didn't turn, too afraid of what he might see. He'd always thought of himself as a pragmatic man, but this woman held far too many temptations. So he kept his eyes fixed firmly ahead and stared into the water, wondering what the hell he was doing here.

'Well, I guess we should try it?' Madison suggested, after a few seconds of silence. Then Connor saw a flash of tanned skin and the barest of red bikinis before she hit the water with a splash, and after a few long strokes bobbed up in front of him, her hair wet and her eyes shining. 'Aren't you coming in?' Madison was observing Connor with a quiet intensity as she floated in the water, waving her hands and looking every bit the alluring mermaid he knew her to be.

'This is a terrible idea,' Connor murmured to no one in particular as he dived, expertly hitting the water, before gliding up beside her.

'Look up,' Madison demanded as she floated on her back, her painted pink toes pointing upwards. 'The stars are incredible. Honestly, I've been all over the world, but I've never seen anything quite like that.'

Connor complied, studying the sky for the first time. The glass panels were completely clear and offered an uninterrupted view outside. Madison swam closer and Connor felt the faint brush of her skin as she pointed into the darkness. 'Even when I was in Australia the sky didn't look like that.' Tiny pinpricks shone between larger circles of light. Connor knew the stars and planets, knew all the constellations – if pushed he could probably reel off their names. Despite that, he'd never studied them, or spent more than a few seconds appreciating the beauty of the sky.

'They're nice,' he agreed, knowing the words were inadequate. But he didn't have the language in his head, couldn't think of the right terms for the simple act of enjoying a view.

'Nice.' Madison laughed out loud, the noise echoing like music around the empty pool. 'Connor, they're absolutely stunning.' She kicked off into the water and swam a couple of laps, her bright pink fingernails arcing through the air. And Connor watched her, feeling like a spectator – a man sitting on the outside with no idea how to join in. Until Madison dived and bobbed up beside him, her eyes dancing with humour. 'Are you actually going to swim, or did you just come to look? Because if you're busy calculating what materials you might need for the cafe, or thinking about what you've still got to do at The Hideaway, I might just have to admit there's no hope for you.'

Connor shook his head, his eyes catching on Madison's face. Her cheeks glowed, and her long hair clung to her face, fanning over her tanned shoulders in gorgeous brown waves. 'I'm appreciating the view,' he admitted quietly, watching her face. Knowing, despite his better judgement, that he'd just taken another step towards madness. Perhaps due to tiredness, or some crazy need to prove Georgie wrong and show he was nothing like their father – that there was a lot more to him than work.

Madison flushed but didn't look away. 'So will you swim? Let go of whatever it is that's putting that sad expression on your face? Perhaps even smile?' Her voice turned husky. 'Because this is a beautiful place, and we've got it all to ourselves.' She glanced around the still-empty pool. 'It seems a shame to waste it.'

Connor pushed off the bottom, letting himself float on the surface. He lay on his back, opening his eyes so he could appreciate the sky. The stars shimmered, perhaps giving their approval, but somewhere in the darkness, Connor knew his father was probably shaking his head.

'Swim with me, Connor.' Madison eased away from where they'd been standing and dived underneath the water again. She really did look like a mermaid. All tanned limbs, long trailing hair and a world of temptation. He saw a flash of red bikini as she slid to the surface and into front crawl. Connor hadn't swum in a pool for years. In the summer he'd often go for a quick few strokes in the sea – another of his father's habits he hadn't managed to shake. But swimming had never been fun and it had never looked so elegant.

Connor swam to the side, quickly catching up with Madison and overtaking her. He let his hands slip through the water and tried to clear his mind, doing ten laps in quick succession. Until Madison gently grabbed his foot and tugged, bringing him to an abrupt stop.

Madison grinned and swam closer so their legs brushed. 'Having fun?' she asked, a teasing light in her eyes.

'Yes,' Connor said simply, because it was the truth. The headache had gone. His shoulders felt looser and the kinks of the last few weeks had already begun to work their way out of his system.

'You look different.' Madison studied him. 'More relaxed.' She moved away again and dived, leaving Connor wondering what she was planning next. Suddenly he found himself being pulled under. Beneath the water Madison looked ethereal, and even without goggles Connor could see the lean shapeliness of her body, the two tiny scraps of material forming her bikini. He tried to look away but his eyes were caught – like the original sailor being led to disaster, he'd been snagged in Madison's trap. She grinned and began to swim away, but Connor reached out and caught her ankle, pulling her back towards him. She floated to the surface, and he followed her, bursting through the water to gaze into her smiling face.

'Are you playing, Connor?' Madison asked, delighted.

'I've no idea. Perhaps, yes,' he answered, because in all honesty he still had no clue what he was doing here, and the simple act of touching Madison's ankle had made him feel more out of depth than the water they were swimming in.

'Good.' Madison's eyes sparkled with humour and something else Connor didn't recognise. 'Then let's add a wager. Whoever gets to the other side first buys the ice cream.'

'Ice cream?' In March – surely she wasn't serious?

Madison giggled, and the sound hit Connor's solar plexus, filling it with warmth and an unexpected desire to connect. She glanced at the edge of the pool. 'Let's say best of three so you have a chance – but I'll warn you, I've been known to cheat and I always win.' Laughing, she dived suddenly, disappearing into the blue depths. Surprised, Connor paddled for a couple of seconds before plunging under the surface and following her.

Madison could really swim. Faster than Connor had expected, and it took him a few quick strokes to catch up. He caught her ankle, pulling gently so in a couple more kicks he overtook her, reaching the other edge of the pool first, but they broke the surface at the same time. 'You're a quick study,' Madison said, her eyes approving. 'For a man who never plays, you catch on fast. So that's one for you and two to go.' She smiled again and Connor guessed what was coming next, so swam in front of her so she couldn't dive under the water.

'How about we go after a count of three?' He started to tread water as their bodies drifted towards each other.

'We could say that,' Madison said with a quick snort of laughter. 'But you'll need to move out of my way.' She let her eyes drift downwards, noting perhaps that they were almost touching, their bodies playing a game of cat and mouse in the tiny sliver of liquid space. Connor swam backwards as awareness skipped across his skin. He moved to the edge of the pool and grabbed on, facing the other side, ready to win.

'One, two, three,' Madison muttered, giving Connor no time to prepare before she dived and began swimming away.

'Cheat.' Connor laughed, following her – slower this time. He admired Madison's form as she slid through the water. But as he swam after her, doubts began to creep into his mind.

What am I doing here? There was so much to do in the cafe, more in The Hideaway, and hours of paperwork waiting at home. He didn't have time to play with a beautiful almost stranger, a woman who within a matter of days had managed to burrow her way into his mind.

Who knew what she'd be capable of, given time – or how long she'd even be around?

Connor slowed and swam to the other side, surfacing next to her. This time Madison wasn't smiling.

'You stopped.' She searched his face. 'And somehow I've lost you. Where have you gone to, Connor Robertson? You were laughing a few minutes ago and now you look sad. You're thinking about work?' she guessed, shaking her head. 'You're thinking about work while you're here…' She swept a hand around the pool, taking in the sky. 'Don't you know how to let go?'

'No,' Connor admitted simply, watching the confusion and hurt skitter across Madison's face. Coming here had been a bad idea. He'd been raised on a regime of hard work. One evening in this woman's company wasn't going to change that.

'Don't you want to?' Madison asked, moving closer. 'I've known you a lot of years, Connor, but I've never seen you laugh like you did a few minutes ago. I've never seen your face light up like that. It looked good on you…' She let the words come to a stop as she watched him.

Connor's heart thumped as he scanned Madison's expression, his head a mass of confusion, his body burning with a fierce need. 'And if I give in to it, where will it lead?' he asked, knowing his voice sounded all wrong.

'Honestly, Connor, who cares?' Madison asked sadly, letting herself float so close that their legs touched. Connor stayed put, letting himself drift, until their bodies intertwined as the power of the water – or perhaps simple attraction – took over. Then he could feel the warmth of Madison's breath, feel the heat of her body, and had to fight to stop himself from drawing her to him. 'Because I don't. I've liked you for a very long time, even when you could hardly bear to look at me,' she whispered. 'Even when you broke my heart at the age of seventeen by calling me a flibbertigibbet. I've admired you and wanted to get to know you better. And now you're here with me, only you're not…'

Madison's voice dropped on the last word and Connor felt her begin to retreat, gliding backwards away from him. In less than a minute he knew she'd get out of the water and change before they spent a quiet, uncomfortable drive back to The Hideaway together

– and he'd lose this chance of getting to know this woman who confused him so much.

'I am,' Connor found himself saying, found his hand reaching out to hold hers. He didn't want to spend the rest of his life sitting on the outside looking in. Didn't want to spend it craving things he'd never give in to. He wasn't his father's son. He wasn't a man too afraid to feel anything except contempt.

Madison looked perplexed at first, then her eyes lit up as Connor pulled her gently towards him, until their bodies tangled again. Her skin was smooth and warm and every bit as soft as he'd imagined. She looked into his eyes and swallowed, her dark eyes questioning. 'I am here,' Connor said quietly. 'I'm as present as you, I just don't find it as easy.' He stopped talking as she wrapped her legs around his waist. Wondering if he was right to give in to these feelings – knowing it was already too late.

Chapter Twenty-One

Madison slid herself nearer to Connor, relishing the hardness of his hips and the slight brush of hair from his chest. She took a chance and slipped one arm onto his shoulder, easing herself forwards so their noses almost touched, and noticed those wary eyes that fascinated her so much darkening. He looked conflicted but didn't move away. Instead his eyes dropped to her mouth and she swallowed.

'Well, this is unexpected,' she murmured, determined to lighten the mood. Determined to lift the dark unhappiness from Connor's expression.

'Not entirely,' he said after a long sigh. 'I think this may have been coming since you got off that ferry.'

'Destiny?' Madison asked with a hint of humour – a man like Connor wouldn't believe in such things.

Instead of dismissing it, which she'd been expecting, Connor shook his head. 'Inevitability. I'd call it the law of physics – we all know opposites attract.'

'Well, if it's science, I'd say there's no point in fighting it.' Was Connor actually going to kiss her? While she could see lust in his eyes, there was a huge dose of hesitation – or perhaps sanity – there too. Connor looked at her silently, and for a heart-stopping moment

Madison thought he was going to retreat. Then he must have made his decision: he moved the hand that was still resting on the side of the pool onto her cheek, so he could tip her head and take her lips into a kiss.

Madison wasn't sure what to expect from Connor's kiss. He was a practical man – a man who worked hard, who'd had his fair share of lovers – so she guessed he'd know what he was doing technically. But she didn't expect the flare of heat that licked her insides as soon as their mouths touched – or the expert way Connor fanned the flames. His kiss was gentle, thoughtful, as though he could see right into her head. He eased her mouth open with his tongue and she let him, wrapping both arms around his neck so their chests meshed – setting a whole host of goosebumps off on a feverish march across her body.

Madison had imagined that the kiss would be warm, that it would make her tingle. She hadn't known his mere touch would set off a volcano inside her, or make her want to drag Connor to the nearest horizontal surface so she could have her wicked way with him. She pulled back slightly as she began to tremble, but couldn't back away entirely. Instead she looked into his eyes.

'Cold?' Connor asked, a slight smile playing on the edges of his lips, as if he knew exactly what she was experiencing.

'Surprised,' Madison admitted. 'I wasn't expecting you to be quite so skilled.'

'At kissing?' Connor's face lit up, taking Madison's insides with it. 'I may have spent most of my life working, but there are some things I found time for. And I believe if you're going to do anything in life, you ought to do it well. I've found with a bit of practice, there's not much you can't learn to be good at.'

Madison bit back the stupid burst of jealousy triggered by his words. 'So if it's all about practice, do you think we should try it again?'

Connor smiled, his eyes creasing at the corners, his face losing some of the seriousness Madison had got so used to. He didn't reply, but he did pull her nearer, and then their lips were touching again. Madison slid her hand up into Connor's thick dark hair and tightened her legs around him. Within seconds she was moving, squirming, sighing, while Connor lit her from the inside out, kissing her again slowly – all warmth and quiet control. Which, on some subconscious level, annoyed Madison because Connor obviously wasn't as lost in the kiss as she was – but that was probably a good thing as she was obviously losing her mind.

It was only the loud noises from the changing rooms, the quick blast of a shower, that had them drifting gently backwards away from each other – although Madison couldn't quite bring herself to let go. Perhaps because after all these years she finally had Connor where she wanted him, and he wasn't pushing her away?

Connor looked over Madison's shoulder and gave her a wry smile. 'We're about to have company – I'm thinking no one's going to mistake this for swimming.' He looked down at their intertwined bodies and Madison unlocked her legs from around him, feeling the loss of heat immediately. She gripped the side of the pool, breathing heavily, and tried to concentrate on slowing her heart.

How had that happened? She was supposed to be the free spirit, the sensual one. How had a man like Connor Robertson reduced her to jelly and made her feel so out of control?

'Are you okay?' Connor asked softly, his gaze searching. 'Because you look shocked, perhaps a little off balance, which is something I wouldn't have expected from you.'

'Me neither… perhaps I just need a banana to stabilise my vitamin levels?' Madison joked, hiding her confusion with humour. 'I guess we should get out,' she suggested, as two women appeared from the changing rooms, chatting to each other as they set their bags down on a couple of loungers, unaware of what they'd interrupted.

'I guess we should.' Connor watched her intently.

'We've got our massage booked in half an hour.' Madison cleared her throat, avoiding Connor's eyes as she climbed out of the pool, picking up her towel and wrapping it around her.

She turned to watch as he swam a couple of quick laps before making his way slowly from the pool. He looked every inch the dark-haired Adonis, a man very much in control. While she was trembling – more from emotion than cold – wondering exactly how far she'd fallen already, despite the fact Connor barely seemed affected at all.

'*Ohhh*, thank you,' Madison hummed, as her massage therapist finished the hour-long massage by sliding her fragrant hands slowly across her back, before stepping away. On the massage table beside her, Connor didn't make a sound, but she knew his therapist was just finishing working on his back too, because of the quiet slide of her feet as she moved around him.

They were both lying on their front, wearing nothing but underwear with fluffy white towels covering their bottom half. The lights had been dimmed, but not so much that you couldn't see the white walls or candles burning in each of the four corners. The air was filled with a variety of scents, some of which Madison could identify – frankincense, jasmine, rosemary and peppermint, mixed with almond oil and the smell of fresh laundry.

Madison tried to close her eyes again but as soon as she did, her head filled with Connor and the way he'd made her feel in the pool. She hadn't said much in the half hour between getting out and arriving for their massage, or for the whole hour they'd been having it. But Madison had felt suddenly shy around him, unsure of what to do, while Connor had returned to saying nothing.

'So we'll leave you both here for about ten minutes – just stay lying in this position.' The massage therapist eased the towel up to cover Madison's shoulders so she wouldn't get cold. 'Feel free to chat, or to fall asleep. Just relax if you can – this is all part of the treatment. If you get up too fast you won't feel as rested when you leave.'

'Okay.' Madison closed her eyes and the room fell silent as the therapists left. 'So did you enjoy that?' she asked Connor, wondering if by some miracle he'd actually fallen asleep. He hadn't said a word during the whole massage – aside from a few quiet groans as the therapist had worked on him. She opened her eyes again, but couldn't see Connor's face because it was turned towards the wall.

'I… yes.' Connor turned his head so he could look at her. 'I've never understood the fascination with therapies of any kind – seemed to me they were a waste of time. But…' He wriggled one of his bare shoulders and Madison tried not to stare at the perfect muscles as they flexed, or think about how it had felt when she'd had her hands wrapped around them earlier. *Around him.* 'I feel more relaxed, and the ache has gone.' Connor's lips curved. 'What did you think? You made a lot of noise – most of it sounded painful.'

'Ah.' Madison blushed, remembering her moans of pleasure as the therapist had worked out the kinks in her back. 'I loved it. I hope all that groaning didn't disturb you?'

'No.' Connor's eyes darkened. 'I liked it. I like how you take pleasure from things and aren't afraid to show it. If I'm honest, I don't really know how. I've only just begun to realise that might be a fault.'

'Sounds to me like you're dangerously close to trying some yoga,' Madison joked, charmed by Connor's words and the quiet admission she knew wouldn't have been easy.

'Perhaps.' Connor looked serious. 'This evening has been fun – more fun than I expected, so thank you, for forcing me into it. Perhaps I can see a little of Georgie's point of view – even if I don't entirely agree with it.'

'Georgie will come around – if she doesn't, I guess there's not much you can do.'

Connor closed his eyes.

'Will the business be okay, if Georgie doesn't work with you?' Madison asked quietly.

'It'll survive. I was just hoping for some company.' Connor opened his eyes again and Madison could see tiredness, and perhaps a hint of vulnerability there too. But before she could reassure Connor, he added, 'Besides, I've still got Jesse…'

'And you've got me too,' Madison admitted, knowing she was taking another huge step towards the edge she was in danger of hurtling over. 'I mean, not at work.' She paused, gauging his reaction. 'But if you need someone to talk to, or to have fun with…'

'Thank you.' Connor dipped his chin without lifting his head from the towel. 'I've been offered a few ears recently, but I might just take you up on the fun.'

'And the yoga?'

Connor laughed, a quick burst that lifted Madison's heart. This sad man with the serious eyes who took too much onto his shoulders was beginning to change in front of her. 'Why not?'

'Oh, Connor Robertson,' Madison said, feeling excited because she was finally making headway with him. She lifted her chin from the towel and rested it on her hand. 'I may yet get you doing the dragon pose.'

And whatever happened, Madison would do everything she could to build on the friendship they were forming now. To help relieve the tension around Connor's eyes – and lighten the darkness around him.

Chapter Twenty-Two

Sprinkles – the little ice cream parlour at the dock – was open, even though no ferries were due until the morning. But there was still a small queue of people outside and a couple walking along the seafront, eating cones covered in drizzles of chocolate. Beside Sprinkles, The Rock Shop was also open, and a few customers milled around inside, their hands filled with postcards and seashell creations. Next to that, an outdoor clothing shop was running a sale, and a young child toddled out wearing a dark blue fleece that still had the price tag on. His parents ran out of the store behind him, carrying the empty shopping bag and following the child, giggling as he headed down the seafront. Surf & Ride was closed, but a man was looking at the timetable in the window, making notes on his mobile phone. Madison pulled her light coat tight around her shoulders and shivered.

'Cold?' Connor asked.

'My hair's still damp – I'll be okay in a minute,' Madison replied, pointing to the sparkling string of lights hanging from the lamp posts, bobbing in the wind and framing the seafront. 'They're new. Makes it seem almost magical here, doesn't it?'

Connor looked surprised. 'I've never noticed them – I hardly come down to the dock. They're… pretty, I suppose.' He took a few moments to drink them in, shrugging off his jacket and handing it to her. 'Here, take this.'

'I'd say no, but I'm too cold to be polite – thanks.' Madison slipped her arms inside the dark leather and smelled the familiar scent of sawdust and paint – this time there was a hint of rosemary and peppermint too, a lingering memory from the massage. She hugged it tighter.

'I'm really not hungry.' Connor frowned at the queue, which had thinned to a couple of people.

'I can't believe you're turning down the chance of a Sprinkles ice cream.' Madison felt Connor's forehead, ignoring the tingles that flitted across her skin. 'Are you sick?'

'Is it really that good?' Connor looked doubtful. 'Because I've a beer in the fridge, and a chocolate bar at home, if Georgie hasn't eaten it.'

'You haven't tried any?' Madison squealed. 'Seriously, you've lived on Sunflower Island your whole life and never had a Sprinkles ice cream?'

Connor frowned. 'You're looking at me like I'm mad.'

'It's pity!' Madison exclaimed. 'I'm looking at you with pity. This is like having one of the Seven Wonders of the World on your doorstep, and deciding never to visit it. I knew you worked too hard, but I had no idea your life was so… joyless.' Madison shook her head and grabbed Connor's hand, holding on and tugging them both to the end of the queue. 'Connor Robertson, I'm about to introduce you to a whole new culinary experience, so you'd better prepare yourself.'

'Does it involve vegetables?' Connor grumbled. 'Because I'm really not prepared for that.'

'This is a vitamin-free zone, which is why I'm so surprised you've never been. There's no menu. You choose whatever takes your fancy. I love peanut butter and chocolate. If I'm feeling crazy I ask for a sprinkling of space dust.'

Connor looked at Madison blankly. 'What's wrong with vanilla?'

'There aren't enough hours left in this evening to explain.' Madison laughed, tugging Connor forwards again as the queue shortened. A couple left the shop holding matching cups filled with luminous orange and blue ice cream, and the crease in Connor's forehead deepened.

'Is that actually edible?' he said playfully.

She loved Connor like this, Madison realised, watching his mouth tip into a smile as he turned back. He was looser, so much less uptight. If he'd just kiss her again this evening would be perfect. 'There's only one way to find out.' Madison giggled, almost bumping into Finn as he walked out of the shop holding an enormous cone with about ten large flakes sticking out of it.

'You're here?' Finn looked surprised.

'We're… getting ice cream,' Madison replied.

'Ah, a date. We're out on one too.' Finn smiled as Amy appeared beside him. She was holding a small cup of chocolate ice cream. Her hair was up, she'd done her make-up and she wore the sparkly black heels Madison had admired the week before. 'We were going for a drive along the coast but this woman needed something to cheer her up. I'd normally get flowers, but Sprinkles was closest and everyone knows ice cream's the only way to mend a broken heart.'

'I'm fine.' Amy patted Finn's arm. 'I'm out with the most eligible bachelor in town – why wouldn't I be happy?' Madison could tell her friend didn't mean it from her crumpled forehead.

Finn shook his head, his expression light. 'Because you're in love with someone else? Don't sweat it. I'm enjoying your company, regardless of your crappy taste in men.' He grinned. 'Besides, I've been wanting to come here for a while.' He smiled at his ice cream before nodding to Madison. 'Enjoy the rest of your evening – try to do at least one thing I would.' Finn waggled his eyebrows as he and Amy walked away.

Madison tugged Connor's hand again and they entered the tiny room. Sprinkles could barely fit more than two people at the counter at a time and the walls were covered with about a million shelves, filled with bottles of silver and gold sprinkles, bowls, candles, sparkles and chocolates in all shapes and sizes. It felt like Aladdin's cave, or a scene from a *Harry Potter* movie. Behind the counter, a woman dressed in black wore a bright white apron with 'Dreams do come true… especially if they're made of ice cream' printed on the front.

'Madison. You're here.' The woman beamed, the wrinkles on her face smoothing out as she smiled. She squeezed herself out from the behind the counter so she could give Madison a hug.

'Mrs Blake.' Madison hugged the woman back, her head disappearing into her shoulder. Whenever she was home, Madison always popped in for an ice cream, and they'd developed a friendship over the years.

'Remember I told you to call me Laura.' Laura grinned and ran a hand over her grey hair, held in check by a white net. 'Goodness, look at you – you're even more beautiful than the last time I saw you. Where are your aunt and uncle? You usually come together.' Laura moved back behind the counter and picked up a cup. 'You don't like cones, I remember. Is it a peanut butter and chocolate day again?'

'With oodles of sparkles and a sprinkle of space dust, please. My aunt and uncle are on a cruise in the Caribbean, taking a well-earned rest.' Madison looked at the array of ice cream tubs behind the glass – they were yellow, blue, green, brown… one was even black. Colourful and delicious looking, there was so much to choose from. A thousand memories slammed into Madison. As Laura said, she used to come with her aunt. They'd walk along the seafront, talking rubbish for hours. She'd always hated leaving Sunflower Island on the ferry, because the last thing she'd see as they'd pulled away from the dock was Sprinkles, reminding her of all the things she was leaving behind.

'Did your aunt ever tell you I got the idea of selling ice cream from her? I used to visit the cafe at The Hideaway when she worked there as a teen. They only served cakes, but she would sneak ice cream in from the kitchen and make sundaes. We tried them all out. Sandy even helped me create the flavours when I first set up my business.' Laura laughed. 'Some of them were awful.'

'Didn't my uncle once invent a rhubarb and liquorice flavour? He was always making up ridiculous dessert combinations for us.' Madison giggled. 'That story's a Hideaway legend.'

'It tasted like an old boot.' Laura shuddered. 'That will never be repeated in my shop. I'm sorry,' she added, noticing Connor for the first time. 'Who's this?'

'A friend of mine.' Madison blushed.

'A date?' Laura looked delighted. 'He's gorgeous. Hopefully he'll be enough to tempt you to stay on the island for good this time.'

Madison cleared her throat, embarrassed. 'Connor owns Robertson & Robertson Builders. He's doing some work at The Hideaway, fixing up the cafe and redecorating for a Grand Opening we've got planned at the end of this month. We've just been to Lake Lodge together…' She paused – she didn't know how to explain the relationship, especially after their time in pool.

'Of course, I should have seen the resemblance to your mother. You really do look like her – same eyes and mouth. I knew Vanessa Robertson. Such a wonderful woman. I remember your father being head over heels in love with her, even in school. He always kept himself to himself, but Charles came alive when they were together. I hear he was never the same after she passed.'

'I really couldn't say,' Connor said stiffly.

Laura must have read his mood, because she began to scoop Madison's ice cream into a bowl, humming softly to herself. She handed the dish over before turning back to Connor. 'I'm sorry I made you feel awkward. It must have been a difficult few years.'

'I don't remember,' Connor said simply. 'My father never talked about my mother.'

'I didn't see him after she died and of course I've never met you. I heard he became a bit of a recluse. I'm guessing he took it badly – Vanessa always was the lighter side of that relationship. But then, opposites do attract.' Madison didn't look at Connor but knew her cheeks had reddened. 'Do you fancy some ice cream?' Laura continued. 'I've got all the usual flavours, plus a few of the unusual ones too.' She swept the scoop over the display. 'Raspberry, lemon, chocolate chip, banana… alternatively, curry or avocado. There's even Hawaiian pizza – it's vegetarian. I make that ice cream specially for one of my regulars.'

'I think that might be a little more than Connor can handle as a first-timer,' Madison joked. 'I'm hoping he'll go for some space dust, perhaps a scoop of banana.' She eyed him thoughtfully, taking in his suddenly tight shoulders, the hint of tension around his eyes – which had appeared as the conversation had turned to his parents. 'How about a scoop of avocado to go with it?' she asked, aiming to make him laugh. When Connor stared at her, Madison chuckled. 'Okay, you choose.'

Connor scanned the flavours. 'I'll have strawberry with a scoop of Hawaiian pizza – you can add the space dust, because I've got to admit to being intrigued.'

'Wow.' Madison's mouth stretched into an O. 'I guess the pizza shouldn't surprise me, but that's an odd combination.'

Connor shrugged. 'They don't have pie.'

'In that case, Laura, please add a scoop of avocado to mine.' Madison handed her bowl over. 'It wouldn't do for Connor to be more adventurous than me.'

They watched as Laura scooped Connor's ice cream into a green cup before adding avocado to Madison's bowl, then sprinkled them both with a healthy pinch of space dust. As Connor tried to pay, Laura shook her head. 'On the house. I've no idea how I avoided bumping into you all these years, but I'm glad I finally have. You remind me of your mother – playful.' She nodded. 'Fun, but at the same time thoughtful.' Laura squeezed out from behind the counter again to give Connor a quick hug, which he accepted awkwardly. Then she turned to Madison. 'And you come back soon, missy – no leaving the island again without saying goodbye. If you're ever looking for a little more adventure –' Laura pointed towards the counter – 'remember I'm here.'

'I will.' Madison gave her friend another quick hug before walking outside, past the long queue of people that had formed behind them, waiting impatiently in the darkness.

'You have a knack for making friends,' Connor admitted. 'I've always envied that.'

'I just talk to people. There's nothing clever about it. Making friends is easy – it's keeping them that's hard, especially when you're always moving around.' They headed to the seafront in silence, taking in the swaying sparkly lights. Madison dug out her spoon and took a quick bite.

'It's hard to believe so many people want to buy ice cream at the beginning of March.' Connor picked up his spoon and dug in too. 'Okay, now I understand,' he said. 'I thought the pizza flavour was a joke, but it's actually very good. I might even try the avocado next time.'

'You're weakening. I knew there was a health nut underneath that tough exterior,' Madison teased, enjoying the look on Connor's face as he dug into the colourful dessert. He wasn't thinking about work or his parents.

'If you served something like this in the cafe, you'd be an instant success. I'm guessing people can't get hold of Laura's ice cream without driving all the way down to the dock?'

'The cafe?' Madison asked vaguely, eating another spoonful of ice cream.

'Perhaps Laura sells it to other businesses?' Connor suggested.

'Yes, she has. I think she still does,' Madison replied, as space dust exploded in her mouth along with understanding. 'Of course, I can't believe I didn't think of it. Connor, you're a genius.'

'I am?' He looked up from his half-empty bowl.

'That's exactly what we need – having ice cream and making special desserts and sundaes will bring tons more people to The Hideaway. It'll make all the difference. You're brilliant. And we can get it in place for the Grand Opening.' She jumped up and down on the spot, doing a quick, happy wiggle, and Connor looked at her, amused.

'You do know you're in a public place, right?' he asked, making her laugh.

'One thing I've learned in life – aside from how to book a plane ticket – is we all need to let our hair down sometimes, Connor. Even you.'

Connor looked amused. 'Is that another roundabout way of persuading me to try yoga?'

'Why not?' Madison grinned, digging the spoon into her ice cream again. 'You've proved you can be adventurous. Just look at your choice of ice cream.'

'And look at yours,' Connor said, his tone lowering as he watched her.

'You can try some if you like?' Madison nudged a little onto her spoon and offered it to him. Connor wasn't the type to share food – she knew that already from the way he held himself back from people – so she was expecting him to say no. She wasn't expecting him to take her hand and guide the spoon towards his mouth, or to pull her closer as he did so.

'Tastes… okay,' he observed, watching her. 'For a vegetable. Now it's your turn.' He dug into his pizza flavour and held the spoon out. Madison opened her mouth and tasted. The flavours danced across her tongue. There was sweetness from the pineapple with a savoury undercurrent, followed by a popping of space dust that fizzed across the roof of her mouth.

'Interesting.' She licked her lips, noticing Connor's eyes following the movement.

'I'm going to say thank you again,' Connor said seriously. 'For bringing me here. For introducing me to a new culinary experience.'

'And what Laura said about your mother?'

'Perhaps for that too. I wasn't lying when I said my father never talked about her, so the insight was... enlightening. Perhaps it helps to explain why he was the way he was.' Connor traced a rough finger down the side of Madison's face. 'You have a way of bringing lightness into the world that's difficult to ignore.'

'Oh... well.' Madison was tongue-tied but she didn't look away, even as Connor leaned down to give her an unexpected kiss. He tasted sweet and her insides warmed as he gently ran his tongue across hers. She tried to edge closer, but their ice cream bowls bumped, making them both step back. Connor watched her for a beat, his eyes intense, and Madison shivered, pulling his coat tightly around her.

'I guess we should go home.' Connor looked disappointed. 'You're cold.'

Madison checked her watch. 'It's only eight thirty. I'm not ready for tonight to finish,' she confessed, feeling her cheeks heat. 'But I'm not sure where we can go next. There are loads of people at The Hideaway and I don't want to get in the way...'

'Georgie's at my house.' Connor frowned. 'The atmosphere there is bordering on hostile.'

'What about my studio? I mean, the heating's on and there's a kitchen, mugs and a kettle. I could probably make us a hot drink – we could pick up milk and teabags on the way? It'll be an excellent opportunity for us to compliment your paintwork again.'

'No dragon pose?' Connor teased, watching Madison. Like he was waiting for something – perhaps poised for them to take another brave step?

'Are you ready for that?' Her voice deepened. But she didn't look away, even as Connor smiled suggestively.

'After swimming under the stars, a massage and ice cream – who wouldn't be? You're changing my world, Madison Skylar – why stop now?'

Chapter Twenty-Three

What had possessed him to do this? Connor opened his eyes to find Madison beaming at him. There was some kind of hippy music playing in the background, and he could swear he smelled camomile tea brewing somewhere, even though they hadn't put the kettle on.

'We'll begin sitting.' Madison pointed at one of the dark blue mats on the floor before sinking smoothly into a cross-legged position. Her face looked serene and beautiful, in sharp contrast to the oozing mass of nerves that had taken up residence in Connor's head. Despite that – or perhaps because of it – he found himself dropping to the floor so he could sit on the mat facing her. He crossed his legs, feeling a stretch through his calves.

'I always like to start my sessions with a few deep breaths,' Madison explained, watching Connor with an unreadable expression. 'I'm guessing you're going to think I'm crazy. But it's surprising how many of the little things we don't pay attention to in our lives.'

'Workloads, schedules?' Connor said, taking a deep breath in and filling his lungs.

'Breathing.' Madison smiled. She'd changed into a set of clothes she kept in one of the wardrobes upstairs. Now she wore a red vest top that followed the curves of her body, and black yoga leggings.

Connor's jeans were loose and he'd stripped down to his long-sleeved T-shirt. The outfit wasn't perfect, but Madison had told him it would work. She took another deep breath in before letting it out, and Connor found himself doing the same. 'Feel the tension leave your body with each breath,' Madison encouraged softly. 'Forget about what you're supposed to be doing – put aside your to-do list. It'll be easier to relax.'

Connor didn't know about that. His shoulders felt tight and he was finding it difficult to concentrate, with her sitting on the floor opposite him and that incredible view of the stars outside the window framing her slim, strong body. But he did as he was told, relaxing a notch as the air slowly left his lungs.

'We're going to start with child's pose – give it a try, don't strain your shoulders and if anything hurts, stop.' Connor watched as Madison knelt onto her knees before slumping forwards with her arms in front of her. She took a long breath in and let it out before turning her head to look at him and grinning. 'This is great for grounding yourself. Can you try it?'

'Not without feeling ridiculous,' he murmured, moving onto all fours before sinking down and deciding he'd officially lost his mind. He could feel the stretch across his shoulders but it wasn't unpleasant. Perhaps Madison was right and the constant ache there was due to tension rather than anything sinister?

'Does it feel okay?' Madison asked, sounding concerned.

'Yes. Will this take long?' Now he was here, back in The Hideaway, the reality of what he was doing was messing with his mind. He should be working in the cafe, or at the very least doing some paperwork.

'Clear your mind,' Madison soothed, placing a soft hand onto Connor's shoulder, making the muscle under the surface go wild. 'I can see the tension here despite all the relaxation this evening – this won't take long, and it'll work a lot better if you give in to it.'

'I don't know what that means,' Connor said, feeling both confused and turned on.

'It means stop thinking,' Madison answered softly, taking another deep breath. 'I love being here, knowing there's nowhere else I need to be, nothing that needs doing. I'm not saying forever,' she added quickly, so his impatient comment died on his tongue. 'Just for the next few minutes. I'm at peace with the here and now. Try it: three breaths. See how it feels.'

Connor closed his eyes and filled his lungs before letting the breath out slowly. He could hear Madison next to him and ached to look. As he let out a breath, he found himself relaxing again as the air left his body, taking a little of the tension with it.

'Now move upwards and get on all fours,' Madison ordered quietly, as Connor sat back on his knees. 'This is tabletop. Rise up, like this, see – we call this one cat.' She curled her spine and moulded her body like an angry cat arching its back, then dipped it down again, doing the movement a couple of times in quick succession. Her arms were tanned and her slim body looked strong and agile. Connor let his gaze trace Madison's skin. He'd never realised how flawless it was, or how sensual such slow, peaceful movements could be. Madison stopped suddenly and turned to look at him. Her face went bright red. 'You were meant to copy me, do it at the same time.'

'I...' Connor cleared his throat. 'Did you learn all this in Thailand?' he asked, making conversation, trying to get his errant body back on track.

'I learned in India, but I've done courses in a few other countries.' She flashed a quick smile. 'And you're distracting me. This isn't a spectator sport. To get the full benefit you need to participate.'

'I feel ridiculous,' Connor said, getting on all fours and mirroring the catlike movement. Despite that, the stretch across his back felt good. He could feel Madison's eyes on him as he completed a few sets before pushing back onto his knees again. Her cheeks were still red, only now she looked flushed rather than embarrassed. Was he having the same effect on her as she'd been having on him?

'That's...' Madison swallowed, waving a hand in front of her face. 'It's hot in here,' she added. 'Do your back and shoulders feel all right? There are a couple more warm-up exercises I'd like you to try before we move into some of the basic poses.'

'It's fine.' Connor watched Madison as she nodded, looking strangely shy. She moved onto her hands and knees, then stretched her legs out behind her so her straightened torso was held up by her hands and toes.

'This is a basic plank. From here you walk your hands backwards and stretch upwards.' She stuck her bottom in the air and moved her hands towards her feet so her body moved into an upside-down V shape. 'This is downward dog. You've probably heard of it – pedal your feet up and down like this to warm up your legs.' Madison lifted her heels one after the other so she looked like she was walking. The movement was smooth and strangely graceful.

'You look good,' Connor admitted. Unused to offering compliments, the words felt odd on his tongue. 'I can tell you've been doing this for a while.'

'It's the one thing I've stuck at through the years. Good thing too, as it turns out. It makes me feel peaceful and grounded. Whenever I feel like I don't know what to do next, or if I'm lonely, I do a yoga session. It always helps.' She turned to look at him, her head still upside down, her hair trailing like a waterfall past her ears, down towards the floor. 'And I've no idea why I told you that, except I hope you have a similar experience. I know you need to find a place to escape to that doesn't involve work. A place where you can let go and be happy.'

'I escape when I run.' From everything, except thoughts of his father. Connor tore his eyes away from Madison and got himself into a plank position before moving his hands into the correct place. Now his head was pointing to the floor while he faced his knees. 'I feel ridiculous,' he murmured again.

'You need to move your legs.' Madison knelt beside Connor and he stilled, more aware of her than ever. She guided his leg into the correct position and sat watching while he tried to copy her. 'How does that feel?' she asked quietly. There was tension in her voice. Connor couldn't tell why, but awareness skidded through him, making it hard to concentrate.

'My legs feel odd, like they're in the wrong place.'

'You need to move this leg further to the left, here…' Madison edged closer and tried to ease it into another position, bumping her shoulder against his arm, making his body tense as he reacted to her.

He cleared his throat. 'Where exactly?'

'Here.' As Madison moved again, Connor did the same. Trying to read her mind, he let his leg slide towards her, feeling it shake as he held himself upright. 'That's a little too far,' Madison said, coming even closer, pushing against Connor as she adjusted his arm.

'Let me try,' Connor grumbled, jerking his leg, beginning to lose his balance as Madison tried to adjust him again. 'That's not going to work…' He didn't have time to right himself as his leg went out from under him and he found himself falling sideways, losing his footing as gravity took over and he toppled.

'I'm sorry,' Madison shrieked, trying to grab Connor's arm. But it was too late, and before she could help, he landed on his side in an untidy pile. 'Are you okay?' Madison leaned over as he rolled onto his back, her long brown hair trailing on his chest. The top of her T-shirt fell forwards, exposing the hint of a red lacy bra.

'I'm fine. I didn't hurt myself.' Connor lay on the floor and looked upwards at the newly painted ceiling. 'Well, this is relaxing, more like the massage. I might prefer it to yoga – perhaps you can add it to your routine?'

Madison looked into his eyes. Hers had deepened to a dark brown in the dim light. Combined with her hair, which had all but fallen out of the untidy knot on her head, she looked sexy, beautiful and a little dishevelled. 'This is becoming a habit. Does anything hurt?'

'Why, are you planning to kiss it better?' Connor responded softly, wondering what the hell had got into him. Maybe it was just the result of this evening, spending so much time with Madison? Or perhaps he'd spent too long fighting this attraction – and was finally ready to give in to it?

'If you like…' Madison looked surprised, but her gaze stayed locked with his. Connor's heart thumped. He should walk away now, he knew that. Get up off the floor, grab his shoes and run – from the dangerous feelings she was stirring inside him, the reckless wants and needs filling his heart. Because despite how he was feeling, there was still the small matter of him keeping the truth about The Hideaway being for sale from her, which made him feel dishonest. But instead of doing the right thing, he found himself reaching up and taking Madison's hand so he could tug her down until their faces were almost touching.

'My lips hurt,' Connor said.

Madison laughed softly. 'If you're hurting, then it's my fault. I really ought to make it better.' She leaned over tentatively and traced her lips slowly across his mouth – just the merest of touches, but enough to set off a rocket in his body and head. 'Enough?' she asked, pulling back.

'No,' Connor replied, wondering if he'd ever get enough of this woman. He knew he was making a mistake, even as he placed a hand on the back of Madison's head so he could gently pull her towards him. He knew deep in his heart he'd probably regret it. Despite those doubts, or perhaps because of them, he blanked his mind, desperate to be free of the guilt whispering to him about schedules and deadlines, of failing to live up to the legacy he'd been left. And he let himself fall, pulling Madison towards him again, until their lips met and he could barely think at all.

Chapter Twenty-Four

Connor Robertson was kissing her. That was all Madison could think as she let him pull her nearer, moving one leg up and over his torso until she straddled him, fulfilling a teenage fantasy that had begun to come true in the pool. She let her fingers run through Connor's thick, brown hair as he kissed her, letting her body dip down so she could lie across his torso. Now they were chest to chest, she could feel his hard muscles through her vest, could feel the power of his arms as he wrapped them around her back.

Only they weren't close enough. Not by a long shot.

Madison moved her arms lower to reach for the bottom of Connor's T-shirt, surprising him – he broke off their kiss to stare into her eyes. 'You sure about this?' he asked, scanning her face.

'Never surer.' Madison lifted the T-shirt to the middle of Connor's chest, exposing smooth, tanned skin and a trail of dark hair that travelled like an arrow from his belly button, before disappearing into the top of his jeans. She'd seen his body in the pool, but being here in her studio it felt more intimate.

'I know you won't want to answer but… is there anyone else?' Connor asked, and Madison stopped tugging at his clothes.

'No…' She paused, thinking about Seth and the open relationship she was in the process of ending because there was no future in it. 'Not really, not anymore, and in all honesty… it's never been like this.' She sat up, still straddling him, her eyes skimming the bottom of his chest. Was he going to change his mind? Throw her off, disappear back into the cafe to hide himself in work? Or would he give in? 'In truth, I've never wanted to feel like this with anyone else.' Her voice dropped as she tried to explain, tried to put into words her thoughts. The same ones she didn't understand herself. 'You know I've had… feelings for you since I was fifteen.'

'I remember you from then.' Connor's eyes flickered across her face, his expression unreadable. 'I'm not sure why. I noticed you, but you were too young… Besides, I didn't have time for girlfriends – I was always at work.'

'You're not working now.' Madison's eyes lowered to Connor's belly button again, dropping to the top of his jeans, where their bodies met.

'I'm meant to be doing yoga.' A slight smile lifted Connor's face.

'I'd rather do this.' With that, she tugged at his T-shirt again, only this time he didn't stop her. Instead he helped as she pulled it over his head. Madison stayed where she was and gave herself a chance to look at him, to take in the muscles and hard planes of his body, the breadth of his shoulders and chest. There wasn't an ounce of excess flesh on him, just firm muscles and tanned skin that told of months toiling outside – and a long scar running across his shoulder, probably from a work injury. Madison grasped the belt on Connor's jeans and began to undo it, before he stopped her by putting his hands over hers.

'I may be out of practice, but I'm pretty sure this works better if we both get undressed,' he said quietly. 'If you let me move out from under you, I could even help?'

'I'm happy to do it. The point of this session was for you to learn to let go and relax. There are no schedules here, no expectations for you to do the work.' Madison grinned as she tugged at her vest before throwing it up and over her head, savouring the way Connor's eyes lit up, then slowly dropped to her bra.

'Red?' he asked.

'In China I learned the colour means good fortune and happiness. It may just be superstition, but I wear red a lot.' Connor smiled as Madison reached slowly behind herself to unclip the bra, before throwing it onto the carpet. Her body tingled as his eyes darkened, skimming her skin.

'Good fortune and happiness – I'm not superstitious, but tonight I'll agree with that,' Connor said, pulling Madison down to his chest again. This time it felt different: they were skin to skin. Closer even than when they'd been half naked in the pool. Connor kissed Madison again, the connection surprising her. Now their kiss wasn't slow, studied or planned out as she'd come to expect from him. And it was no leisurely journey or meandering road either. This kiss felt urgent. As though Connor had decided they'd wasted enough time already.

Connor's fingers slid down Madison's back, the calluses on his hands rough against her skin. They stopped for a beat at the top of her yoga pants, before slowly sliding underneath the waistband. He continued to kiss her gently as he explored, taking full advantage of the roomy, stretchy Lycra as he skipped his fingers across her knickers, stroking further downwards across her bum cheeks. Madison moaned against Connor's mouth, found herself squirming against his groin as he continued to explore, before he rolled suddenly onto his side, taking her with him, and laid her gently backwards.

'Now the jeans have to go.' Madison laughed, wasting no time as she tried to sit up and undo Connor's belt, pushing his trousers and boxers over his bottom onto his thighs, where he took over, pulling them off. Then it was her turn. Connor peeled Madison's yoga leggings down, taking her lacy red knickers with them. The fact that they matched her bra was clearly lost on him, as he tossed the bundle of clothes across the room into an untidy pile. Then he sat back down onto one of the mats, leaning against the wall before reaching for her.

This time when Madison straddled him, they were skin against skin with nothing in the way. She let herself sink down, looking into Connor's eyes, feeling her heart judder as she found him watching her, seeming troubled – haunted, perhaps, by ghosts from the past?

'Stop thinking,' Madison demanded as she leaned forwards to kiss Connor again, and he seemed to wake up. He slid his hands slowly from her hips upwards, gently feathering the skin until everything pulsed.

'You really want to do this?' Connor trailed kisses downwards, hitting Madison's collarbone in seconds before easing her backwards so he could continue tracing a slow, sensual path.

'It's not me who's been holding back,' Madison ground out. 'And since I'm naked, sitting on your lap, I'm guessing you've got my answer. How about you?'

Connor sighed as he dragged a tongue across one nipple, sending Madison's thoughts and hormones skittering. 'This is happening fast. And I've never been one to rush into things,' he admitted, kissing a measured path to the other nipple. 'But once I've made a decision, I don't back out.'

'Good to know.' Madison smiled, letting herself sink even lower. 'Does that mean we can stop talking?'

'For a flibbertigibbet you're not very romantic.' Connor laughed and licked the other nipple, sending all of Madison's senses and reason flying again. How could one man manage to take such a hold over her body? Make her feel and want things she'd never experienced? Madison grabbed at Connor's hair, holding him to her as he continued to lick, suck and stroke. He was hard beneath her – as she moved up and down Connor moaned, and she reached out a hand to move him into position.

'Impatient,' Connor teased, moving backwards so he could look into Madison's eyes as she thrust down, her insides stretching as she took him inside her. He stilled for a second, keeping the connection, before joining her in a slow, steady rhythm. Up and down. Deepening the link between them.

Madison's insides were on fire – her body felt like liquid. She'd never felt like this. All her relationships had been fleeting, born of necessity while she was growing up, because she never knew when she'd be moving on. Even Seth had had the air of transience, a friendship honed through short breaks and a recognition that they'd never be permanent. She'd never let herself get close to anyone. Never let herself feel like this. But with Connor she couldn't help it. From the age of fifteen she'd wanted him, for reasons she'd never understood. And now that wish was coming true.

As they continued to move, Connor watched her. His eyes were so dark now – the blue-green irises had all but disappeared as his pupils dilated. His hair was a mess from where she'd run her hands through it, and his mouth – so often clenched with tension – had relaxed.

Madison felt herself building, knew soon she'd fall. Their pace increased, as if Connor could read her mind. She let her eyes flicker closed. Then in one short sudden burst, she exploded, and Connor joined her, shattering into tiny fragments before fluttering back down. Madison rested her head on Connor's shoulder, listening as his fast breathing slowed. Would he pull away now they'd got so close? Or would this mark the change in their relationship she'd been hoping for?

Chapter Twenty-Five

I am an idiot, Connor told himself for about the thousandth time, as he walked hand in hand with Madison towards The Hideaway, noticing for the first time how bright the stars were. It was as if this one short evening had brought him to life, making him taste, feel and see things as he never had before. Beside him, Madison's hair tumbled around her shoulders, catching the moonlight on the tips. The lights were on in the guesthouse, which meant Dee was still up, and perhaps the guests were too – eating cake, playing games or chilling out in front of an open fire. Connor looked at the building, squashing down the layers of guilt that had taken up permanent residence in his stomach.

Guilt at not coming clean with Madison despite their evening together, of raising her hopes about saving The Hideaway for her aunt and uncle – even though he knew there was none. Guilt made worse by what they'd just shared – something he hadn't planned on, but had blown his mind anyway. There was no way he could continue to keep things from her now. Despite what Dee and the Skylars wanted, he had to come clean. He just didn't know how.

'Are you okay?' Madison asked suddenly, brushing wild hair from her eyes. 'Sorry, I phased out. I didn't realise I was so tired.'

'It's okay. It was an amazing evening,' Connor murmured.

'I hope you're not regretting it?' Madison sounded concerned and Connor found himself shaking his head because – despite the guilt – he couldn't imagine having done anything else.

As they drew closer to the guesthouse, the front door opened and Dee and Stanley walked out, followed by a man Connor didn't recognise. Madison sighed and then gasped.

'Seth?' She sounded annoyed. 'What are you doing here?' They came nearer, and Connor hung back as the man approached Madison with a huge grin on his face. He was tall, with blond hair cut short and muscles that told of long hours spent in the gym. In two long strides, he'd wrapped Madison in his arms and was spinning her around in front of the house. Connor took a step backwards, shocked by the intensity of the jealousy that shot through him.

'Mads.' Seth laughed, putting her down. 'I thought I'd surprise you.' He grinned, holding a hand out to Connor. It took everything Connor had not to ignore it. Instead he shook it, quickly letting go. 'Hi, I'm Madison's boyfriend, Seth.' The man didn't come out and ask who Connor was, but he had the air of someone staking his claim. *Boyfriend? Seriously?* Connor really should have expected it: Madison was hardly the traditional type. Despite knowing that, ice penetrated his veins, sliding through his blood until his emotions were paralysed.

Which was probably a good thing.

'It's getting late. I've got stuff to be getting on with.' Connor didn't look at Madison as he spoke. He steeled his heart, determined not to show her how he was feeling. How could he have been so stupid? He knew what Madison was like – a leopard didn't change its spots. Just look at his father, look at Georgie… This was what you got when you let your guard down.

'Oh, *ahhhhh*…' Madison looked horrified as her attention switched between Connor and Seth. 'I really should explain.'

'No need.' Connor shook his head, marching down the driveway in the direction of the road before Madison could say any more.

He wasn't in the mood for explanations of any kind. Besides, he had paperwork to do. Lots of it. And a pile of beers in his fridge he might just make a dent in. So he continued to stomp away, wondering what the hell had got into him this evening, and how long it would take to get the memories of the dark-haired mermaid, who'd tasted so sweet, out of his mind.

Chapter Twenty-Six

'Who was that?' Seth asked, as Connor headed down The Hideaway's drive in the direction of his home. Madison closed her eyes and shook her head, trying to block out Connor's expression as Seth had introduced himself. Two steps forward and a million steps back – that seemed to be the mantra for their relationship, no matter what she did.

'His name's Connor. I've known him for a while,' Madison answered, hearing irritation in her voice and trying to hide it. 'What are you doing here?' She looked up into Seth's face, at the cropped blond hair and sharp cheekbones she knew so well, feeling a familiar tug of affection, but nothing like the mind-numbing attraction and confusion that overwhelmed her every time she got near to Connor. Dee took Stanley's hand and swiftly disappeared inside The Hideaway, no doubt attempting to give them time alone. Madison pulled Connor's coat around her shoulders, realising she hadn't returned it, feeling suddenly cold. 'Shall we go inside?' She didn't wait for an answer. Instead she trudged into the hallway and closed the door.

'Thought I'd surprise you. I said I wanted to catch up?' Seth looked puzzled, his light blue eyes clouding. 'I knew you'd be bored by now, so we can spend a couple of days together and mix things up. Maybe you'll want to come back with me to Amsterdam after?'

'I'm working, and I told you I want to stay,' Madison grumbled, exasperated. Why did no one believe her? Of all the people she'd met on her travels, Seth was the one who knew her best, yet even he didn't seem to know her at all. She could hear voices from the sunroom, so made her way towards the door leading to the kitchen, knowing from the quiet tap of footsteps that Seth had followed. She switched on a light before flicking the knob of the kettle. 'You want some camomile tea?'

'Please.' Seth stood next to the long breakfast bar with his hands in his pockets, looking both handsome and out of place. Madison had never imagined him at The Hideaway. They'd always met in other places – hotels, campgrounds, on boats, in cities. Never anywhere she'd lived permanently or cared about. And it felt wrong. *He* felt wrong and she wasn't sure why. Had she always felt this way? Had they always just been a convenience to each other?

'I'm in the way.' Seth looked put out. 'I got the sense that guy – Connor – wasn't that happy to see me?'

'He doesn't really do happy – I wouldn't take it personally,' Madison explained, putting teabags in two mugs so Seth couldn't see her expression.

'You're seeing him?' Seth asked gently, sounding out of sorts. 'I know we've always agreed we're not exclusive, so I don't want to tread on any toes.' He talked quickly, obviously trying to get the words out.

'Yes, no, I've no idea. We're – I don't know what – just friends,' Madison admitted. Now Seth had arrived, Connor probably wouldn't ever talk to her again.

'I could speak to him?' Seth offered, walking around the kitchen to look out of the window, avoiding her eyes. 'Explain our relationship?'

'Can you?' Madison cocked her head. 'Because now I've taken a step back, I'm not sure I can explain it myself.' She poured water over the teabags and handed a mug to Seth.

Seth frowned, putting his hands in his pockets. 'I care for you, Mads.'

'I care for you too, but I'm sorry, I don't want to do the friends with benefits thing anymore. I don't want to lose your friendship, but I need more… I want something different.' She sipped from the mug, burning her tongue.

'I thought keeping things casual suited both of us. This feels sudden…' Seth looked unhappy.

'I think it's been coming for a while,' Madison admitted. She just hadn't known it until recently. 'How long do you plan on staying?'

'I thought a few days, if that's okay?'

Madison nodded because she couldn't really say no.

'Are you sure you're happy with this, Mads?' Seth asked, looking bemused. 'You've never wanted anything but casual, never craved a permanent home – we always said we never would.'

'*You* said that.' She hadn't said anything. 'I want different things. This is a new beginning for me. I've been running for most of my life – it's time I found somewhere permanent.' Madison sipped some more of the hot tea, relishing the burn now as it slid down her throat.

'Running?' Seth asked.

'I never felt like I belonged.' Madison glanced around the room. 'But this place is different. I can't explain why. It's always been different.'

Seth looked around the kitchen, a line appearing on his forehead. 'It looks ordinary, exactly what we said we never wanted. But if you're happy... do you want me to leave?'

'Of course not. You can stay in one of the guest rooms. I'm going to be working but you can do a yoga class, go for a walk. I'm pleased to see you, Seth. It'll be good to catch up.'

'It'll be good to spend time with you too – I've...' He paused. 'Missed you.'

'I've missed you too, but don't expect me to change my mind.'

'We'll see.' Seth's expression turned thoughtful. 'Remember, I've known you a while too, Madison Skylar. I know all about the ache in your blood, the need to move on. This place looks cosy, but not very exciting. I'm guessing a few more weeks and you'll be climbing the walls and booking that ferry out of here. And when you do, you'll know where to find me.'

Would she?

'We'll see,' Madison echoed, sipping more of her drink, feeling unsettled. Hoping Seth wasn't right. Knowing – whatever happened – she had to make things right with Connor first.

Chapter Twenty-Seven

It was dark in the cafe. Probably because it was only 6 a.m. Connor put the lights on before taking a step backwards. Jesse had obviously finished the counter last night – it gleamed – and the oak shelves had been given another coat. The walls looked dull in comparison, a combination of dirty brown paint and multiple chips reaching down to bare plaster suggesting someone may have once been throwing darts. In the kitchen, Jesse had cleaned the brushes and lined them up beside the can of varnish. Connor hadn't seen the boy this morning – he'd still been in bed. But after tossing and turning for most of the night, he'd thought he might as well get up, call Jaws, go for a run and get started. If for no other reason than to force the image of Madison and Seth out of his head.

Dammit, he needed a strong cup of tea and at least three pies. He'd probably head into town later and treat himself. He heard the sharp tap of heels on the stairs leading into the cafe from outside and braced himself for Madison – somehow, he knew it was her before she'd even appeared.

'You're up early.' He busied himself with the tile cutter without looking at her. He heard Jaws go to greet her and cursed the traitorous dog under his breath.

'Couldn't sleep,' Madison murmured, plonking a mug of tea at his side before kneeling to give Jaws a tummy rub. 'I brought you a peace offering. I'd like to explain about Seth.'

'There's no need,' Connor said gruffly. 'I'm a grown-up. I know what happened in the yoga studio was a mistake.'

'It wasn't for me,' Madison answered after a long pause. 'Seth and I are friends… okay, we've been more than that. But it's always been casual. That sounds bad,' she added, when he fixed her with an incredulous glare.

'Casual?' Connor ignored the sharp stab of jealousy and picked up his tea to take a sip. It was exactly the way he liked it, which inexplicably made him annoyed.

'We get together sometimes. We've been friends for years. It's never been serious and it's over now. I'm not even sure what he's doing here.'

'Aren't you?' Connor shook his head. For a woman of the world, Madison didn't understand much about men. 'I think your Seth might feel differently.'

'No.' As Connor turned to look at Madison, she flushed deeply. Her hair was tied up on her head again and she'd applied no make-up. She wore old jeans and a loose shirt that looked like it might belong to her uncle. She'd obviously dressed in a hurry but she'd never looked more beautiful to him. 'You're wrong. He's got other girlfriends – women – he sees. We have fun, no strings. I've never felt strongly about him.' She looked confused. 'Sometimes it's nice to have company. Especially when you're far from home and alone. We met in Amsterdam and then kept in touch after. I know I don't admit it, but I get lonely…' She took a breath, looking embarrassed.

'Sometimes I crave the company of a friend. But Seth's only that. He's a wanderer, he doesn't want to settle down.'

Connor shook his head and swallowed the rest of the tea in one, wishing it were beer or something stronger. Did Madison really not understand the effect she had on people? She clearly had no idea what she was doing to him. 'You've spent your life surrounded by people,' he said, exasperated. 'I've watched them fall at your feet. Follow you around like puppies.' His eyes dropped to his dog, who was practically drooling on the floor, showing his belly and hoping for another tummy rub. 'How can you not know the man's in love with you?'

'He's not – that's ridiculous,' Madison started, before nibbling her fingernail. 'We're just friends… He's never wanted more. We want different things – he's never been interested in permanence.'

'Seems to me you're the one pushing Seth away – not the other way around,' Connor said gently. 'Perhaps like you do with everyone in your life?'

'You're wrong. That's not what I've done with my aunt and uncle.'

'Isn't it?' Connor looked at her intently. 'Then why are you always leaving?'

'Because for a lot of years, I didn't know how else to live. I don't mean to push people away – that's not what I'm doing with you.' Madison pouted but didn't say any more because there was a crash from upstairs as someone opened and then slammed the door, before loud footsteps headed down to join them.

'Seth.' Madison sounded surprised. The man in question rubbed his eyes. His hair stood up on the top of his head in wisps, and his clothes – a dark blue sweatshirt and black jeans – were rumpled. 'How did you find me?'

Seth yawned. 'Dee mentioned the cafe was in the process of being renovated. I woke up and thought I'd take a walk and check it out. I heard voices when I got outside.' He glanced at Connor's empty mug. 'You got tea down here?'

'In the kitchen.' Connor pointed to his left. Aside from putting up tiles and painting, they'd finished the kitchen off a couple of days before, which meant they could at least make themselves hot drinks, and there was a microwave to nuke pies. 'Or there's coffee and biscuits.'

'I'll make us drinks,' Madison offered. 'Any camomile?' She gave Connor a half smile that made his insides pitch forwards.

'Georgie gave Jesse a load of stuff to bring down – there might be something herbal in there. I haven't checked the cupboards.' Connor watched Madison disappear into the kitchen, then picked up a tile and marked it up. He had work to do this morning. He hadn't got up early to chat.

'It looks good in here.' Seth walked up to the counter to join him. 'I can see this place will be quite something when it's finished. You do renovation work a lot?'

'I do whatever comes my way,' Connor admitted, putting a square blue tile in the cutter.

'You known Mads long?' Seth walked down the counter so he could check out the shelving.

'Since she was fifteen. She hasn't changed much.' Connor frowned as Seth walked around the back of the counter to get a better look.

'You do great work,' Seth murmured. 'I'm not very good with my hands.'

'You staying long?' Connor muttered, unable to stop himself. He had an image in his head of Madison and Seth that he couldn't quite get rid of.

'Not anymore – I got a call from a friend late last night. She's in Paris so I'll be leaving this evening.' Seth glanced towards the kitchen with a sad smile. 'It's a shame. I was hoping to persuade Mads to join me when I left.'

'She's planning on staying.' Connor could hear the jealousy in his own voice.

Seth glanced towards the kitchen again. 'If you've known Madison for as long as she says, you'll know how many times she's said the same. I've an inkling this place won't keep her long. Nothing else ever has. I'd spare yourself some pain…'

Connor was saved from answering by Madison bringing in their teas and a plate of biscuits. As she put them on the counter, Connor avoided her eyes, taking another mental step backwards from the feelings she was bringing out in him.

Chapter Twenty-Eight

'It's looking good down here.'

Connor looked up – startled by the unfamiliar voice – as he finished laying the last blue tile, completing the small patch he'd begun in the kitchen hours after Madison and Seth had left. There were now only the walls to paint, ready for the Grand Opening – but wow, there were a lot of them. The man Connor recognised as a guest of The Hideaway stood in the doorway, staring at him. He wore a dark grey suit and held a clipboard against his right thigh.

'Can I help?' Connor rose to his feet and dusted his hands lightly across his jeans.

'I've been waiting to speak with you. My girlfriend and the other guests are out walking and I've been wanting to see how the work on the cafe is progressing without an audience. I'm seriously considering putting in an offer on The Hideaway. I had a few conversations with the Skylars before they left for their cruise. Dee said now might be a good time for you to answer some questions. I'm David O'Sullivan. I own Lake Lodge. We haven't formally met, but you helped us off the beach last Friday – and I hear you've done some work for my site manager as well.'

Connor glanced behind David into the cafe. Jesse had popped out to walk Jaws ten minutes earlier and the room was empty and silent.

'You've been staying here?' Connor murmured. 'Isn't that a little... odd?'

'Leaving today.' David nodded. 'I like to scope out the places I'm thinking of buying in advance. It's good business. I thought I'd stay a week to see how the place runs, its strengths and weaknesses. It was my girlfriend's birthday, so I killed two birds with one stone. Sophia favours cosy and homey rather than sophisticated.' David shrugged. 'None of us is perfect.' He looked around the kitchen with a frown. 'I'll get in a surveyor, obviously, but I wanted to pick your brains. How are the buildings structurally?'

'The place is sound.' Connor folded his arms, feeling like a traitor. What was Dee thinking, sending the man down here?

'So it's just about the revamp. I can see everywhere needs a lick of paint.' David looked thoughtful. 'And the cafe is looking better already. When do you think you'll finish?'

'We're still agreeing timings,' Connor replied, feeling uncomfortable. It was bad enough keeping the fact that The Hideaway was up for sale from Madison, without giving inside information to a prospective buyer. He busied himself clearing up some of the stray pieces of tile he'd discarded. 'I really don't know at the moment. It's not in my hands.'

David frowned. 'I'm hoping it won't be opening soon. I can see The Hideaway is picking up business. A couple of Lake Lodge's customers have even talked about booking in. The yoga retreats and walks were a good idea. With a cafe opening, it's bound to get busier. I don't want the Skylars changing their minds about selling up, or raising the price.' He chuckled, clearly oblivious to the fact that Connor was mentally giving him the evil eye. 'This place will be a great complement to Lake Lodge. Owning both means I'll dominate the hotel business on the island.' David walked to the counter and ran an eye across the wood. 'Beautiful workmanship. I've got to hand it to you, you know your stuff. The main building is a bit of a state though – I'm wondering how much work will need to be done. I've got a few ideas, some walls we could lose, and the kitchen could be modernised.'

'Not much needs doing. It's only cosmetic. I've been hired to redecorate, so you won't need to worry about that.' Connor frowned and picked up the tile cutter, throwing it into the corner with some of his other tools. The man didn't even sound as though he liked it here. 'If it were me I'd leave the rest alone – The Hideaway has its own charm. It would be a mistake to pull the guts out of it.'

David nodded slowly, looking unconvinced. 'Perhaps shabbiness is part of its character. The place is comfortable, I will say that. I haven't slept so well in years. And the food is incredible.' He grinned. 'I may just poach Dee and transfer her to Lake Lodge to redesign my menus.'

'That'll be a little like ripping the soul out of the place, won't it?' Connor cleared his throat, feeling irritated and even guiltier for having this conversation.

'There'll be plenty of character left when I've finished with it. I won't make too many changes, at least not at first.'

'What about the rest of the staff?' Connor asked, turning to look David in the eye, although the man avoided him by ducking behind the counter to take a look around.

'The girl Amy's okay, and the cleaners do a passable job. I'll need to bring in a new yoga teacher, someone to run the walks who really knows the area. With the right kind of advertising, competitive rates…' He turned back to Connor so he could wink. 'I've been lowering the prices at Lake Lodge recently to keep the guests flocking to us – if I do the same here, we'll be fully booked in no time. Aside from a couple of small B&Bs, which I'm already undercutting, there's barely any other competition on the island.'

Connor started, surprised by David's admission. No wonder The Hideaway had been losing so many guests. It seemed underhand, but Connor knew his dad would have seen it as good business. 'Why change Madison? She's doing a great job teaching yoga and the walks are popular.'

'I like my own people. I know Madison's amiable and easy on the eye, but I've been asking around and the word is she's prone to leaving on a whim. I need my staff to be reliable. I'll give everyone plenty of notice, and there are always housekeeping positions over at Lake Lodge – we're used to a fast staff turnover there. No one has to worry about losing their job. We'll find alternatives. It's all part of my negotiations with the Skylars.' David took a long look around the room. 'Someone will be in touch soon about you doing more for us at Lake Lodge. I've got a few big projects on the horizon – they'll add up to a lot of business.'

Connor let out a deep breath, rubbing his thumbs across his temples because he could feel a headache starting again. He really should say no, should say he couldn't help. But at the back of his mind he could hear his father's voice nagging him not to be an idiot. Telling him how much that kind of contract was worth – perhaps enough to get the business solvent? So Connor dug reluctantly into his pocket for a card. 'Get someone to call me for a quote.' The words caught in his throat but he shook them off. This was business. Madison would understand. But even as he handed the card over, he knew in the back of his mind she wouldn't.

For all he knew though, Madison could be heading off on the ferry to join Seth before she ever found out.

.

Chapter Twenty-Nine

Connor stood on the shoreline. The sea was rough this morning, and the spot where they'd laid his father was foamy and white, reminding him of a rabid dog.

He watched the waves roll in and out, thinking about his conversations with Madison and David the morning before, and kicked a stone, watching it bounce three times on the water's surface before it disappeared. Jaws ran next to the waves, barking until Connor kicked another for him to chase.

'Here again?' Finn's voice came from behind, startling him.

'I could say the same thing.' Connor didn't turn, but knew Finn was coming closer from the crunch of his feet on the sand. 'Is walking on the beach a new habit of yours, or are you following me?'

'Couldn't sleep.' Finn sighed without elaborating. 'And you're much more entertaining than the TV. Is your dead father talking to you again?'

Connor closed his eyes. 'I'm contemplating life,' he answered, feeling guilt like a lead weight on his chest. He began to walk slowly, following the edge of the sea up the beach, hearing Finn follow.

'Any answers? Asking for a friend.' Finn's tone was light, but Connor heard an edge beneath it.

'It's a lot simpler if you don't let people get close to you.' Rain began to fall lightly in the air and Connor pulled up the hood of the old coat he'd put on earlier – Madison still had his favourite – feeling the droplets slide down his fingers. Behind him Finn cursed and stopped for a moment, probably to pull up the hood of his own coat.

'That's your father talking,' Finn said eventually, catching up so they were side by side. 'Although in some ways I agree. Is this something to do with Madison?'

'Yes… no,' Connor started. 'I'm really not looking for company.' He stopped for a moment to glare at the water. The waves were high, deep blue and angry. Where the sea met the horizon, the sky looked cloudy and dark, a mix of cotton-wool layers in greys and blacks. He barely paid attention normally, too intent on pounding the sand so he could get back to work.

Why was he here today, feeling conflicted, when by all accounts Madison was probably already packing for her next trip, ready to follow Seth to who knew where, regardless of what she'd said? 'Do you think we're destined to become our parents?' Connor asked, wondering if he'd actually said the words he'd been thinking out loud. But after hearing about his mother from Laura – how losing her had closed his father off from people – he had to wonder if he'd joined the same path. The rain drummed onto his coat, spraying droplets over his face.

'Well, I'm not a milkman and I hate jazz, so in my case no. If you're thinking of your father, Connor, I have to say – what do *you* think?' Finn picked up a stone and tried to skim it across the waves but missed. He picked up another and tried again.

'Some say I work too hard.' Connor swallowed, his eyes fixed on the horizon. When Jaws laid a fresh pebble at his feet, Finn was the one to pick it up and throw it. 'Others that I'm cold. Or I put work before everything that matters.' He thought of his conversation with David, of the meeting he had at Lake Lodge later, of how he'd fallen out with Georgie by trying to force her to stay at university so she could join the family business – and winced. 'Perhaps they're right.'

'Some might say you're trying to live up to an expectation, or to prove a ghost wrong. I'd say maybe it's not just your father driving you. You were always focused – even at school you were voted least likely to be found smoking behind the bike sheds.'

'While you spent most of your childhood there?' Connor asked.

'Ah, the simplicity of a misspent youth.' Finn laughed. 'I'm not saying there's anything wrong with being driven. We need people like you to get things done. It's just, work shouldn't be everything.' He paused and threw another stone – this time it bounced three times and he cheered. 'Have you ever thought it might be time to let your hair down? There's a quiz in my pub next Saturday, perhaps you should take some time out? Play hooky from your schedule – come and join us.'

'I tried letting my hair down.' Connor thought of Madison in the pool at Lake Lodge, their time in the yoga studio before Seth arrived to make a mockery of it. 'A pint of bitter and a few questions on sport aren't going to fix this,' he snapped.

'Fix what – what's really bothering you? Spit it out.'

'I didn't ask for an ear.' Connor's temper flared again. 'And I'm not looking for a friend.'

'You've never looked for anyone – maybe that's your problem?' Finn picked up another stone and hurled it hard as the rain turned more severe. Soon Connor's clothes would be soaked through, but he couldn't bring himself to care. 'And perhaps you're getting a friend anyway. God knows you need one. Think of it as accepting a good deed, or an opportunity to unburden yourself, knowing my lips will stay sealed. It's the promise of a barman – silence is engraved across my soul.'

'Bullshit.' Connor laughed, feeling the tightness in his chest lighten. 'I will say I'm angry. I've spent a lot of years trying to live up to expectations, feeling like a failure anyway. Now I'm wondering why. But at the same time I'm still treading the same path – driving the people I care for away – because I don't know how to do anything else.'

'Putting yourself out there is painful, Connor – you're only human, don't kick yourself for it.' Jaws laid a rock at Finn's feet this time, surprising Connor. Even his dog seemed to be swapping sides. 'And if this is to do with Madison, don't give up on her – or yourself – yet.'

'It's easier being alone,' Connor admitted. 'Perhaps my father had that one right. At least you don't disappoint anyone, and they can't disappoint you.'

'It's a lonely road you're on,' Finn said, coming to stand beside Connor and looking at the darkness on the horizon again. 'I know because I'm on it too. But I can't help but wonder if you should rethink the direction you're going in. Sometimes we walk away from the things we need most, because we're too afraid of what having them might mean.'

'What do you mean? Do you think I'm scared?' Connor asked, surprised.

Finn looked at Connor sadly. 'I think you'd be a fool not to be. My question is, are you brave enough to try letting someone in?'

Chapter Thirty

The air's warmer, Madison thought, pulling Connor's dark leather coat off her shoulders and carrying it over her arm. After she'd said goodbye to Seth at the ferry the evening before, she'd spent an hour in The Hideaway sunroom, reading a book. It had felt comfortable and familiar, but she couldn't get Connor out of her head, or the feeling that he was still annoyed with her. Which was the reason she'd decided to head for his house after her yoga session this morning, on the pretext of giving his jacket back.

'He's not here,' Jesse shouted from underneath the bonnet of a green sports car. Madison couldn't see his head, but she could tell it was Jesse from the style of loose jeans he always wore. 'I know it's you, Madison,' he added. 'I can tell from the sound of your feet.'

'My feet have a sound?' Intrigued, Madison walked away from Connor's house, towards the car, which was parked in the gravel driveway. It looked shiny, and very expensive – not that she knew much about those things.

Jesse stood suddenly, banging his head on the bonnet. 'Ow.' He rubbed his forehead and turned around to face Madison. He looked tired, and a trail of grease decorated his nose.

'Are you okay?' Madison moved closer so she could check Jesse's head. 'Doesn't look like anything's broken.'

'Aside from my heart.' Jesse frowned. 'Sorry. I heard about Amy dating Finn. Someone spotted them out in his car the other night and texted me the good news. I can't believe she's moved on so quickly.'

'I think she's trying to take her mind off you. It's not serious – this is Finn we're talking about.' Madison looked back at the house. 'Where's Connor?' Her heart skipped as she said his name.

'He's gone to a meeting at Lake Lodge – headed off early with Jaws after his run, looking grim. I'm taking a few hours this morning and we'll catch up with the painting later. I worked late last night – the car's been making strange noises and…' Jesse paused, looking at the pile of tools on the driveway. 'It's funny. I used to spend hours under this bonnet, but I've not looked at the engine since I split with Amy. And somehow it doesn't feel the same even now. So I'm asking myself, why did I waste so much time looking at this –' he nodded at the car – 'when I had a living, breathing woman at home?'

'Familiarity? Habit?' Madison suggested, pleased that Jesse might finally be seeing the light. 'It's easy to lose sight of what's important when you've got it under your nose. Sometimes we do the same thing over and over just because we're used to it, or we're convinced it's right. It takes something to change before we realise what we're doing is wrong.' She paused. Maybe that was what was happening to her?

Jesse nodded. 'Perhaps. Look –' he gazed at the car – 'do you want to join me on a drive? I feel like we haven't caught up since you got home and I need to check if the engine sounds better.' He slammed the hood shut, secured a slim, brown leather belt that stretched around the bonnet, then wiped his fingers on a rag from the pile on the floor. The car looked even more beautiful now, with its shiny silver grille at the front and big round headlights that looked like eyes.

'Why not. I don't need to take out our walkers until this afternoon.' Madison glanced towards the house again.

'Connor won't be back for hours and Georgie went into town earlier. You can leave the coat with me,' Jesse offered, reading her mind.

'I'd rather give it to Connor myself, thanks. Holding it hostage is probably the only way I'm going to get him to talk to me.' *So I can explain again about Seth.* Jesse looked like he was going to ask why, but Madison waved the question away and opened the passenger door, climbing inside as Jesse jumped in too. He fired up the engine and they headed out of the driveway, onto the road that would take them past The Hideaway. The car had a stunning interior, with a shiny walnut dash covered in bright white and red dials.

Jesse put his foot down, and the engine purred. 'Sounds better, but I'll take a quick whizz into town to check. Amy used to come for drives with me when I first got the car, but for some reason she stopped.'

'Can we drop in at The Hideaway, so I can let Dee know where I'm going? She worries and I don't have my mobile,' Madison explained.

'Sure.' Jesse steered the Morgan through a narrow, leafy lane and they were at The Hideaway within ten minutes. When they arrived, Madison hopped out of the car with Connor's coat, but before she got to the front door it swung open.

'Two more guests booked in today – they'll be arriving this evening.' Dee beamed, her face filled with excitement. 'You'll have a full house on your walk tomorrow. Apparently, they'd booked into Lake Lodge, but changed their minds after hearing about your adventure walks. I didn't know where you'd got to. I've been dying to share the news.'

'I went for a walk to Connor's. How did they hear about The Hideaway?' Madison grinned.

'Georgie was chatting to someone in the pub. They asked when the Grand Opening is, too. Stanley thinks it would be a good idea to drop some leaflets around the island when we've confirmed the date, and he'll upload something to social media too. If Georgie can get people interested with just a chat, imagine what real publicity could do.' Dee's cheeks glowed at the mention of Stanley. 'While I've caught you, there's a quiz at The Moon and Mermaid on Saturday – we were thinking of making up a team. I've got someone to cover here, so Amy and I can go with Stanley. Do you want to join us? We haven't been out since you arrived home.' Dee's eyes flicked to the Morgan. 'See if Jesse can come? It's about time we did something to throw him and Amy together.'

'Do you think that's wise?' Madison asked, imagining them in a public place.

'No. But things have been so good here recently and Amy is enjoying her job more. It's worth a try. Sometimes relationships needs a little help to get back on track.' Dee looked at Madison intently.

'I'll ask. Would you pop this inside for me, please?' Madison handed Connor's coat to Dee, ignoring the comment, which was obviously aimed at her. 'Jesse's taking me for a spin, but I'll be back in plenty of time for the walk.'

'Don't get lost.' Dee smiled indulgently. 'Things have changed so much since you came home. I don't want to lose you again.'

'I'm going nowhere,' Madison promised, heading to the car. When she climbed in, Jesse fired up the engine again and they drove out of the driveway. After a couple of minutes, they passed The Moon and Mermaid, where Finn stood on a ladder, erecting a banner advertising the quiz across the front of the pub.

'We're organising a team,' Madison said, as they joined the road that would take them across the island into the main town. The sky was brightening and sunshine peeped between the clouds. 'Do you want to come along?' She took a chance. 'Invite Connor and Georgie too?'

'I'll ask. Georgie's usually up for anything, but don't count on Connor. Is Amy going to be there?' Jesse didn't take his eyes off the road, but Madison saw his hands tighten on the steering wheel.

'Yes. Dee's arranged cover at The Hideaway.'

'Then count me in.' Jesse nodded. 'Amy won't be happy, but it beats being ignored. Besides, I'm not planning on leaving her alone with Finn.'

Madison sat back, content to stay silent. 'This is a beautiful car,' she said eventually. 'Last time I saw you, you were driving a battered old Ford.'

'It belonged to my grandfather,' Jesse said as they hit the main Sunflower Island High Street, passing Merlin's Travel Agents, The Red Velvet Bakery and the nail bar, Tips & Toes. 'We used to be close, until he had a big falling out with the rest of my family – I never saw him after that.'

'What happened?'

'He fell for a woman half his age. Drove a rift in the family that never healed.' Jesse shook his head. 'I was only ten, but I missed him for years. I couldn't believe it when he left me the Morgan. This car means the world to me.'

'Does Amy know that?'

'I'm not sure.' They hit traffic and drew to a gentle stop outside Magic Charm Jewellers. 'Amy loves that place,' Jesse said sadly. 'She was always looking in the window. I never thought to ask her why… I can't believe I was so stupid.'

'I remember her admiring an emerald ring once,' Madison said. 'You know her favourite colour's green?'

Jesse's laugh was empty. 'I do now…' He paused. 'Did you mean it about the thing with Finn not being serious, or were you just trying to make me feel better?'

'I meant it.' Madison smiled when his expression brightened. 'Amy loves you, but I think she's looking for more…'

'More what?' The traffic started to move and Jesse edged the car further up the High Street.

Madison cocked her head. 'I suppose you need to show her what she means to you.'

'How do I do that?'

'If you really want her back, that's what you need to figure out.'

'I guess I will…' Jesse nodded, looking thoughtful.

Chapter Thirty-One

'So, there's a lot of people to talk to and I need you to focus.' Stanley handed out leaflets to Madison and Georgie as he looked up the High Street. He glanced at the clipboard in his hand and ticked something off. 'I want you both to do this side of the High Street – see if shop owners will display leaflets about the Grand Opening. We want a lot of guests at this event if we're going to make a big enough splash. I'll see if I can interest the *Sunflower Tribune* in the story. I know they do articles on local events and I'm wondering if we can drum up coverage. Meet back at The Red Velvet Bakery in a couple of hours?'

'Sure…' Georgie said slowly, as Stanley headed in the opposite direction. 'I'm still not sure why we're doing this now when the cafe isn't even finished,' she confided in Madison. 'The Grand Opening's in less than a fortnight and Jesse and Connor have been working day and night for the week, but I'm not sure they're going to finish in time. I might not be talking to Connor, but I'm worried he's working too hard. I offered to help, but he refused – he said he's happy to do it with Jesse.'

'I'm sure they'll be fine.' Madison glanced down the High Street, trying to ignore the churn in her stomach that was telling her they might have bitten off more than they could chew. Had she pushed Connor into this? He'd been working so hard she'd barely seen him. And despite repeated attempts to drop off his jacket over the past five days, they hadn't talked. Maybe he was still upset about Seth? She'd explained that things between them were over, but Connor seemed to be avoiding her anyway. 'It's only painting.'

'Weeks of painting.' Georgie frowned. 'Take it from one who knows. And then there's still all the furniture to put back, stock to buy, licences to sort. And what about the main event – your legendary ice cream sundaes?'

'Amy's sorting the paperwork – the licence is already in place,' Madison explained, hoping her friend had managed to renew it. 'She's hired a man with a van to pick up the furniture from storage – and the stock will get delivered the day before. I've talked to Laura and she's happy to sell her ice cream to us on a regular basis. I've arranged for the first batch to arrive just after the freezers, and I've already paid for it.' By dipping into her emergency travel fund – this was worth it. 'I just need to create a menu and print it out. We'll be fine.' Madison looped an arm through Georgie's, sounding a lot more confident than she felt. 'As long as we can get enough people to come along, which is why we need to hand out these leaflets.'

They wandered down the High Street. The first shop they came to was Magic Charm Jewellers, and they both stared inside. An emerald ring, just like the one Amy used to admire, twinkled in the centre of the display, reminding Madison of her conversation with Jesse – would he ever figure things out? And how mad would Amy be tomorrow night when he turned up at the quiz?

'I'm not sure I'll still be here for the opening.' Georgie stared blankly into the window. 'I've been here for two weeks and nothing's resolved with Connor. He won't see things my way, and he's working most of the time, or heading off for meetings that I know nothing about. I've tried talking to him about the business. But last time he said if I was planning on travelling, he wasn't sure why I cared. In some ways he's becoming more like our father. I'm worried – he's closing himself off. I've never seen him act this distant before.'

'Is he okay?'

'Who knows? It's not like Connor communicates.' Georgie drew a broken heart on the window of the jeweller before rubbing it out.

'What are you going to do?' Madison asked.

Georgie shrugged. 'Leave. It's not like Connor wants me around, and it's not like he listens when I talk to him.'

'So you're giving up?' Madison squeaked. 'Does that mean you've already booked your ferry?'

'I can't bring myself to do it. My course tutor has emailed to ask when I'm coming back to uni. To be honest, jumping on a ferry seems so much easier than having to make a decision…'

'In some ways it is,' Madison admitted. 'That's what I've always done, but I wonder now if that was the best solution. Running from something that's hard to fix or painful is easy. The problem is, one day life catches up with you – or you get bored of running.'

'You think I should make it up with Connor and finish my course?' Georgie sounded cross. 'You're meant to be the free spirit. I was relying on you not to give me any advice.'

'I call it learning from experience. I think you should figure out exactly what you're running from before you make a decision.'

Georgie let out a deep breath. 'That's a good question, but I've already figured it out. Every time I come here, Connor looks tired and wrung out. Even having you around hasn't changed that. Dad was the same. If I do the course and come home, is that my future too?' She screwed up her face. 'He's so unhappy, but as soon as something comes along to change that –' Georgie raised an eyebrow at Madison – 'he finds an excuse to push it away.'

'No one's life is mapped out, Georgie. We all get to make choices. Maybe yours will be better than your brother's and your dad's? You don't have to become like them.' Madison checked her watch. 'We've only an hour and twenty minutes to drop these leaflets off – if we don't, Stanley may murder us. Let's talk about this again later.' Madison opened the door of Tips & Toes, the nail salon she and Amy used to visit together, and a familiar wave of chatter surrounded her as she walked inside. The owner, Julie Harris, jumped up from her chair.

'Madison Skylar. You're back!' Julie exclaimed, giving Madison a hug before grasping her hands to examine them. Julie had beautiful long fingers and pointy, sparkly pink nails. 'And not a moment too soon. I heard you were home for a visit. I can't believe it took you so long to come and see us.' She tugged Madison towards a chair. 'And Georgie Grayson, what a treat.' Julie gave Georgie a hug too. 'Do you want your nails done?'

Georgie nodded and they both sat down. Madison put the pile of leaflets on the table beside them.

'You're opening The Hideaway Cafe again?' Julie scanned a leaflet as she picked up a bowl, filling it with soapy water and asking Madison to dip her fingers in it. Beside them, a woman with blue hair did the same for Georgie. 'I used to go when I was younger. The grapevine's buzzing with gossip. I hear The Hideaway's been quiet because of Lake Lodge, and you've been helping to turn things around. That new owner has been undercutting everyone on Sunflower Island, even me.' Julie's eyes widened. 'The spa is offering manicures at half price. It's no way to treat local businesses – that man should be careful or he'll have no friends. I'm already hearing tales about people refusing to book in there because of the way he treats people on the island.' She sighed, gently pulling Madison's fingers from the water and drying them. 'I've also been told you've been spending time with a certain builder…' she continued. 'Connor's a looker, but his father was a heartless man and they say the apple doesn't fall far from the tree – you'd better be careful of that one.'

'Connor's nothing like he seems.' Madison jumped to his defence. 'He's dedicated to his job, that's all. He's really… nice, once you get to know him.'

Julie's eyes sparkled and Madison wondered if she'd just been teasing her. 'Nice, *eh*… I suspected as much.' Julie filed Madison's nails and continued to probe like an expert interrogator. 'Tell me about your plans for the cafe.'

'We're planning a Grand Opening in a week and a half. That's why I came. I wondered if we could leave some leaflets? We need as many people as possible to attend. I want the place to be heaving when my aunt and uncle return.'

'I've a soft spot for The Hideaway, a lot of us do. Leave as many leaflets as you like, and count me in as a guest. Whatever you need, I'll be there for you.'

'Thank you.' Madison's eyes filled. 'You've no idea how much your support means.'

'Ah, love.' Julie squeezed Madison's shoulder. 'We look out for each other on Sunflower Island. And you're part of the family – always have been, doesn't matter how many times you leave.'

'I'm not going anywhere,' Madison promised. Whatever happened with Connor or The Hideaway, she *was* home for good and she was never leaving again.

Chapter Thirty-Two

Connor sneezed as he entered The Moon and Mermaid, walking behind Georgie – who still wasn't talking to him – and Jesse, who'd inexplicably dressed up in his smartest T-shirt and jeans. The pub was heaving, and tables covered every inch of the floor. The bar was ten people deep and Connor groaned, glancing back at the exit. His head ached and his throat felt sore – he wasn't in the mood for this, wasn't even sure why he'd come. Finn had asked, Jesse too, then Madison had dropped off his coat while he'd been at the builder's yard, leaving a flyer about the quiz in one of the pockets. He'd screwed it up and put it in the bin, before finding the leaflet an hour later on his bed, carefully smoothed out. *Probably Georgie's doing.*

And now he was here, wondering why the hell he hadn't thrown it away again.

'Madison!' Georgie screeched, marching across the pub at speed, creating a pathway through the hordes of people. To the left of the bar Stanley, Amy, Dee and Madison sat at a table piled with drinks, crisps, bits of paper and pens. Madison hugged his sister before looking up at him with a grin, making something in Connor's chest hum.

'I'm glad you made it. We've already chosen our team name. We're the Sunflowers,' Madison murmured, tapping her fingertips on the seat beside her. She wore a pair of fitted jeans tonight and a red T-shirt that hugged her curves in all the right places. Connor's eyes dipped to the delicate skin on her neck, remembering how smooth it had felt when he'd been kissing her, before he realised what he was doing. He still felt wary, despite Seth leaving and Madison's assurances about their relationship being over. He'd been avoiding her, but somehow wanted to be around her again, if for no other reason than to find out how she felt.

'Why are *you* here?' Amy asked loudly, interrupting as Jesse pulled out the chair next to Dee.

'I was invited,' Jesse replied. 'You know I love quizzes… We always used to make a great team.'

'That was before,' Amy growled, glaring at Dee.

'Besides, there's nowhere else on Sunflower Island I'd rather be right now,' Jesse added, staring at her. Amy had dressed up tonight, in a green top that seemed to make her skin glow. When Finn came to kiss her hello, Jesse glared.

'I can think of at least one place,' Amy grumbled, flashing a false smile at Finn, then picking up her cocktail and swallowing a mouthful without elaborating.

Before Jesse could ask what Amy was talking about, Tom the barman came to kiss Madison on the cheek, making Connor's insides twist. 'Madison, I'm so happy you're here. Let me know if you need any help tonight – I've got an inside track to the answers.' Tom winked as he cleared their empties and headed for the kitchen.

At the bar, Finn picked up a microphone and hopped onto a chair so he could shout above the music. 'I'm glad to see you all here at our monthly quiz night. Some of you, I know, have never been.' Finn waved his microphone in the direction of Connor. 'So I'll give you a brief introduction. Tom – my lovely new assistant – will be available this evening for drink refills and food orders. Keep them simple, people. The chef's sick and Gillian from The Red Velvet Bakery has agreed to cover, so it's pasties, pies or sandwiches to go with your Pink Flamingos tonight.' A couple of people cheered and Finn waited for them to settle. 'Coincidently, the first round is on food and drink. Ten questions: if you want me to repeat any, wait until the end.'

As Finn asked the first question, Dee took a piece of paper and began scribbling. 'I think we've got this round sorted, folks.' Stanley grinned, sipping from his pint as his eyes stayed firmly on Dee, who must have been aware because her cheeks flushed pink.

'Did you get your coat? I dropped it off yesterday.' Madison eased herself closer to Connor so she could be heard above the crowd. 'I'm sorry I held on to it for so long – I kept hoping I'd catch you.'

'I've been busy.' Connor sipped his pint, ignoring his sore throat and the way awareness skipped across his skin.

'Georgie says the painting in the cafe kitchen and bathroom's coming along – I know you're doing the main room next, but she mentioned there was a lot of it. Do you need any help?'

'No.' Connor shook his head, thinking about the work David was planning to offer him at Lake Lodge. It would be difficult to fit it all in, but if he started early and finished late, he should be able to manage it. He certainly didn't want Madison hanging around, messing with his head again – he'd learned that lesson the hard way. 'Jesse and I have it covered.'

Frowning, Madison picked up her Pink Flamingo and sipped. 'Are you still mad about Seth?' she asked suddenly. 'If you are, I understand why. But you have to know he's gone and… well… we really are just friends.'

Connor gulped his drink as words – conversation – escaped him. He wasn't mad. He wasn't sure how he felt.

'And I don't regret what happened,' Madison continued, a line appearing on her forehead that Connor suddenly wanted to smooth away. 'I just hope you feel the same way.'

'How are the bookings coming along?' Tom appeared back at their table, trying to make conversation.

'Good, thanks.' Madison cleared her throat. 'You might have seen the leaflets we've been distributing for the Grand Opening. I'm guessing the cafe will be ready in time?' Instead of looking at Tom, Madison fixed Connor with a searching gaze. His eyes dropped to her mouth but he jerked them up as Georgie elbowed him in the ribs.

'You need to concentrate,' Georgie whispered. 'Next round's on science and nature, and the rest of us are crap at that.'

Connor pulled a piece of paper towards him as Finn asked the first question. 'Who can speak to the dead?' At the bar, Finn grinned.

'That's not a science or nature question,' Georgie grumbled.

'It is in my quiz,' Finn laughed.

'Fine, it's a medium,' Georgie whispered to the team.

Connor wrote it down as someone passed the table, patting him on the back. 'Good to finally see you out,' the man said, before taking a seat three tables down. When Connor looked closely, he recognised his postman, Sid Sutton. He looked around the room, taking in the people at the tables, eating, drinking, laughing. His father never went to the pub – all his drinking had been done at home – so Connor hadn't either. Once again, he wondered why.

'Name three hormones that are released in your body when you're attracted to someone,' Finn asked loudly, winking at Connor. At the back of the room, near the entrance, there was a loud laugh as a group of women from The Sunflower Island WI began to whisper. Connor recognised Clara Devine, a local woman who made gin in her back garden, because his father had fallen out with her once.

'Oh, I know that.' Georgie grabbed the paper and began writing. 'There's testosterone, dopamine… I can't remember the others.'

Stanley beamed at Dee. 'How about serotonin?'

Georgie wrote it down. Across the table, Amy glared at Jesse, who was drinking his pint, seemingly oblivious. Stanley patted Dee's hand before pecking her on the cheek, making Dee giggle. Had Connor missed this romance, too intent on work again to notice what was going on around him?

'They make a cute couple,' Madison observed. 'I wasn't expecting Dee to fall so fast – she's never been a romantic – but I think it might be the real thing.'

'I'm not sure I know what the real thing looks like,' Connor admitted, his voice dropping.

'Respect, admiration, attraction, chemistry…' Madison sounded wistful.

Connor swallowed but didn't look at her. 'Have you felt that with a lot of people?' he probed, mentally kicking himself for asking.

'Not… until recently.' Madison fell silent – was she talking about him? Connor's heart thumped deep in his chest, arousing feelings he'd spent his life trying to suppress. Around them, the room buzzed and Connor watched Tom work the tables, taking orders and delivering drinks, glancing at Madison now and then, looking a lot like Jaws did when he followed her. Connor hadn't wanted to come tonight, had no idea why he had. But somehow – despite the headache and sore throat – he was glad he was here, even if he still didn't know what to do about Madison. Was Finn right – was he scared?

The round finished and Finn stood on the chair again. 'Next set of questions are on sport. I know we've got some experts in here, so this one's going to be difficult. Pens at the ready.'

Amy frowned at Jesse, pushing the paper towards him. 'You might as well do this one by yourself – I'm not sure any of us are as qualified.'

'What's that supposed to mean?' Jesse looked puzzled.

'Which 100–1 outsider won the 2009 Grand National?' Finn shouted from the bar.

'That's Mon Mome.' Jesse quickly wrote down the answer.

'You know that, but after five years together I'll bet you don't even know my favourite colour.' Amy rolled her eyes and finished her Pink Flamingo as Tom arrived to replace it.

'It's green.' Jesse didn't look up from the paper.

Beside Connor, Madison sighed. 'I'd forgotten how much I love these quizzes. I used to come with my uncle when I was home. He's really good, and of course he knows everyone.'

'I've never been,' Connor admitted, finding his eyes drawn to Madison's hands. He remembered her sliding those nails down his back when they'd been in the yoga studio, and briefly closed his eyes, trying to get his wayward body back on track. The round finished with only Jesse contributing answers, and Finn rang a bell, indicating everyone should settle.

'Next round's my favourite: pot luck. There's something for everyone – music, geography, general knowledge, even politics. Good luck, teams.'

Amy took the paper and a pen as Finn began. 'How many flavours of ice cream does Laura serve at Sprinkles?'

'Oh, I know that.' Amy scribbled 'forty-three'. 'Finn asked Laura the other night, on our date.' She ignored Jesse as he glowered at her.

'Now I'm going to play a piece of music from a movie,' Finn continued. 'You need to name the song, film, composer and what happens when this song is played – there are four points up for grabs.' The pub fell silent as the music began. Someone turned it up and Connor recognised the song.

'That's "We Love to Laugh",' Madison whispered. 'It's from *Mary Poppins*, the composers are Richard and Robert Sherman and when they sing Uncle Albert and Bert levitate towards the ceiling. It's one of my favourite scenes.'

'How the hell do you know that?' Georgie asked, incredulous.

'I love that film. My aunt used to put it on whenever I was sick.' Madison's cheeks reddened at the memory. 'She was always so incredible to me.' The mood changed as a boppier song began playing. Amy snatched the paper and Connor watched Madison slowly sip her cocktail, looking thoughtful.

'Are you okay?' He leaned closer – he couldn't seem to help himself. No matter how many times his brain told him to move in the other direction, his body kept pulling him back again. Was this the Madison effect? Like the pull of gravity, was she impossible to break free from? And did he really want to anymore?

'When was the Morgan 3-Wheeler first built?' Finn asked. Jesse grabbed the pen and wrote down '1909'.

'Tell me the date we first met?' Amy asked suddenly.

'Um.' Jesse looked thrown. As he tried to remember, Connor recalled the moment he'd first seen Madison. It had been the summer, sometime in June. Her eyes had been lively, her skin tanned, and she'd looked like something from a faraway land that simply didn't belong on Sunflower Island. She'd come to talk to him and he'd told her to go away – perhaps he'd been afraid even then?

'The third of December.' Amy stood suddenly, glaring at Jesse. 'I've no idea why I expected you to remember. It's been a long day. I hope you lot don't mind if I call it a night.'

'I'll walk you.' Jesse pushed back his chair, but Amy shook her head.

'I'll come.' Madison stood too. 'You're staying at mine so we can go together.' When Connor began to rise, Madison shook her head. 'You stay and finish the quiz, we'll be fine.'

But after Madison left, Connor couldn't settle. He could still smell lemongrass, remember the softness of her skin, how her laughter had filled the pool at Lake Lodge. A thousand memories filled his head and he closed his eyes, wondering if he'd ever be free of these feelings – and if that was really what he wanted after all.

Chapter Thirty-Three

Connor's head hurt – *really* hurt – and his legs felt like jelly. Something licked his face, and he opened one eye and groaned as Jaws whined at him.

'You're hungry?' Connor grunted, trying to turn onto his side so he could get out of bed. *Dammit.* What was the time? He checked his bedside clock and moaned when he saw it was almost half past six. Connor swung his legs over the side of his double bed onto the wooden floor. The heating was on but he shivered, feeling cold and sick. What time had he got home from the quiz last night? The pile of clothes by his bed suggested it was late. He hadn't eaten at the pub because his head had been throbbing, and the thought of food made his stomach churn. *Still does.*

'Another ten minutes,' Connor whispered, lying back on the bed and pulling his duvet up and over his feverish body. 'Then I'll feed you, we'll go for a run…' The words trailed off as he fell back to sleep.

☆

'He didn't get out of bed and he's boiling.' Jesse's voice filled Connor's head and he squeezed his eyes tighter. He'd only been asleep for five minutes – what the hell was the boy doing here?

'Why are you in my bedroom? It's still early.' Connor moaned. 'Is something wrong?' He tried to sit up, but his body wouldn't cooperate.

'Stay where you are!' A voice demanded. Was that Georgie? He must be delirious because even after last night she was barely talking to him. God, his head hurt. Connor tried to roll his shoulders but they ached too much.

'Don't be ridiculous.' Connor's throat felt raw. 'I've got to run, then there's all that painting.' *All that painting.* For a moment he remembered. They had days of it, had hardly made a dent. Plus, someone at Lake Lodge was getting in touch soon about a new contract.

'You're not working today – you're not fit to go anywhere,' Georgie soothed. 'Dee's made you some lemon and honey – it's got a dose of paracetamol in it. Drink up and go back to sleep.'

'Jaws needs walking and I have to get to work.' Connor tried to sit up. Why did he feel so weak and why did everything hurt?

'You've got the flu.' Georgie read his mind. 'Dee said it's been going around, and remember when you arrived home soaked to the skin from your run last Friday? It's no wonder you're sick, considering that and how hard you've been pushing yourself. Forget Jaws, I already walked him. Jesse's going to start work at the cafe and I'll help. You need to rest.'

'I need to get up.' Connor tried to lever himself into a sitting position and failed. Beside the bed Jaws whined, then eased himself onto the floor. Connor had never felt so bad – his body didn't feel like it even belonged to him. He closed his eyes. If he had a quick nap he'd be fine.

☆

A door closed downstairs and Connor woke, checking the bedside clock. It was almost eleven. Jaws jumped to his feet, wagging his tail, ready to play, but all Connor could do was groan as he tried to move. His bedroom door opened, and Jesse and Madison both came flying in. Madison was dressed in her yoga outfit – she'd probably just finished a class. Jaws bounded across the room to greet her, his tongue lolling as his tail wagged.

'What's happened to your dog?' Jesse stopped by the bedroom door, looking surprised. 'He usually barks like a maniac or tries to bite people – that's all he's ever done with me and I've been living with you for almost four months.'

'I call it the Madison effect.' Connor's voice came out husky. He watched as she knelt down to pet the Boxer behind his ears. Some of her hair slipped out of the knot on her head and tumbled over her shoulder, and something inside him ached to run his fingers through it. If he wasn't so weak he might have followed through. 'Get close enough and she'll probably do the same to you,' he added.

Jesse snorted. 'How are you feeling?'

'Fine,' Connor mumbled, trying to move.

'Stay where you are.' Madison marched across the room so she could push Connor back on the bed. 'Jesse's come to tell you he and Georgie have everything under control at the cafe. I'm here to make sure you don't get up.' She felt his forehead and frowned. 'You're on fire.'

'I need to paint.' Connor swallowed. 'Or we won't be ready for the Grand Opening.'

Madison paused. 'We will – I've no idea how, but somehow we'll make it happen. This time, Connor Robertson, it's not all up to you. You need to concentrate on getting better.'

Connor closed his eyes. 'Why are you here?' he repeated, as he fell back to sleep.

☆

Two hours later, Connor woke to find Madison standing beside him, holding a tray. She placed it on the floor, encouraging him to sit. 'I made you vegetable soup, and here's Dee's special medicine. There's water by the bed – drink, you'll be dehydrated.' She felt Connor's forehead again.

'You should steer clear, you don't want to catch this,' he murmured.

'I'm immune to bugs.' Madison flashed a smile. 'All those vegetables. You really should try it. How are you feeling, honestly?'

Connor was about to say 'better', but the words died on his lips as Madison sat on the bed and gazed at him. 'Rubbish.'

Madison smiled. 'I didn't expect honesty.'

'I didn't think you'd still be here – I've been expecting you to take off after Seth,' Connor admitted, sipping some of Dee's concoction. It tasted okay, and the lemon and honey soothed his sore throat.

'So now we're both surprised.' Madison watched as he ate some soup. 'Can I ask you something?'

'Sure.' Connor put the spoon down – he wasn't in the mood to eat.

'Have you forgiven me for Seth? I've wanted to ask, but you've been too delirious to understand.' She winced suddenly. 'Actually, don't answer that. I'm being unfair, cornering you when you're sick.' She got up suddenly and looked around the room.

Connor watched Madison turn her back to him. Had he forgiven her? He wasn't sure. Or perhaps he just wasn't quite ready to take another chance on her yet.

'Can you get into that chair?' Madison changed the subject, pointing to the soft blue armchair in the corner. It had belonged to Connor's mother. He rarely sat in it, had no idea why he'd kept it.

'Why?' he croaked.

'So I can change your bed. It's damp because of the fever.'

'I'll do it.'

Madison laughed softly. 'I'm sure you'd try. And being this helpless must be driving you nuts. But for once, let someone else take over. If you really want to get back to work, you need to rest. I've watched how hard you push yourself. Getting sick was only a matter of time.'

'I never get ill,' Connor grumbled, irritated. His father hadn't had a sick day in his whole life – yet another stick he used to beat Connor with.

'Perhaps this is your body's way of telling you not to do everything yourself?' Madison pushed the duvet back and helped Connor to his feet. He felt weak, but managed to move to the other side of the bedroom. When he sank onto the chair Madison wrapped him in a blanket as he began to shiver. 'I've had an idea about getting the cafe finished. I've made a few calls and there are people willing to help. We could have a painting party.' Madison flashed a smile. 'Give everyone cake in return for labour.'

'That's… I'll be fine by tomorrow.'

'And if you're not? You've an island of people willing to assist, friends who care for you – didn't you see that in the pub last night?'

Do I? Connor didn't answer because he didn't know what to say.

'Do you want to shower?'

'No.' He wouldn't be capable of standing by himself, would probably faint if he tried, and if Madison offered to help… Connor didn't want to think about it. If he could forget about Seth and they got naked again, he planned to at least be conscious. 'I need to rest. You do what you need to while I get better. I'll be back at work tomorrow.'

Madison stayed silent as she changed the sheets and guided him back to bed. Within minutes Connor fell asleep.

☆

'It's Wednesday. The cafe's meant to open next Tuesday,' Connor grumbled, as he sipped more of Dee's lemon and honey drink. He'd been in bed for three days and still wasn't better, which was driving him crazy. Georgie had been working with Jesse on the painting but they were still way behind schedule. He closed his eyes, ignoring the pain beating behind them.

'I've got it covered,' Madison soothed. 'People are coming on Saturday to help with whatever isn't finished.' She held up a hand when Connor tried to protest. 'Concentrate on getting better, then you can start bossing everyone about.'

'I'm bored.' Connor sighed. 'Lying in bed is boring.'

Madison smiled, getting on the bed to sit cross-legged facing him, as Jaws watched them from the floor. She wore her yoga pants again today and some kind of orange top that was two sizes too large – it must have belonged to her aunt. She'd barely left his side for the last few days and he'd begun to look forward to her visits. 'Do you want to watch a movie? I'll keep you company. Stanley's leading the walk this afternoon, so I can stay.'

'That's not necessary—' Connor began.

'He's doing it anyway. That's what people do, Connor, when they care about each other.' Swallowing, Madison looked away.

'Georgie's got a tablet, and I know she has Netflix. We could choose something now?'

Connor sat up. He felt a little better, but when he'd tried to get out of bed this morning his feet had almost gone out from under him.

'Aunt Sandy always put on *Mary Poppins* when I got sick.' Madison grinned. 'Ms Poppins managed to get Mr Banks flying a kite, and he's an even worse workaholic than you.'

'I've no desire to fly a kite. But I'll watch the movie.' Madison moved beside Connor and he tried not to look, more aware of her than he'd ever been. She rested the tablet on a pillow between them. As the film began, he rolled his eyes. 'This is ridiculous.'

'That's why I love it.' Madison giggled. 'Relax, Connor. Once Dee's special drink kicks in you might even sing along.'

Connor smiled, feeling lighter. Madison was doing it again, crawling under his skin, making him feel things he had no control over. Despite his better judgement, his reservations about Seth and what every sensible bone in his body screamed, he knew he couldn't fight the feelings anymore – he was in very real danger of falling for her again.

Chapter Thirty-Four

'I can't believe I agreed to this,' Connor muttered, as Jesse placed another dust sheet on the floor of the cafe. It was early, but people would be arriving in the next half hour ready to help with the painting. Connor had been out of bed for twenty-four hours but still felt weak. At least now he was well enough to work – thanks to Madison.

The cafe counter had been covered with old clothes, and on top was a mass of paint pots, brushes and aprons that Madison had found in Dee's kitchen drawers.

'We need help to finish up. We're running out of time,' Jesse explained, as the door upstairs slammed, and Madison and Amy walked down. Jaws bounded across the floor to greet them, his tail wagging frenetically.

'I'm ready to help,' Madison said, coming to join them. Connor had only seen her the day before, but his heart still leapt as she approached. He nodded at the counter.

'Everything is out. I thought you could all start in the corner over there?' He pointed to the left of the room, opposite the kitchen, where the bulk of the tables would sit beside the bar. 'Jesse and Georgie have painted both bathrooms, half the kitchen, and prepped all the walls in the cafe. How many helpers are you expecting?'

'I spoke to Julie and she's drummed up at least six customers from Tips & Toes, so with us, probably eleven.' Amy avoided looking at Jesse, who sat watching her.

'When are they arriving?' Connor asked.

'Soon.' Madison inspected the paint pots. 'You chose yellow!' She sounded delighted.

Connor looked embarrassed. 'Seemed fitting as we're on Sunflower Island. And since it's dark down here I figured the colour needed to be bright.' Plus, when he'd got to the builder's yard this morning he hadn't been able to bring himself to pick up the grey paint like he had for the bathroom and kitchen – instead he'd filled his basket with yellow. Was that more of the Madison effect?

'Do you have any music?' Madison's eyes danced around the room as she walked the length of it, spinning suddenly in the middle so she could take in her surroundings. 'It's like a dance floor when it's empty, isn't it? We had a disco here once, didn't we, Amy?'

Her friend laughed. 'When your aunt closed it for a spring clean – I remember. Your uncle piled all the chairs and tables to one side and you made me meet you in the dark. I'm sure Dee knew what we were planning, because she left out loads of snacks.'

'And torches.' Madison chuckled.

'I always had the best times with you.' Amy sighed. Connor could imagine it, could see young Madison dancing in the darkness, swaying to the music and losing her head. What would he have been doing at the time? Working, studying, keeping things tidy and right – staying out of his father's way while becoming just like him? Dammit, he wanted to kick the idiot he'd become. Thank God Madison had arrived to help him see the light.

'There's a speaker in the corner – I'm not sure if it works.' Connor watched as Madison headed towards it.

'It does,' Jesse said, stirring paint in one of the pots and watching Amy with a thoughtful expression. 'Georgie and I have been using it. It'll work off your phone.'

'I've got some tunes to get us in the mood for painting.' Madison dug out her mobile. 'I always work to music, don't you?'

Charles Robertson had favoured classical when he'd been decorating. At a push, a punishing opera. Anything light or lively had been banned. Ever since he'd been working alone, Connor had preferred silence – until now he hadn't realised how boring that was.

Madison put on a dance track and bobbed to the tune as she picked up a paintbrush. Seconds later she was swiping paint onto one of the walls, her strokes slow and careful despite the frenzied beat.

'Hello.' At the top of the stairs three pairs of feet came into view. Seconds later Stanley, Georgie and Sophia were in the cafe, looking around.

'This is amazing.' Sophia's eyes shone as she stared up at the ceiling. 'Amy told me what you were planning. I had a day off so I came to help. David's working again.' She screwed up her face. 'It's a shame. He'd get a real kick out of this renovation.'

Or would he be pricing it up in his head, Connor wondered, figuring out how to get his pound of flesh that much cheaper? Or trying to sabotage their efforts so they didn't get the cafe open in time. *Jeez* – guilt gnawed in his chest. They needed to get the cafe open, to stop the sale in its tracks before Madison found out.

'Are you hoping to paint the whole cafe this afternoon?' Sophia asked.

'Whatever we don't do today we'll finish tomorrow. You didn't need to come.' Madison put her paintbrush on the side and went to greet everyone, hugging them warmly. 'But I'm glad you have.'

'What's the plan?' Georgie asked Connor.

'Can you do the edges? If you could work in teams – Madison, Amy and Stanley over there. Georgie, Jesse and Sophia in that corner. When everyone else arrives they can join you.' Connor went into the kitchen so he could continue where he'd been painting before he got sick. He could hear the music pounding in the other room and found himself swaying in time, wondering what the hell had got into him. *Maybe I'm still delirious.* He picked up the paintbrush and began to paint. Five minutes later, someone prodded him in the back.

'Reporting for duty, friend.' Finn's green eyes sparkled as he inspected Connor's work. 'I'll tell you now, I'm only here because Madison asked. That and because I was promised at least one slice of Dee's chocolate cake. Was the yellow a deliberate choice, or did someone see you coming?'

'Madison likes yellow,' Connor bit out.

'So the wanderer's struck again. I'm glad you changed your mind,' Finn admitted. 'Love happens to the best of us apparently.'

'To you?' Connor asked, ignoring Finn's assumption and picking up a spare brush from the counter so he could hand it to him. If the man was in his space, he might as well do something useful. 'There will be cake later, but only for those who paint,' he ground out, turning back to the wall and dabbing more yellow onto it.

'I was in love once. Not something I care to repeat.' Finn sighed, shrugging off his jacket and heading to the opposite end of the cooker. 'I'd advise you to steer clear of engaging your heart, but that look on your face tells me I might be too late.'

'If you're looking for conversation, perhaps you should go find Amy?' Connor grumbled.

Finn laughed. 'From the looks I got when I arrived, Jesse will stab my eyeballs out with a paintbrush if I go anywhere near her. Besides, Amy's not interested in me – she's head over heels with the boy-child. I wonder if he'll ever grow up and figure out how to win her back.' Finn handled the brush like an expert, finishing the edges around the cooker in no time.

'And you know that how?' Connor asked, intrigued. He'd never been able to read people, had no idea what they wanted unless they asked. It was a skill Madison had in spades.

'The curse of the barman: I've seen it all before. Amy wants commitment. She needs a sign from Jesse that he's going to put her above everything else. If he can't do that, I'm not sure he's worthy of her.'

Connor shook his head. 'I'll take your word for it.' He looked up to find Finn watching him. 'I hope you're not about to share some of your sage advice with me.'

Finn smiled wickedly. 'Since you're making me paint, I figure you deserve it. Give Madison a chance – the girl's a gem and you don't deserve her, but she seems to like you anyway. Let your hair down, allow someone in. Don't become your father. I can see signs of life emerging. Don't let all those years of living with a bastard win. Oh, and come to the pub again. I was right: takings were up when you came. Try a Tuesday, that's always a slow night for me.'

Connor laughed, a quick short bark that surprised him. What was happening to him? 'I'll think about it.' He shook his head and leaned forwards to paint again as the song in the other room changed, flipping over to a lively dance track he'd probably heard before but didn't recognise. 'But only if you finish painting at least one of these walls.' Content, Connor continued to paint, surprised by the warm feelings these people were bringing out in him. So used to being alone, to keeping himself locked in, it was a revelation to be surrounded by a crowd. They were chatting, some dancing, transforming the dull brown walls into something colourful and bright. And Connor could see the place changing, see light emerging, as if somehow just having Madison down here had brought out the sun.

And if she could change a place like this, a dusty old cafe in need of an update, perhaps she would do the same for him?

Connor heard the sound of footsteps as more people arrived. He recognised Gillian from The Red Velvet Bakery and a couple of familiar faces from the builder's yard. Beside them, surrounded by a team of women, Julie from Tips & Toes beamed at the group and picked up a paintbrush.

How did Madison do it? Bring so many people into her world, create connections like she'd known them forever? Madison greeted the new crowd as though they were family, handing out brushes and directing them into different corners of the room. And Connor held back because he didn't know how to do anything else.

'She's quite something when she's got the bit between her teeth, isn't she?' Finn said behind him. 'I can understand why you'd fall for her.'

Before Connor could respond, the door slammed again and Dee lumbered down the stairs, holding a huge tray laden with plates of food. There were sandwiches and crisps, pies of various colours and sizes, carrot and chocolate cakes, a bowl of strawberries and another with sliced cucumber and tomatoes. 'I brought the workers food.' She grinned at the crowd. 'And doesn't it look busy in here? There are a couple of others who texted me earlier and said they'd be coming to help. I've got urns of tea and coffee, which I'll bring down in a minute. This is amazing.' Her eyebrows rose. 'Really amazing – I never expected so many of you to turn up.'

'We've got Madison to thank for it,' Connor admitted. 'I'll help with the drinks.' He followed Dee up the stairs, closing the door to the cafe behind them. 'We need to tell Madison, Dee. I feel like a liar. I got a text from David this morning saying the plans to sell up are progressing.'

They picked their way along the leafy pathway around the main Hideaway building, heading into the side door that led to the kitchen. 'I know.' Dee shook her head. 'But it's only a fortnight until the Skylars are home – who knows what they'll decide once they see how much progress we've made. I'm feeling bad myself, but perhaps things will change once they return? They adore that girl. Maybe Madison being here to stay might change their minds?'

Four large flasks sat on the kitchen counter, as well as cups and containers of milk and sugar. Dee placed them into a couple of large carrier bags and handed one to Connor. 'Selling up was always a last resort. Jack didn't want to do it but when Sandy got ill, he knew they wouldn't have the energy to turn The Hideaway around. Now bookings are up and the place is thriving, maybe they'll decide to hang on?'

'And in the meantime we continue to lie?' Connor muttered, knowing there was little choice.

'I'd rather call it withholding the full picture,' Dee said, stroking a hand through her bob, looking guilty. 'Or doing what's right. Besides, if we tell Madison now, how do you think she'll react?'

'Badly. I know I would.' Sighing, Connor headed back to the basement with Dee. His only hope was that Madison would never find out.

☆

'Have you seen Amy?' Jesse joined Connor in the kitchen two hours later and looked around the room, frowning when he realised they were alone. 'She was in the cafe ten minutes ago and now she's disappeared. So has Finn.' Connor shook his head and for the first time, he saw fear in Jesse's expression.

'Amy's not interested in Finn. If they left together, it'll be a coincidence. I know he had to get back to the pub for a delivery,' Connor explained.

Jesse blew out a long breath and picked up a brush, swiping it across one of the walls. 'Every time I see Amy I get more confused. It's like she's looking at me, expecting something – and I don't know what.'

Connor shrugged. 'Mind-reading isn't one of my superpowers, but Amy's dropped enough hints about you not paying enough attention to her for even me to pick them up.' Connor continued to paint as Jesse went quiet, wondering why he was getting involved. But somehow over the last few weeks he'd realised that holding back, not connecting with people, was a miserable way to live.

'She has?' Jesse looked confused. 'I don't understand... I know she loves Pink Flamingos, and her favourite colour's green.' He paused. 'Because Madison told me.' He grimaced before nodding. 'I don't know the date, but I remember we met on the first day it snowed, six years ago in December, just after I moved here. I know because when the snowflakes settled in her hair they glittered and she looked like an angel.' He swallowed. 'I've never told her that.'

'Why?' Connor asked, even though he already knew the answer.

'I was afraid,' Jessie admitted. 'What if she thought I was stupid? Besides, she should know how I feel about her.'

'I've known you years and I'm not sure I do,' Connor said. 'I know you love football, golf, hockey, rugby, and more recently, your car...'

Jesse paled. 'None of that matters without Amy.'

'Then I guess you need to show her that.' Connor turned back to his painting, knowing, as he said the words, that Jesse had already left.

'Are you alone?' Georgie joined Connor ten minutes later, immediately picking up Jesse's brush and dipping it into the paint. 'This is fun. All those years of decorating with you – and Dad when he'd let me in the same room – and I can't say I've ever enjoyed it. It's been surprisingly refreshing working with Jesse. And everyone's doing a good job in there, despite the noise. Mind you, Dad would have had a coronary seeing the place like that.'

Connor watched as Georgie dabbed the brush at the edge of one of the white kitchen cupboards. She was a natural – careful, precise. It was almost like she'd been born to it, which he supposed she had. The music changed and Connor heard laughter in the other room.

'I've been thinking about what I'm going to do next.' Georgie spoke without looking at him. 'I've been dithering… but spending time working with Jesse and Madison while you were sick, having fun at the quiz night last weekend, even being here today, it's helped me make up my mind.'

'You're leaving.' Connor kept his voice light and his face devoid of emotion. 'Of course,' he added, because wherever Georgie went, he didn't want to lose her. 'I understand we don't have the same ambitions. I didn't get it at first. You need to know you have my blessing whatever you decide, that there's always a home for you here. I don't want you to think I'm like Dad – expecting you to be like me.' He swallowed, his heart beating faster as he tried hard to put his feelings into words, trying to think of the kinds of things Madison might say. 'But I'll love you, whatever you choose to do.'

'Oh, Connor.' Georgie's face brightened and she dropped her brush into the paint pot before launching herself at him. 'I didn't think I'd ever hear you say that. The thing is…' She hugged him tighter and Connor found himself wrapping his arms around his sister too. He'd miss her, miss the promise of having her working with him. But if being around Madison had taught him anything, it was that he wasn't his father, and he didn't have the right to control someone else's life. 'I've told my course tutor I want to go back.'

'Okay.' Connor closed his eyes before opening them again. 'Sorry, what?'

'I'm leaving on the ferry this evening…' Georgie paused. 'I'm going to finish my degree.'

'Okay… Sorry, I don't understand. I thought you had your heart set on travelling?'

'I don't have my heart set on anything, Connor.' Georgie smiled up at him. 'That's the problem. I'm looking for something, but I've no idea what. Travelling sounded exciting, but after being here for three weeks, I'm not so sure. Being on Sunflower Island can be amazing – Madison helped show me that. And you being sick meant I had a chance to work at my own pace, and I enjoyed it. If I leave I'm just running away. I need to keep my options open, at least until I figure out what I really want – like you and Madison have. Perhaps I'll be back here in the end, working alongside you at Robertson & Grayson Builders.' She laughed when Connor raised an eyebrow at the name change. 'Or I'll become a travel bum. Whatever happens, I've realised I'm not ready to decide – but running away isn't going to solve anything. I do know I'm glad I have you as a brother.'

'I'm glad to have you as a sister too.' Connor pulled Georgie towards him so he could hug her again.

So Madison had struck again – exactly where Connor had least expected it, letting light in, changing his world – and suddenly, just like that, he knew it was already too late: there was no escape now. He'd fallen for her.

Chapter Thirty-Five

'That's another booking. Makes five over the last two days. We're almost full for the next three weeks. Word is spreading, Madison. The man this morning asked specifically about your adventure walks. I've no idea how you're going to keep getting everyone lost, but this is working. I can't believe you made it happen.' Amy walked around the breakfast bar in The Hideaway kitchen and gave Madison a big hug, before pulling up a bar stool. 'If only you could fix my love life as easily.'

'I'm guessing you'll have better luck sorting things out with Jesse if you actually talk to him.' Madison put a cup of coffee Dee had just made underneath Amy's nose. 'How are things going with the plans for the Grand Opening tomorrow?'

'The furniture's arrived from storage already. So have the cutlery, cups, plates and fridges, and the rest will be here later. Connor and Jesse are supervising the deliveries and I'll put it all in place.' Amy ticked an imaginary list off on her fingers. 'I've got the building regs signed off thanks to a nice man at the Town Hall, and Stanley persuaded the press to come to the Grand Opening. I've sorted out the shifts for the cafe – between me, you and Dee, we can keep it ticking over, at least until the Skylars decide if they want more staff.

I'm so excited. It's an amazing new beginning. And it wouldn't have happened without you, Madison. I'm so glad you came back.' Amy hugged her. 'What are you doing?' Amy stepped back for the first time to take in the breakfast bar. It was piled high with all kinds of goodies – bananas, chocolate drops, hundreds and thousands, space dust, chocolate chip cookies, edible glitter, chocolate sauce and whipped cream.

'We're waiting for Laura's ice cream so we can design our desserts. These bits and bobs were in the cupboards – I've no idea how Dee manages to store all this stuff.'

'Where's Dee?'

'Phoning Laura – the ice cream should have arrived by now.' Madison tapped her fingers impatiently on the counter.

Their conversation was interrupted by Dee, who ran back into the kitchen looking pale. 'There's a problem,' she said. 'A very *big* problem. Laura's had a disaster at home. Her big freezer packed up last night. She was running late and didn't realise till just now. All the ice cream's melted. She can't replace it by tomorrow. We've nothing to put into our sundaes.'

Madison looked at the open doorway, thinking about the envelope of money in her bedroom. A month ago she'd have already been packing. Instead she took a long breath. What would Connor do? 'We need a plan B,' she said slowly.

'Good.' Dee smiled. 'For a minute I thought you were going to skid out of that doorway and make a run for it.'

'Not this time. We've got all this stuff.' She pointed at the breakfast bar, feeling suddenly animated. 'I know it's not as exciting as a Sprinkles ice cream, but it's a start. We need to make something fun and different, so people aren't disappointed. Have you any ice cream in the fridge, Dee?'

'Only vanilla and chocolate. Lots of it, admittedly, but it's boring.' Dee looked despondent. 'Sunflower Supermarket doesn't stock much else. It's hardly the culinary experience we've been promising. We need at least five desserts for the opening. I was going to photograph the sundaes and Stanley said he'd knock up a temporary menu. He's already designed a logo. People are going to be so disappointed if all we have to offer are vanilla and chocolate cones.'

'We'll offer more than that.' Madison pulled up her sleeves. 'I remember having an ice cream sandwich in Australia.' She got a plate and slapped down two cookies, before filling one with strawberry jam and the other with peanut butter. She added a few chocolate drops and hundreds and thousands, before finishing with a small dollop of vanilla ice cream and placing a biscuit on top. The result looked colourful, but would it taste good? 'Dee, please can you take a picture?' Madison stood back as the cook whipped out her mobile and photographed it. 'Would you try it, please? I'm not sure I'm brave enough.' Madison pushed the plate towards Amy and folded her arms, feeling tense as she watched her friend take a bite.

'That works.' Amy nodded vigorously. 'Actually it's really good, better than I expected – what shall we call it?'

'The Hideaway Sundae Sandwich?' Madison suggested. Amy polished off the rest with gusto as Madison wrote the name and ingredients on a small pad.

'I'm thinking we might need more taste testers or I'm going to be sick.' Amy rubbed her stomach.

'I'll get Connor.' Dee disappeared outside, heading for the cafe before Madison could respond. Then The Hideaway's phone started ringing and Amy slipped out too, leaving her alone. She scanned the ingredients, wondering what Connor would like – he'd lost weight when he'd been ill and she needed to build him up.

Madison sliced a banana, grinning as she placed it on a plate, then added chocolate ice cream and layered on a dollop of whipped cream. She added a scoop of space dust and hundreds and thousands, repeating the ingredients again, building the dessert into a towering beast. By the time Connor opened the door and walked in, the ice cream sundae was huge. She picked up Dee's phone from the side and took a photograph.

'Dee said to tell you she's gone to speak to the supermarket about ordering more supplies. I heard about Laura's ice cream. That looks great – is it for me?' Connor smiled, watching Madison as he walked up to the counter, making her skin tingle. 'I see you added a banana.'

'It's the only healthy thing about it.' Madison handed Connor a spoon so he could test it. 'It's called The Hideaway Fundae, and I made it for you.'

Connor scooped ice cream into his mouth and swallowed. 'Tastes good,' he said gently. 'You… keep surprising me.'

Madison's stomach lurched. 'In a good way?'

'Yes.' Connor stared at her. 'I'm sorry for the way I behaved when Seth arrived. He… threw me, and I should have believed you when you said you were just friends.' When Madison tried to interrupt, Connor held up a hand. 'We both know I'm crap with words, so it's probably better if I get this out.' He eyed the dessert. 'Hopefully

I'll manage something coherent before this melts.' He looked into Madison's eyes. 'I've missed you. More than I expected, more than I ever thought I'd miss anyone, and I'm sorry I doubted you. You're here – still here – despite me pushing you away.' He stepped closer and ran a thumb across Madison's cheek, making her heart hammer. 'I want to say thank you, for getting me help to finish the cafe, for looking after me when I was sick, and for helping me understand how empty my life was without anyone in it.'

Madison swallowed. 'Am I in your life?'

Connor smiled. 'I hope so.' He leaned over to stroke his lips gently across hers, starting slowly, letting the sensations settle before he took it deeper. Madison couldn't wait – she'd stood on the side-lines waiting for Connor to make up his mind. Now he'd decided to let her into his life, she just wanted him closer. She kissed him back, gripping the collar of his shirt, taking the kiss from warm to red-hot in seconds… until a door slammed and someone cleared their throat.

When Madison glanced up, Jesse was standing in the doorway looking embarrassed. 'Is Amy here?' he asked as Connor stepped backwards, letting Madison go.

'She went to answer a call. I'm sure she'll be back soon.' Madison's voice was unsteady.

'Can I wait?' Jesse's eyes roved over the ingredients and widened as they took in Connor's dessert. 'That's a whole new level of unhealthy.' He squinted at it more closely. 'It looks good though.'

'We're testing sundaes for the Grand Opening,' Madison said as her body settled. 'Laura can't get her ice cream here so we're having to get creative. Do you want to pull up a chair?' Madison ignored her knees, which were still wobbling. 'Perhaps you'd like to be one of my tasters?'

Jesse nodded.

'I thought you wanted the morning off?' Connor asked.

'I did. I mean, I have. But I've done what I needed to get done and now I've come here to finish it,' Jesse replied as Amy burst into the room.

'Four more bookings – we'll be turning people away soon! Oh.' Amy's face dropped as she spotted Jesse. 'It's you.'

'Before you leave again, I need you to listen.' Jesse hopped down from the bar stool and walked around the table to join Amy. 'It took me a long time to understand what I'd done to you. I have to admit to being a little dense.' He shrugged. 'It's a fault of mine, but I'm willing to mend it.'

'Right. Okay…' Amy looked at the floor.

'The thing is, I get what I did wrong and I know why I hurt you. I've always been distracted – by sport, the car. I took you for granted. I guess I had a lot of growing up to do. I never explained what my grandfather's car meant to me. It was my last link to him, a link I never realised I needed – but that's in the past. I know a stupid car can never replace you.' He pulled a box from his pocket and opened it. 'I sold the Morgan, spent the money in Magic Charm on this ring – Claire says hi. I know green's your favourite colour – and it'll remind me of the car. I want to remember my grandfather and if you wear this, I always will.' He dropped onto one knee. 'Will you marry me, Amy Walters, wear this ring and be my wife? I've spent far too long without you in my life.'

'Oh, Jesse.' Amy's face dropped as she stepped backwards. 'You shouldn't have. I mean, yes, but you can't sell the car.'

'I already have.' Jesse slid the ring from the box, and took Amy's left hand so he could put it onto her fourth finger. 'That car was a beautiful thing, but it's just metal and paint. It won't keep me warm at night, it doesn't laugh and it's crap at conversation. I don't love it, I only love you.'

Amy gazed at the ring. The emerald sparkled under the kitchen lights and the band glittered gold. 'This is beautiful, but you need to take it back…' She slipped the ring off her finger and handed it to Jesse, placing her hand over his when his face dropped. 'Oh, I want it, but you can buy me a cheaper one. Dammit, I'll be happy with one from a cracker. You shouldn't have to give up what's left of your grandad to be with me. All I needed was this…' Amy tapped Jesse's heart with her fingertip, stepping closer. 'All I needed was for you to put me first.'

'I don't understand.' Jesse looked confused as Amy gave him a soft kiss.

'It doesn't matter,' Amy said gently. 'I do.'

As Amy and Jesse left the kitchen hand in hand, Madison glanced at Connor. He was watching her with the strangest expression on his face.

'You free for dinner tonight?' He smiled when she nodded. 'Come to my house at seven, come alone and bring dessert.' He took a quick bite of his sundae, grinned and nodded goodbye.

Chapter Thirty-Six

Madison had enjoyed a million adventures in her life, had been to a thousand places. But her stomach had never been in so many knots, and she'd never felt as excited as when she knocked on Connor's door that evening. She'd brought a bag of bananas, space dust, a carton of chocolate ice cream and a huge smile.

Jaws started to bark and Madison could hear the slap of his tail as he wagged it, then the door opened and Connor was standing in the doorway, dressed in dark jeans and a button-down shirt she didn't recognise. He looked handsome and a little embarrassed.

'You look… clean.' His tone was playful. 'And very pretty – I like the dress.' Connor's eyes slid downwards to take in the satin black number Madison had bought on the internet. It hugged her figure, ending just above the knees, exposing just the right amount of cleavage. She wore a sparkling red choker around her neck and had finished the outfit off with a pair of black heels, borrowed from Amy.

'I'm feeling lucky tonight.' Madison grinned and Connor stepped backwards so she could walk inside, then she dropped to her knees to pet the dog.

The first thing Madison noticed was that the house smelled delicious – a combination of cheese, garlic, pasta and herbs. Connor led them into the kitchen. The room had changed since she'd last visited, when Connor had been sick. The plant had moved to the kitchen counter for a start – also, it was alive. Madison went to look at it. 'A miracle?' She grinned at Connor. 'I didn't think even *you* were capable of those?'

He laughed. 'A replacement. It's basil – I'm trying to impress you tonight. Besides, I needed some for our meal.'

'What are we having – don't tell me, pie?' Madison opened the freezer so she could put the ice cream inside.

'Bruschetta followed by vegetarian lasagne.'

'Vegetarian lasagne?' How had he managed to choose her favourite meal?

'Don't get too excited, I've never made it before. I got Georgie to email me a recipe. I told her we'd be safer with a pizza, but she insisted. I never knew so many vegetables existed in the world.' Connor shuddered. 'Would you like a glass of wine? I thought we could eat in here.' He pointed to the kitchen table, which he'd already laid. A candle burned in the centre and a couple more glowed on the windowsill. Madison held back, her stomach fluttering. Connor had gone to a lot of trouble. All these years it had been her pursuing him. It was… strange, having it the other way around.

'I'm going to dim the lights.' Connor fiddled with one of the switches. 'It's not purely to be romantic – although that's part of my plan. But if it's not too light in here, there are some incredible views of the stars – it's one of the reasons my dad built the kitchen here.' The corner of his mouth tilted upwards. 'I can't say I've ever watched them, but since I'm trying to embrace a new side of myself thanks to you, I thought we could stargaze while we eat tonight?'

'Love to.' Madison looked around the kitchen for glasses, trying to stay collected because she was in serious danger of hurling herself at this man. 'Shall we pour the wine?'

'Let me.' Connor filled the glasses. 'Do you want to sit? Dinner will be a few more minutes and I've things to get ready, but I thought we could… talk while I'm cooking?'

'Talking's good.' Madison pulled out a chair and sat watching Connor as he got a salad from the fridge and put it on the table between them. 'Where's Jesse?' Madison stroked Jaws as he joined them, resting his head on her knees.

'At Amy's. I think the ring did the trick, although by all accounts they spent the afternoon returning it and buying the car back.' Connor shook his head. 'I can't say I understand, but I'm figuring love doesn't have to make sense – expecting it to is a route to madness. I'm guessing he'll move back in with her before the week is out.'

'Will you mind?' Madison sipped some wine as Connor busied himself taking the slices of bruschetta from the fridge, placing them on plates and adding basil. Madison smiled – a few weeks ago Connor ate from takeaway boxes. Now he was using garnish.

'No.' Connor stopped to look around the kitchen. 'Perhaps… I've grown used to the company. This is a big house for just me and Jaws.' He glared at the dog, who was now lying on his back, begging Madison for a stomach rub. 'And I really don't know what you've done to bewitch my dog, but I'm guessing if I'm not careful he'll be leaving me for you.'

'You'll have to up your game, try some adventure walks, or maybe yoga?' Madison joked as Connor placed the starters in front of them. 'This is impressive.' She picked up her knife and fork. 'I had no idea you could cook.'

'Neither did I…' Connor looked puzzled. 'Surprisingly I enjoyed it. I've learned cooking is relaxing when you make time for it.'

Madison sliced some of the bruschetta and ate a little, chewing slowly. The tomatoes were juicy and the garlic complemented them perfectly. 'This is good.'

Connor ate a chunk of the toast. 'Not bad, considering it's almost the first meal I've ever made from scratch.' He washed it down with wine. 'I think I'll try making a pie tomorrow – but I might put beef in that.'

'You seem different.' Madison studied Connor. His shoulders were relaxed and the tension around his eyes had almost disappeared.

'Perhaps I'm loosening up. Letting go of my father's lessons, putting life before work – I have you to thank for that.' Connor tilted his wine glass in Madison's direction. 'You've changed too.'

'How?'

'You're still here – despite my predictions and your setbacks – and you've changed this place for the better. Now the whole of Sunflower Island is rooting for The Hideaway and everyone's talking about your adventure walks. After the Grand Opening of the cafe they'll be talking about your sundaes too. You've really made a difference. I…' Connor paused. 'I'm not good with words, but I admire what you've done. You took a setback and turned it around, when in all honesty I thought you'd run.'

Madison sipped her wine, warmed by the compliment. 'I still think my greatest achievement was getting you to try yoga.'

'I'm not sure about the yoga.' Connor leaned closer. 'But I…
enjoy spending time with you. You're not what I expected when
you first came home.'

'I'm not?' Madison leaned closer too, until their glasses clinked.

'No… you're a thousand times more.' Connor's eyes dropped
to the dip between Madison's breasts. 'Is that red underwear?' He
looked delighted.

'I really can't remember, perhaps we should check?' Madison
raised an eyebrow, nodding at the oven. 'If you lower the tempera-
ture, you can leave a lasagne cooking for hours.'

'Well, that's better than pizza,' Connor said softly, taking Madison's glass and leading them both into the sitting room – stopping
for long enough to turn down the oven. 'I'll put the guard over the
fire before we go upstairs.'

'Or we could stay here,' Madison suggested, walking to the
window. The view was beautiful. You could see for miles – over
the fields to a galaxy of stars with a full moon beyond. Connor
placed a soft kiss on her shoulder, sending her nerve endings
into a spin.

'In front of the fire…' Connor traced Madison's shoulder with
his mouth. 'It's not Amsterdam, but it's different.'

Madison turned and put her hands onto Connor's shoulders,
running them slowly down his sides. 'I don't want Amsterdam,
or Paris, or anywhere else,' she said, as he caught her hands and
stepped closer, kissing along her collarbone. Madison dropped her
head back, losing herself to the sensations. She felt his fingers at the
zip of her dress seconds before it pooled at her feet.

'Red.' Connor smiled at her underwear.

'I told you it was lucky. Now I want to look at yours.' Madison giggled, reaching up to undo the buttons on Connor's shirt before tugging it off. The belt came next, followed by his jeans, which joined the rest of their clothes on the floor. Then he was standing in a pair of black boxer shorts. Madison let her eyes trail upwards, past strong legs, narrow hips and broad shoulders, until she reached his face.

'I've never invited a woman here,' Connor confessed, his voice silky and warm. 'Because it never felt right – but you feel right, Madison Skylar.' He ran a finger lightly down her spine, making her shiver. 'Why do you think that is?'

'Science?' Madison's breath shortened as Connor's hands continued to explore, running from the sides of her waist across her stomach – making her suck in a breath – before drifting slowly to the top of her knickers.

'I'm wondering if it's destiny.' Connor's hands glided to the fastening on Madison's bra and her knees wobbled as he unclipped it.

'Destiny?' Madison gasped as Connor stroked the bottom of her breasts with his fingertips. 'I thought a man like you didn't believe in such things?'

'I believe in a lot of things now,' Connor admitted. 'I've spent too long living life in my father's shoes, looking at the world through his eyes, being miserable. I never believed there could be another way.' Connor captured Madison's mouth, pushing the bra from her shoulders.

Madison didn't know what was happening. On one hand she knew where she was standing – in Connor's house, in her underwear, being warmed by a roaring fire, probably being stared at by Jaws.

On the other, she was having an out-of-body experience as Connor's kiss deepened and she began to lose awareness of everything around her. *Except for him.* She wrapped her arms around his neck and pulled him closer. Connor's skin felt warm and firm. He moved her backwards – until she was closer to the fire – and shifted to his knees, pulling her down until they were facing each other.

The fire felt hot and the flames crackled, but it was nothing compared to the heat in Connor's eyes. He slid his hands down Madison's sides again, stopping at her knickers. Then he pushed them over her hips to her knees, where she finished sliding them off. But when Madison started to pull Connor's boxers down, he took over.

'Control freak,' she teased.

'Old habits.' Connor traced a finger down Madison's face, pausing as it reached her chin, then continuing downwards. 'This feels like a new start for this house – it's never felt completely mine until now. I like having you here.' He kissed her ear, moving lower. 'Especially now I know you're not leaving.'

'Not until I've had my lasagne,' Madison joked, shivering as Connor laid her back, following her down until they were both naked on the rug in front of the fire. Then Madison took control, straddling Connor suddenly so she could lean down and look into his eyes. 'I'm home, Connor Robertson. I've been home since I saw you on the dock. I've been searching for this place for years, on some misguided adventure – trying to find the place I belonged, desperate not to get in the way, or to connect with anyone because I thought I'd be safer.' She bent down to kiss him gently on the lips, and Connor traced a path across her back and stomach before feathering down to the warmth between her legs. 'And now I'm here, where I should always have been – with you.'

'Connecting,' Connor whispered, pushing Madison up before pulling her back down – joining their bodies. They moved up and down as the fire roared beside them, and the moon threw slivers of silver light into the sitting room. Madison could feel her body coming alive, every nerve ending tingling. Her breath came in short pants and she closed her eyes. They moved faster, skin against skin, heat against heat. Until they exploded and Madison let herself fall, hugging Connor to her chest, knowing she was finally home – and nothing was ever going to get in the way of that again.

Chapter Thirty-Seven

It was still dark and the moon was high when Connor crept out of the house with Jaws. He'd left Madison asleep by the fire, wrapped in a fluffy blanket, surrounded by plates of half-eaten lasagne and an empty bottle of wine.

It took only ten minutes to find his way to the water's edge and the place where he'd left his father. Connor stood for a moment, taking deep breaths, choosing his words.

'I've come to say goodbye,' he murmured, feeling a weight lift from his chest. 'It's been a long time coming, but I've realised you were wrong.' Connor rolled his shoulders, feeling looser. Water lapped the edges of his shoes and waves pounded in the distance. 'I'm not a failure. I never was.' He shook his head sadly. 'I've spent my life trying to prove myself to you. I realise now I never could.' He looked at the horizon, wondering if a ghost could actually hear him and whether it mattered. 'You hated me – I've never understood why. Now I've realised it's really not important. Perhaps I reminded you of my mother? Or maybe it was just the way you were made. I do know I was headed down the same path – pushing friends, colleagues and family away in favour of work, especially the people who love me. I'm lucky a wanderer came along to guide me in another direction.'

Connor thought of how Madison had looked this morning – her hair spread out like a wild thing on the rug as she'd quietly dreamed – and smiled.

'I never saw her coming, never thought she'd stay. But she has, and knowing her has changed me. So, I'm here to say goodbye – and to wish you the same peace wherever you are. Be happy, let it fill your world, because at the end of the day, it's all that really matters.'

Connor stepped back again, away from the water's edge, watching the waves swirl and sway, sucking whatever was left of his bitterness away. If anything of his father had remained over the past year – memories, duty, guilt – they were long gone now.

It was time for his new beginning. And the first thing Connor had to do was come clean with Madison about The Hideaway being for sale. But when he crept back into his house, ready to watch the sunrise, Madison had already left.

☆

Connor wrapped his towel tighter around his hips and brushed water from his forehead, putting down his mobile after listening to the message – he'd been in the shower after his run, had heard the phone buzzing, but even a quick sharp sprint hadn't got him there in time.

A few weeks ago, the message from the general manager of Lake Lodge offering him the contract for the building and maintenance at the hotel would have had him grinning – it was exactly the work he needed to turn the business around. Instead he pulled out one of the oak chairs around the large table in his kitchen and sat with his head between his hands.

He couldn't accept it. He knew he couldn't. Somehow, having Madison in his head over the last few weeks had taught him a few life lessons.

Connor picked up the mobile and returned the call. When the answerphone picked up he breathed a sigh of relief. 'I'm sorry, Mr O'Sullivan... David. Something's come up and I'm afraid Robertson & Robertson Builders is no longer available to take on the contract at Lake Lodge. I wish you the very best finding another firm to work with.' He put the mobile down, feeling a weight lift off his chest. Knowing he'd just taken another huge step away from the life he'd always known, towards the woman he loved.

When Connor's mobile rang again fifteen minutes later, he was dressed and looking for the keys to his truck, determined to find Madison before the celebrations at the cafe kicked off.

'Dee?' He headed to the front door with Jaws at his heel, relieved it wasn't David calling to ask him to reconsider.

'I need a favour,' Dee explained, sounding harassed. 'There – no, put the bunting up there.' Her voice was muffled. 'Sorry Connor, I know you've probably got loads to do, but I need someone to pick up about a hundred tons of ice cream from the Sunflower Supermarket in half an hour. I would go, but it's not going to fit in my car. Also, we need to be fast – they've promised to pack it in ice boxes, but my car's not exactly known for its ability to get from zero to sixty in less than six months.'

'Now?' Connor grimaced. He wanted to speak to Madison – for some reason, the urge to confess was eating at him. Maybe because of what they'd shared last night?

'If you can.' Dee sounded guilty. 'I know how you feel about taking time out from work, but if as many people come today as Stanley's predicting, we'll be running out of ice cream fast. Chairs over there, no, not there…' Dee continued to bark orders.

'I'll go.' Connor shook his head at the mobile when Dee let out a cry of thanks. 'No problem, I've always time for my friends – I'm a new man now, hasn't Madison told you? I'll pick up the ice cream and bring it straight to you.'

And after that, he'd find Madison Skylar and confess all – he only hoped she'd be able to forgive him.

Chapter Thirty-Eight

The sun shone brightly and the air was crisp and cold. Madison stood back to admire the banners she, Amy and Stanley had spent the morning hanging, with a lot of direction from Dee. 'Grand Opening of The Sunshine Hideaway Cafe' was displayed across the front of the guesthouse, and colourful red, blue, yellow and pink bunting ran along the whole side of the building, leading to the entrance.

Inside Dee's kitchen, about a hundred cakes lined the counters and the aroma of chocolate, vanilla and strawberries filled the room, permeating the air like something out of a fairy tale.

'What time will everyone arrive?' Madison bounced back into the kitchen for the fifteenth time that morning, eyeing up the trays of cakes. She wore black leggings from her yoga class earlier, matching them with a red top that reminded her of Connor. She'd left his house while he'd been on his run this morning. She'd been so excited about getting things ready for today, but hoped to get lucky when she saw him later. 'Are you anticipating the entire island will come?'

Dee grinned. 'According to Stanley we're expecting hundreds, and they'll start arriving in another hour. We've got enough cake and ingredients for your sundaes to feed an army, and Connor should arrive with the ice cream any minute now.'

Madison giggled, spinning Dee around so that her white apron fluttered like a butterfly. 'We've saved The Hideaway! The place is booked solid for the next two months – we might even have to clear out the other guesthouses. And the cafe looks set to be a hit, meaning we'll have even more customers.' She laughed. 'We'll be turning people away soon. I can't believe I thought about leaving Sunflower Island because there wasn't a place for me here. If it weren't for Connor, Amy and you, perhaps I would have.'

'We're happy to have you permanently – it's taken long enough to persuade you to stay. But Madison, don't be disappointed if things don't work out exactly as planned.' Dee looked worried. 'Remember, there's always a home for you here – whatever the future holds – so please don't leave.' Before Madison could ask what Dee was talking about, the front door banged.

'We're home!' a couple of familiar voices rang out.

'What?' Dee and Madison said together.

Madison didn't wait for an answer – instead she charged out of the kitchen into the hall. Her Aunt Sandy and Uncle Jack were standing in the middle of the hallway with four suitcases beside them. They looked tanned, tired and a little shell-shocked as they took in the colourful bunting wrapped around the banisters and up the stairs.

'Madison—' Sandy didn't get a chance to finish her sentence because suddenly Madison was in her arms, then Jack joined in the hug. Madison's eyes filled as she squeezed them both, aware of how little she'd seen them recently – too intent on avoiding connections in case she got hurt. 'I'm so glad to see you,' Sandy said warmly, stepping back to look at Madison. 'We decided to come home after finally getting your email. Your uncle wouldn't let me check it at all for the first few weeks, and when I did the email from you had gone into junk. I only found it a few days ago. Then there was a chance of an early flight, so we took it. I was bored of all that sitting around anyway. I know you love travelling, Madison, but I missed being home.' Sandy looked around the hall sadly.

'Why didn't you call ahead?' Dee asked.

'We wanted to surprise you. I'm so sorry we haven't been here,' Sandy added, looking at Madison again. 'I'm sure Dee and Amy explained the cruise was last-minute – we'd never have gone if we'd known you were visiting.'

'It's fine, my trip was last-minute too. I'm just glad you're back early. We've so much to tell you.' Madison's mood dipped as she considered her aunt. Sandy looked tired, her complexion was paler than usual and even her hair – normally glossy and sleek – looked dry and wiry, which seemed odd after such a long holiday.

'You look wonderful.' Sandy stroked a hand across Madison's cheek. 'Being home agrees with you. How long are you staying for this time?' She glanced at her husband. 'I'm so glad we didn't miss out on seeing you.'

'I'm home for good, I hope – or for as long as you'll have me at The Hideaway,' Madison said shyly.

'You're staying?' Sandy grew even paler, looking around the hallway again.

'If that's okay?' Madison's stomach dropped.

'That's brilliant – I'm sorry, I'm tired. It was an early start,' Sandy explained, as Madison grabbed her aunt's hand and led her into the kitchen.

'I can't believe you made it back for the Grand Opening of the cafe – we've got loads of people arriving in an hour.' Madison knew she was talking too fast, but something was wrong. She could see her aunt and uncle were unhappy. Had she done something wrong, overstepped a boundary, come on too strong? 'We've made a few changes. Come into the kitchen and we'll tell you about it,' she continued, searching for things to talk about.

'A Grand Opening? Slow down.' Sandy followed Madison, looking confused.

'I know The Hideaway hasn't been getting enough bookings.' When Jack looked shocked, Madison added, 'It was obvious when I arrived and Stanley Banks was the only guest. The good news is we're fully booked for the next few weeks. We introduced yoga sessions and adventure walks, and having the cafe open again will be the icing on the cake. Stanley has arranged loads of PR – there are press attending and a lot of Sunflower Island will be turning up to support you.' Sandy and Jack looked dazed. 'You have no idea how much everyone here loves the guesthouse. So much has changed since you went on holiday. I hope you don't mind us taking over – but we wanted it to be a surprise,' Madison finished, watching their expressions. 'I know I haven't been around much to help with things – I want to rectify that. I hope that's okay?'

'You have been busy.' Sandy looked shaky, and Jack quickly pulled up a chair.

'This all sounds brilliant, Mads, and I want to know more. But your aunt's tired – let her sit for a minute. It's been a long journey.'

Sandy slumped in the chair and Dee bustled around the kitchen, getting water and a pile of chocolate cookies.

'Are you okay?' Madison asked, as Connor opened the kitchen door.

'Ice cream's in the truck. Where do you want it?' Connor grinned at Madison, making her insides fizz, but when he spotted her aunt and uncle, he frowned. 'Jack, Sandy, you're home.' Connor's attention flicked back to Madison, then he dropped his eyes and looked away.

'Only just,' Sandy said lightly, standing again so she could give Connor a hug.

'There's no time for hellos, people. We need to get the ice cream down to the freezers in the cafe,' Dee grumbled, heading for the door. 'Sandy and Jack, why don't you go and freshen up, then join us in a while? We'll stash the ice cream, and Madison can make you one of her almost-famous desserts when you're ready.'

'Sure.' Jack looked at Sandy, who nodded. 'We'll see you all in a minute. And Madison…' Jack's smile dimmed. 'There are some things we really need to talk about.'

☆

The cafe looked magical. Amy had hung white fairy lights along the wall to the left of the bar, and behind the counter a till was flanked by shelves of shiny cups, saucers and plates – stacked next to multiple jars of different coffees, syrups and teas. At the front counter, a glass cabinet displayed Dee's delicious chocolate, vanilla, carrot and fudge cakes. To the right, a glass-fronted freezer offered multiple tubs filled with chocolate and vanilla ice cream, next to an array of multicoloured toppings.

'I need to talk to you.' Connor joined Madison at the counter as she arranged the ice cream and toppings, then rearranged the menus for the fiftieth time. He looked worried and Madison stopped, desperate to smooth the creases from his forehead she'd all but eradicated last night. At Connor's feet, Jaws whined – perhaps picking up on the mood.

'Is it my aunt and uncle?' Madison asked, still feeling a little out of sorts as she stroked the dog's head. Her uncle wanted to talk to her and she couldn't imagine why. Unless he wasn't happy she planned to stay? Perhaps she'd been right all along and she really was in the way.

'Not exactly.'

'Work?' Madison took in the light dusting of stubble across Connor's jawline, before running a fingertip across her chin. It felt tender and she shivered, remembering their evening.

'It'll have to wait,' Dee sang out, giving Connor a hard stare as the cafe door opened and what felt like a million people began to descend the stairs. Then it was all hands on deck as everyone seemed to arrive at the counter at once, ready to compliment them on the decor, order drinks or gasp as Madison assembled a spectacular dessert. Within ten minutes the place was buzzing, and Madison stood heating milk for another batch of cappuccinos. Someone – perhaps Connor – put 'Let's Go Fly a Kite' on the music system, and she began to hum along. Madison's aunt and uncle hadn't arrived yet, but Dee, Stanley and Amy were waiting tables, and the room was sprinkled with people gossiping and catching up. There was Laura from Sprinkles, Gillian from The Red Velvet Bakery, Tom from The Moon and Mermaid, Julie and a few familiar faces from Tips & Toes – while Jesse sat at the bar, gazing at Amy as she whizzed around clearing tables, a small emerald ring sparkling on her finger.

'You've done an incredible job.' Finn made Madison jump as he reached across the bar to give her a quick kiss on the cheek. 'And I could have predicted Amy and Jesse would get back together. Shame, I do like that girl...'

'You were never serious about Amy. Far too many fish in the sea,' Madison teased. 'What do you want to drink?'

'I'm here for a sundae. You choose which – I hear you have a gift for the unusual. Perhaps that's the wanderer in you...' Finn leaned his elbows on the counter as Madison dolloped vanilla and chocolate ice cream into a dish, adding Smarties, popcorn and a smattering of space dust before handing it to Finn.

'On the house – for all those Pink Flamingos you keep making me, and for helping with the decorating.'

Finn shrugged. 'It looks good – what do your aunt and uncle think?'

'Don't know, but I'm expecting them any minute.' Madison frowned. 'My aunt looked tired. I hope she's all right.'

Madison glanced across the room, searching for Connor, who was standing with Jaws at one of the side tables, surrounded by a group of men she recognised from the builder's yard. One of them nodded before taking a business card from him. Connor glanced up and caught Madison's eye. Something was off in his expression, and once Madison got out from behind the bar, she was determined to find out what.

'The press are on their way.' Stanley appeared at her side. 'Are your aunt and uncle here? It would be great to have them in the photos. *Oh*, and a dessert would be good,' he added, spying Finn's bowl. His question was answered as Sandy and Jack walked down the stairs, looking around the cafe. Their eyes widened as they took in the rows of customers, who shook their hands and kissed their cheeks as they passed.

'It's like the old days,' Sandy said as she scanned the new yellow paintwork, ice cream cabinet and cappuccino machine. 'Except there are tons more people and no rhubarb or liquorice ice cream.' She shuddered. 'I can't believe you made all this happen, Madison. You've never been so…' She paused. 'I want to say committed, but that sounds rude.'

'Maybe it's true.' Madison nodded. 'You're right, I've not exactly been reliable – and I know I kept leaving – but I'm here to change that. And you should know, this wasn't just my doing. You'd be surprised by how many people wanted to save The Hideaway.' Her aunt and uncle looked at each other and frowned. 'Is everything okay?'

'Of course.' Jack nodded without looking at Madison. 'Although there are a few things I probably need to say.'

'Perhaps we should talk about that later, after the party?' Dee interrupted on her way to the kitchen, holding a tray of empty cups and plates. 'When you've got time to explain properly. Besides, didn't Stanley say the press were due soon?'

'Yes, and it's getting busier,' Stanley exclaimed, coming to join them as another crowd of people walked down the stairs and approached the bar.

'What's going on?' Madison asked, feeling her insides squeeze. Dee and Connor looked unhappy. Her aunt and uncle needed to tell her something. What was she missing? And why was everyone so jumpy? Then more customers arrived, drowning out any chance of a heart to heart. The volume in the room increased and Madison watched Sophia and David approach across the cafe.

'You came!' Madison shook off her bad feeling and gave Sophia a quick hug. 'This is my aunt and uncle. Sophia was a guest of The Hideaway until a few weeks ago. She's a midwife – this is her boyfriend, David O'Sullivan. They came for her birthday.'

Jack blanched as he shook David's hand.

'I hope you had a good holiday?' David asked, his eyes flicking around the room.

'You know each other? Of course, David, you mentioned you'd stayed at The Hideaway before,' Madison said.

'I've known your aunt and uncle for a while,' David explained. 'We had an enjoyable time staying here while you were away,' he continued, looking at Jack. 'The place has a lot of potential.'

'It's very special.' Sophia glanced around the cafe. 'And has more than lived up to its potential already.' She sounded annoyed. 'Madison has done wonders, introducing the yoga and walks, these incredible sundaes. You must be so proud to see the results of her work.'

'It's… an astonishing transformation,' Sandy agreed. 'We weren't expecting so much to change. It's a little overwhelming.'

'I've been recommending The Hideaway to everyone I know.' Sophia beamed, ignoring David as he glowered at her. 'Obviously we stay at Lake Lodge regularly, but there's something about this place I love. Besides, David enjoys a little competition…' She grinned at him.

'Lake Lodge?' Madison asked, taken aback. 'I don't understand.' She picked up a couple of mugs and set them under the cappuccino machine, keeping her hands busy.

'David owns Lake Lodge. Sorry –' Sophia's face dropped – 'David asked me not to mention it.'

'I know you've only just got back from your holiday, but I'm keen to move on with the sale,' David interrupted before Madison could respond.

'What sale?' Madison's hands froze as she turned to pick up the drinks.

'I'm going to buy The Hideaway, assuming we agree on a price.' David nodded at Jack and Sandy. 'I've been speaking to the Skylars since it went on the market. Connor's advised it's structurally sound and I see no reason not to progress.' He glanced around the cafe. 'You've realised some of the potential here, but with the right management there's even more that can be done.'

'You're selling?' Madison whispered, her eyes flicking from her aunt and uncle to Dee and Connor, who'd extracted himself from the group of men to join them. 'You *all* knew?'

'I didn't.' Sophia glared at David. 'I didn't mention that David owned Lake Lodge because he said he wanted to leave work behind completely.' She frowned, shaking her head.

'It's only just gone on the market,' Jack explained. 'After your aunt nearly died, we knew we needed to slow down. There's so much to do here, visitor numbers were dropping, the place had got shabby – we couldn't keep up. It felt like there were no other options…' He paused. 'I asked Dee to keep the sale quiet… I had no idea you'd come home, or that you'd do all this.'

Madison swallowed, unable to take everything in. Her eyes filled with tears. 'Aunt Sandy nearly died?' She knew her voice was wobbling, could hear the emotion even as she tried to hide it. 'When?'

'I had a small…' Sandy paused, looking upset. 'Episode. Back in September. It was a surprise. I spent a week in hospital. It's one of the reasons we went away. I…' She looked embarrassed.

'Small episode?' Dee sounded annoyed. 'Shall we call a spade a spade? I know I didn't say anything, but Madison deserves to know.'

Sandy sighed. 'Perhaps it wasn't so small. I had a heart attack. I was doing yoga in my office, then there was this awful pain in my chest. I was lucky – Dee popped in to talk to me, otherwise it might have been too late. The doctor said it was linked to lots of factors, including stress.' She shrugged. 'There's been a lot going on. We've been losing customers for a while and it got worse when Lake Lodge opened. I hadn't realised how much it affected me.'

'You didn't tell me.' Madison felt numb. She picked up some chocolate sprinkles and sprayed them over the drinks, barely caring where they landed. Everything about Sunflower Island felt like it was slipping away, an illusion disappearing. It was as if she were seven years old, at the airport again, being sent away.

'You were in Thailand – we didn't want to worry you. These things always sound so much worse than they are. I made it to the hospital in time, got some medicine, had a rest. The doctor recommended a complete change of lifestyle, working less and avoiding stress. I'm getting better…'

'We knew you'd want to come home,' Jack continued. 'But with everything being so grim here, we… well, what could you have done?' He looked around. 'A lot, obviously – I can see that now. But we didn't know… we didn't realise. All we knew was how hard you find this kind of news to hear… and how much you enjoy travelling. We've only ever wanted you to be happy, Madison.'

'You could have called me.' Madison shook her head, absorbing the news. The Hideaway was up for sale, her aunt had nearly died – Connor and Dee knew, and no one had told her.

'You've had your own life, love, travelling,' Sandy murmured. 'You've never wanted to stay.'

'That's… that's not true—' Madison's breath caught. Everyone was looking at her and she couldn't breathe. Suddenly she was making her way out from behind the bar, pushing between the bodies of her so-called friends – people she could hardly see. Someone tried to stop her, another wanted a hug, but Madison couldn't stay. She had to get out, up the stairs, to find her way into the light – away from these people she'd believed loved her. The people she thought were her friends.

Had they all known? Had everyone been laughing while she'd been trying to save The Hideaway – the place she'd claimed as her home? She was an idiot – she'd never belonged here, didn't belong anywhere. Seth was right.

'Madison,' Connor shouted from behind her. 'Wait.'

Madison didn't want to – everything inside her screamed at her to run, to head to the bedroom she'd started to think of as hers, and pack. But she waited, hoping it was a mistake, that there was some explanation that would make everything okay.

'I've been wanting to tell you—'

'But you didn't, because…?' Madison snapped, turning so she could look at Connor. In the distance more people were walking towards the cafe. One held a camera – maybe they were the journalists Stanley had talked about? *It doesn't matter now.*

'It wasn't my place, and I know that sounds bad. I talked to Dee – it was up to your aunt and uncle. Besides, we never thought you'd stay.' Connor blushed. 'At least, not at first.'

'So what, you slept with me, let me…' Madison swallowed the lump in her throat. 'Care for you – because it was convenient? Georgie told me you only date tourists. I suppose that means I fell into your normal category.' Madison's chest felt tight. The tears pooling in her eyes were in danger of spilling over. She straightened her back. She wasn't going to cry, wasn't going to show Connor how much he'd hurt her.

'That wasn't it,' Connor said quietly. 'Your uncle asked me to decorate. I knew the place was up for sale, and David came to see me when he stayed at The Hideaway. I couldn't exactly refuse to speak to him.' He swore. 'And that sounds bad – I'm not good at this.' He stared at her. 'You know I'm not good with words. I believe in keeping promises, in doing the right thing, and I made a promise to your uncle – to Dee – to keep this quiet.'

'You did.' Madison pushed aside her emotions. This wasn't the time to let her feelings out. 'You promised your client that you'd fix his guesthouse, respected the sanctity of the deal. I get it. I know how much your work means to you. No doubt you've got more lined up at Lake Lodge…'

Connor looked guilty. 'Not anymore.'

'But you did? Ah, that's just…' Madison's hands shook as she whipped around, following the bunting along the house to the kitchen. She pulled her mobile from her pocket and dialled a cab, barking instructions seconds before the battery ran out.

'You're leaving?' Connor followed as Madison charged up the stairs, heading for her bedroom. Jaws followed behind, but she ignored them both. She pulled her backpack out from under the bed and opened her wardrobe, grabbing handfuls of clothes and stuffing them inside. She paused, looking at the photo album on the floor of the wardrobe, at the picture of her aunt and uncle on the bedside table, then shook her head. She didn't need them. Didn't need anyone. Never had. She was a wanderer, would always be a wanderer. It was the only way to protect herself.

'What about The Hideaway?' Connor watched, his hands by his sides, his voice desperate. 'Who'll teach yoga, take the walks?'

'I'm sure David will find someone.' Connor stared as Madison gathered up her toiletries from the bathroom and dropped them on top of her clothes. Finally she snatched the envelope from her bedside drawer. 'I guess I do need this after all.'

'You're leaving – after everything you've said?'

'I don't belong here,' Madison said quietly. 'I thought I did, but I don't.' Her throat felt raw, her legs were shaking and she wanted to throw up. But she finished packing, waiting for Connor to say something, waiting for him to tell her not to go.

'I'm being the person I've always been. I wasn't lying, Madison. I couldn't tell you the truth. It wouldn't have been…' Connor paused, perhaps knowing the words wouldn't sound right. 'Professional.'

'Ah.' Madison's voice cracked. 'And of course being professional is what it's all about. I forgot that while I was falling in love with you. I forgot what's really important.'

'You're leaving because you're afraid,' Connor said quietly. 'You're doing what you've always done. Running before you get hurt, because running is easier than staying. You're less vulnerable that way.'

'That's not it… You *lied* to me. Everyone did. I've never been part of this place. I've always been an outsider. You've all just proved that.' Tears pricked Madison's eyes again and she swiped at them with the back of her hand. The doorbell rang and she looked out of the window, at the cab already parked outside.

'I'm coming!' Madison held up her hands as Connor moved towards her. 'There's no place for me here.' She picked up her backpack and headed for the stairs, gripping the envelope tightly between her fingers, wondering if Connor would follow. If he'd try to explain, or win her back.

But as Madison raced towards the front door and the cab waiting on the drive, she didn't hear any footsteps behind her – there was no shout and no one begged her to stay.

Instead, The Hideaway stayed silent as she opened the door and half ran, half stumbled to the cab, holding back a sob as she gave a final backwards glance to the only place she'd ever wanted to call home.

Chapter Thirty-Nine

'What are you doing in here?' Finn asked mildly from the doorway of Connor's home office. 'Because there's a party in the cafe that you're partly responsible for – the press are here and no one can find Madison.'

'She's gone,' Connor replied, ignoring the ache in his chest. If he pushed it down for long enough he wouldn't notice it soon. Instead he shoved the papers round his father's old oak desk, trying to remember what the hell he was meant to be doing with them.

'Gone?' Finn asked, scanning the empty room. 'I've got to wonder why, considering you two have been so close.'

'Madison's done what we all knew she would,' Connor said bitterly, checking his watch. 'She's probably buying her ferry ticket now.'

'She walked out on Sunflower Island without saying goodbye to anyone?' Finn looked thoughtful. 'I'm guessing that's not the full story.'

'She was upset.' Connor swallowed the pain burning a hole in his heart. 'I don't know why you're so surprised.'

'Because, *duh*.' Finn shook his head. 'The woman's in love with you. I've never seen her as happy as she's been these last few weeks. So I've got to ask, what happened?'

Connor closed his eyes. 'She found out her aunt was sick and The Hideaway's up for sale.'

'And that you knew all along?' Finn guessed. 'You didn't think to *tell* her?'

'I planned to, but the Skylars came home early and she found out by herself.' Connor shuffled the papers on his desk again. There were quotes here he should have finished weeks ago, invoices to record. Instead he'd been swimming, eating ice cream or practising yoga – basically losing his mind. 'It doesn't matter, it's obvious she hasn't changed.' He stood up. The ache in his head was back and there was a matching one in his chest. He might need to go for a run later – to chase the feelings away.

Finn put his hands in his pockets and looked around the office. 'So your plan is what, to bury yourself in work? Step back from the world and live out your days a lonely old man, like your father?'

'No… yes. It's not me leaving on that ferry,' Connor snapped, thumping the switch on his laptop so he could do some work. Jaws wandered into the office from the hall and sniffed Finn's shoes.

'It's you sitting here, shutting down, when you should be following Madison and begging her not to leave.'

'This isn't a movie, Finn,' Connor said bitterly. 'We're not all going out to fly kites. There's no happy ending for me here.'

'That's your father talking,' Finn said sadly. 'But you've a chance to change that path. I've seen it over the last few weeks, seen you coming alive. Don't shut everything out now.'

'You don't understand.'

'I understand what you're giving up – which is why I'm asking, are you really ready to let her go?'

Connor closed his eyes, remembering the last month, how he'd lived before. But all he could see was Madison – forcing him to eat bananas, getting lost on the beach or flashing her red underwear as she slowly brought him back to life.

And suddenly he knew she couldn't leave. 'You're right.'

Connor didn't wait for Finn, didn't wait for anyone. He hopped up from his desk, grabbed his keys, called Jaws and was on the drive and in his truck in seconds. The passenger door opened and Finn climbed in. 'For moral support,' he murmured. 'Besides, I'm a sucker for a happy ending – beats watching you talking to a ghost.'

They set off, but when they got to the end of the driveway the Skylars were standing in their way. Behind them Jesse pulled up in his Morgan and Amy jumped out. And behind them Julie from Tips & Toes looked out of her car window. Connor slowed and opened his door.

'Where's Madison?' Jack looked inside the car. 'She ran out of the cafe before we could tell her we're not selling. We're not selling to a man who treats the people on Sunflower Island the way David does – and after everything you've all achieved since we left, we just can't.'

'Gone.' Connor's voice flattened.

'Where?'

'To get the ferry. If we don't catch up, we might never see her again.'

'Then you'd better get going.' Jack opened the back door so he and Sandy could hop in next to Jaws. 'Put your foot down. This is an emergency.'

This was it, Connor decided, as he thumped the truck into first and headed out of his drive, taking the fast road across the island. It was time to step into the light and claim the life he deserved – and the woman he wanted to share it with. He wasn't going to let her down again.

Chapter Forty

Connor pulled the truck into the ferry car park and cut the engine. He didn't wait for anyone to follow – instead he started to run with Jaws at his heels, heading for the dock, hoping the ferry was running late because otherwise he knew he'd missed it. But he couldn't think about that. Couldn't think about what it would feel like to lose Madison for good.

'Idiot,' he muttered, as he skidded to a halt on the dock and stood watching the bubbling trail of water left by the ferry. It was too far to swim and there was no other way of catching it. Connor's heart squeezed as he watched the boat disappear into a cluster of dark clouds on the horizon. 'She's gone.'

Rain began to splatter on Connor's jacket, dribbling into his ears and down his collar as he sprinted to the booking office. If he bought a ticket for the next ferry, he might just be able to catch up with her. He dialled Madison's mobile again, knowing already it was dead. Then he stopped running. Because in the distance, standing patiently beside a set of closed white shutters, was a woman who looked a lot like Madison.

Connor walked up to her, feeling his heart hammer with a mix of excitement and fear. Madison was standing with her back to him.

His eyes dropped to her leggings and the flash of a red T-shirt under her jacket. 'Why are you here?' Connor asked slowly, ignoring the clatter of feet behind him signalling that both his dog and the others had followed. He had an audience, but couldn't care less.

Madison turned, her eyes widening. 'I could ask you the same thing.'

'I came to stop you.' Connor moved closer. 'I'll admit I'm stupid – I should have asked you not to leave.'

'But you didn't.' Madison scanned his face, hers expressionless. Her backpack was by her feet and Connor fought the urge to take it so she couldn't run away.

'You stunned me…' Connor searched for the words. The magical combination of nouns, adjectives and verbs that would convince Madison to stay. 'Don't go.' He grimaced. 'I wanted to dress the words up, to make them pretty, but I don't know how…' He swallowed. 'I will say I need you, Madison. Please don't go.'

Madison's eyes brightened.

Connor's attention slid to the ticket in her hands. 'Oh… Did you miss the ferry?'

'No.'

He frowned, looking back at the water, where the boat had all but disappeared. 'So what are you waiting for?'

Madison's eyes sparkled. 'There's no one around – even Sprinkles is closed. I think they're all at the Grand Opening. I'm waiting for the office to open so I can ask someone to call me a cab.'

'Where are you headed?' Connor's heart was in his throat.

'Home.' Madison looked into Connor's eyes. 'I realised something when I got here, when I was waiting for that ferry. I realised there was nowhere else I wanted to go. You were right. I have been afraid. I've been terrified of losing everything. So I've never allowed myself to stay in one place for long. But you showed me how it feels to belong. You showed me how it feels to be loved.' Madison looked down at her hands, and Connor tipped her chin up so he could look into her eyes.

'You're not going?' Connor felt the tightness across his chest ease.

'I'm not going anywhere. My home is on Sunflower Island and I'm never leaving again.'

'I'm sorry, I was an idiot.' Connor stepped closer so he could look into Madison's eyes. 'I put work first because that's what my father taught me. Because it was something I could control. But it's not enough – it doesn't mean anything.' He leaned forwards so he could brush his lips against hers. 'You were only gone a short time but the world grew darker. Without you all the light went out. I want to spend the rest of my life with you, getting lost on ridiculous adventure walks, drinking camomile tea, trying the dragon pose and flying kites. I love you, Madison Skylar – will you stay with me?'

Madison laughed and placed her hands around Connor's neck, jumping up suddenly so she could wrap her legs around his hips. And Connor held on, pulling her closer, knowing he'd never let her go again.

'I love you too, Connor Robertson. I need a man like you in my life. Someone sensible and responsible to keep me grounded, who'll keep me on the straight and narrow, making sure I don't get lost. I don't care if I've lost The Hideaway, because *you* make me feel like I belong.'

'You haven't lost The Hideaway, Madison.' Connor dipped his head and kissed his way across Madison's skin to her mouth, taking the kiss deeper until someone behind them coughed. When he looked up, Sandy, Jack, Finn, Amy, Jesse and half the clientele of Tips & Toes were watching them.

'I'd say get a room, but we're a long way from home,' Finn said mildly. 'I think what Connor was trying to tell you – before he got distracted – is that The Hideaway isn't for sale.'

'That's right, we've taken it off the market,' Sandy added, smiling. 'Please come home, Madison. I promise there's a place for you there. I'm so sorry we didn't tell you about my illness or the sale. You're an important part of our lives, but we never wanted you to feel responsible for us, or that you had to stay… We've always wanted you on Sunflower Island, we just thought your heart lay elsewhere.'

'I did love seeing the world,' Madison admitted. 'But I've realised I love being here – with all of you – more.'

'Then stay!' everyone on the dock shouted, stepping forwards so they could envelope Madison into a huge hug. And Madison hugged each of them back, one by one, until she got to Connor again, and he swept her up into his arms and slowly kissed her.

And at that moment, Madison knew, whatever happened, she'd finally found her way home, to the new beginning she'd been searching for.

A Letter from Donna

I want to say a huge thank you for choosing to read *The Little Guesthouse of New Beginnings*. If you enjoyed it, and want to keep up to date with all my latest releases, just sign up at the following link. Your email address will never be shared and you can unsubscribe at any time.

www.bookouture.com/donna-ashcroft

I loved being on Sunflower Island with the characters from *The Little Guesthouse of New Beginnings*. Everyone was so warm and there was such a wonderful sense of family. I hope you've enjoyed visiting the island and stopping in at the guesthouse too. Were you cheering for Madison as she tried to find her home? And did you love Connor as he gave in to what he'd wanted all along – leaving the lessons from his past behind to swim, try yoga and fall in love? If so, it would be wonderful if you could please leave a short review. Not only do I want to know what you thought – it might encourage a new reader to pick up my book for the first time.

I really love hearing from my readers – so please say hi on my Facebook page, through Twitter or on my website.

Thanks,
Donna Ashcroft

DonnaAshcroftAuthor

@Donnashc

donnaashcroftauthor

www.donna-writes.co.uk

Acknowledgements

I've been thinking a lot recently about support and how far you can go when you have the right people in your life. People who are there, offering the right things at the right times – celebrating wins or giving encouragement when things don't work out. So, I wanted to take some time here to appreciate them.

Thank you to Jackie and Julie, who have always brought sunshine, sanity and just the right amount of wine into my life. To my writing buddy Jules Wake for cheering me on when I've most needed it. To Katy Walker, Sue Moseley, Kirsty Egan-Carter, Hester Thorp, Andy Ayres, Steve Phillips, Bernadette O'Dwyer, Maria Rixon, Chris Evans, Alison Phillips and Amy Deane – your support has been amazing.

To Kirstie Campbell – an author in the making. I absolutely love that you've read my books and thank you for your lovely texts.

To my ultra-supportive partner (and hero) Chris, and my gorgeous teens Erren and Charlie, for believing in me – and for the incredible book cover bunting.

To all the people at ADP, who have bought my books and given me so much support. I can't tell you how much it means to me.

To Natasha Harding for your brainstorming, editing, advice and assistance in helping to guide my stories (while vastly improving them). To Noelle Holten, Kim Nash, Ellen Gleeson and the rest of the Bookouture team for the fantastic covers, blurbs, PR, social media support and everything else you've done. To all the other Bookouture authors – you are an awesome, talented and supportive bunch. I'm so proud to be in such amazing company.

To Katie Fforde for putting me on the right path, just when I most needed it. And to the Romantic Novelists' Association (RNA) for all the incredible work you do. I wouldn't have been published without you.

To my talented sister Tanya Roberts, for the photos you've taken for me to use on social media (and to her husband James for starring in them). To my brother, Peter Ashcroft, who read my books in one sitting, and to my sister-in-law Christelle, for letting him. And to my parents, Janette and Ian Ashcroft, for all their support.

And finally, to the people who have read my books and enjoyed them, many of whom have written lovely reviews – they really do mean the world. Thank you.